PERSEPHONE'S PROBLEM

THE CROSSROADS KEEPER SERIES BOOK 2

SAMANTHA BLACKWOOD

BARGHEST PRESS

ABOUT THIS BOOK...
PERSEPHONE'S PROBLEM

A wayward goddess with a problem and a surprise visit from a trio of divinely dangerous relatives combine to disrupt Alex's plans for a quiet Crossroads Keeper's life.

Persephone knew her affair with the Fae prince wasn't a good idea, but she's a sucker for a handsome face and polite manners. When the prince demands she use her divine powers to help him stage a royal coup, the goddess calls in a favor and dumps the brewing political mess in Alex's lap.

Before Alex can deal with Persephone's boyfriend problem, the Fates descend on the Crossroads to visit with their long-lost relative. Alex soon learns that the magic she inherited from her divine ancestor, Chronos, is vastly more dangerous than anyone suspected ... even the gods.

The Fates have orders to train their newfound Cousin Alex to control her death magic before she kills someone ... or a lot of someones. If she survives her divine relatives' deadly training sessions, Alex will need to use every scrap of her abysmal diplomacy skills to referee Persephone's royal boyfriend problem. If she fails, there will be a bloody battle for the Fae throne, which will endanger her heart family—and everyone else in its path.

Mythical Greek gods, quirky supernatural creatures, a newbie Crossroads Keeper, and a sassy, snarky … and magical pink-eared poodle battle the forces of chaos in this urban fantasy series filled with adventure, humor, a smidge of romance, and newfound family ties.

CHARACTER LIST

MAIN

Alex Blackwood - San Antonio Crossroads Keeper and main character. New to the supernatural world and way more powerful than anyone knows.

Conor - Barghest Hellhound shifter and Guardian of the Crossroads. Friend to Maia and wannabe boyfriend to Alex.

Demeter - Greek goddess and one of the Crossroads creator triune of goddesses. Also Persephone's mother and Hecate's best friend.

Hecate - Greek goddess and founding member of the divine triune who created the Crossroads several millennia ago.

Larry the Kibble Guy - Magical Familiar and Alex's partner. Small poodle with pink ears, a smart mouth, and a crap-ton of magic.

Maia Blackwood - Alex's aunt and the former Crossroads Keeper until her untimely death. She may be a ghost, but she has Alex's back.

Nyx - Greek goddess of Chaos. Daughter of the Titan god of time, Chronos. Mother of the Fates and grandmother of the Oneiroi. Has an evil plan or three.

Persephone - Greek goddess and one of the Crossroads creator triune. Demeter's daughter and Hades's wife. A bit of a flirt, to say the least.

Princess Aine - Exiled Fae princess. Daughter of King Donal and rightful heir to the Fae throne. She has plans but is smart enough to keep them to herself.

The Fates - Three Greek goddesses and Alex's crazy divine relatives. **Atropos:** Dangerous mean girl and scissor-happy lifeline cutter. **Clothos:** Mother goddess and weaver of the Web of Life. **Lachesis:** Nuttiest of the lot. Measurer of the span of each life ... and everything else.

Vincent Ianotti - AKA Vinnie the Vampire. Former human NYC mob boss who turned his life around when he was involuntarily turned. Maia's friend and Alex's honorary uncle.

MINOR

Abel Housemann - Vinnie's right-hand man and leader of his blood harem. Looks like an angel—but definitely isn't one.

Alan Allman - Half Fae, but lives his life without using magic. Mostly. Maia's rekindled love interest and Alex's attorney.

Billy the Squid - Ginormous supernatural squid who lives in Sylvan City's massive lake—when he's not tentacling around town in his favorite cowboy hat. Member of the supernatural posse.

Chronos - Greek Titan and god of Time. Father of Nyx and grandfather of the Fates ... and possibly related to Alex?

Crazy Sam - Cowboy ghost from the Wild West. And yes, he's pretty darn crazy, but a good ghost, at heart.

Danu - Celtic goddess of the Fae. Lazy and more than a bit crazy, but she just might come through in the end.

Flower - Tiny Fae fairy and companion to Princess Aine.

Grenoble - Goblin with a sad past. Larry's best friend and partner in crime.

Grindle - Powerful dark witch and Alex's paternal grandmother. Not a nice witch, at all.

Hades - Greek god of the Underworld. Persephone's husband. A bit of a goober.

Helen Grimby - Wannabe Crossroads Keeper. Alex's mother and Maia's older sister. A nasty piece of work.

Henri - San Antonio Crossroads estate's marvelous French chef.

Manny - Yeti. Sheriff of Sylvan City.

Morpheus - Greek god. One of the Oneiroi, a triune of gods with power over the unconscious. God of nightmares. Always up to no good.

Prince Cair - Son of King Donal of the Fae realm. He's Persephone's latest love interest, but the Prince wants more from her than mere kisses. A royal pain.

Queen Elizabeth I - An ancient Tudor ghost. Friends with Maia. Leader of the Crossroads ghosts and a bit of a royal snob.

Talon Grimby - Necromancer mage and Alex's very much more than dead dad.

Tyre - Indigo Fae warrior. Friend and protector of the Crossroads.

Yselle - King Donal's housekeeper and Larry's old friend.

Sundry other bit players.

1

PLAYING FOR YOUR LIFE

Clotho hurriedly put her cards face-down on the poker table and placed a restraining hand on her sister's madly waving arm. "Atropos, dear, we are guests in this house. I really don't think it's considered acceptable to threaten our host's niece with instant death if she doesn't let you cheat."

Atropos aggressively scissored her fingers in one last snipping motion toward Alex before reluctantly lowering her skeletal arm. "Alex may be our long-lost cousin, Clothos, but I don't want her to think she'll get any mercy from me if she keeps accusing me of cheating at cards." The angry goddess of Fate sniffed in disdain, then subsided into her chair, her attention, along with her deadly hands, once again occupied with her cards.

Those gathered around the poker table for their weekly 'friendly' game breathed a quiet sigh of relief—even the ghosts. As one of the three divine Fates, Atropos's scissors could cut more than just the life thread of living beings; they could also sever a soul's spirit thread, bringing oblivion to any being. Even a ghost.

"Well, that was a close call," Larry whispered. He pressed his furry canine body against Alex's leg, and mind-spoke some advice. *"Might be a good idea to just let her cheat—especially if you want to live to play another day."*

As the poker game resumed, Larry's comforting presence soothed Alex's frayed nerves. She reached under the table and petted his head in thanks, before mind-speaking a reply. *"Yeah, you're right. Lesson learned. Don't challenge a cheating death goddess— even if she is supposedly your cousin."*

Still relatively new to the intricacies of poker, Alex had been observing the game instead of playing, which was how she had noticed Atropos's cheating ways. She may not know the game that well—yet—but she had been paying close attention to the players. When Atropos slipped a winning card from the sleeve of her robe and inserted it amongst the cards already in her hand, Alex's eyes had widened in alarm. And when the cheating goddess had slapped her cards on the table in triumph and reached out to rake in her winnings, Alex had objected without thinking. "Hey! Where'd that extra Ace come from, Atropos?"

Alex had realized her mistake when the goddess's furious gaze pinned her in place, but it was too late to take back her hasty objection. "Um, not that I'm accusing you of cheating or anything, Atropos, but..."

"But you're accusing me of cheating," Atropos had growled at her. "Why, you impudent little—"

Events at the poker table had gone downhill from there. Atropos had jumped out of her chair, pointed directly at Alex, and played snippy scissors with the ancient, rust-covered shears she pulled out of thin air. Only she hadn't been playing. The deadly goddess could take more than an eye out with the pair of scissors clutched in her claw-like hand.

As one of the trio of sister goddesses known as the Fates, each with their own role in the lives—and deaths—of all creation, Atropos's divine duties were the most final. With a snip of her scissors, her job was to cut the life threads of those whose time had come— whether god, supernatural, or human. Less well known was her ability to cut a soul thread as well. This gave her the power to end a being's existence in the afterlife—or anywhere, really.

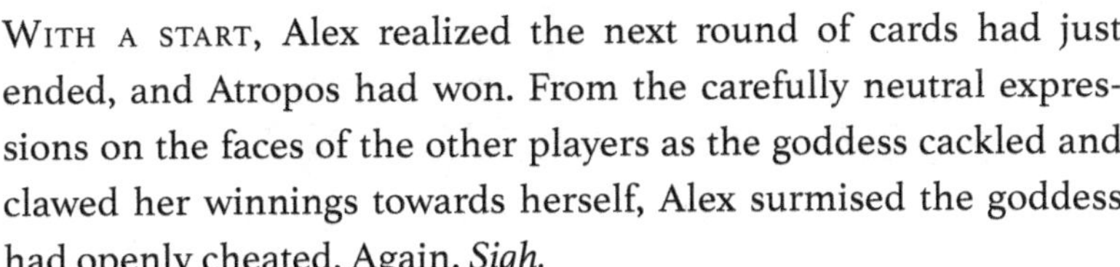

WITH A START, Alex realized the next round of cards had just ended, and Atropos had won. From the carefully neutral expressions on the faces of the other players as the goddess cackled and clawed her winnings towards herself, Alex surmised the goddess had openly cheated. Again. *Sigh.*

THE PREVIOUS EVENING...

The night before the fateful poker game, the three goddesses of Fate had arrived at the Crossroads in a whirl of pleasantries and pissiness ... the latter mainly from Atropos, of course. Before their arrival, Alex had been performing her duties in the Crossroads temple, guided by the ghost of her Aunt Maia. As the former Keeper of the San Antonio Crossroads, before her sudden death several months earlier, her aunt insisted it was her duty to mentor her niece in her responsibilities as the new Keeper.

"Remember, dear, you must trim and light the welcome candles on the altar each day," Maia murmured, watching critically as Alex lit the enormous pillar candles on the altar. "And don't forget to place fresh flowers in the urns each day, as well. You know how Hecate hates wilted flowers. As the divine creator of the Crossroads system, Hecate is very cognizant of her position as a hostess for all beings who use these intersections in the ley lines to travel around the world and between the realms." Maia smiled proudly at her niece. "As her new priestess, and the oath-bound Keeper of this Crossroads, it is now your responsibility to welcome all beings who travel through this Crossroads," she reminded Alex.

Alex nodded absently and fought not to roll her eyes. Her aunt had instructed her on the importance of proper altar care, and of her duties as the goddess's proxy, at least a hundred times over the past several months. Okay, maybe not that many times, she admitted to herself—but it was a lot. She knew Maia was only trying to make up for lost time and ensure she trained Alex quickly on her new Keeper duties ... for her own safety, as well as that of the others who relied on this Crossroads. After all, Alex should have had her entire childhood to learn about her inheritance as a future Crossroads Keeper. And Maia still blamed herself because Alex had missed those experiences, even though it had not been her fault.

"Yes, Aunt Maia, I know—or rather, thanks to you, I'm learning," Alex replied, careful to keep her tone neutral. "But thanks for the reminder." She smiled warmly at her aunt, then reached out to touch Maia's soft cheek, grateful that she could do so. A ghost as recently dead as her aunt should have no substance, appearing almost completely translucent. However, thanks to Maia's brave fight to remain on Earth during their recent battle to save the Crossroads, her ghost had aged drastically. She now appeared— and felt—almost solid, with only a slight wavering around the edges revealing her ghostly state. It usually took a ghost half a millennium, or more, to achieve such a solid state.

Maia sighed at Alex's gentle reprimand, then dipped her head in apology. "I'm so sorry if I keep repeating things, dear. It's important that I—we get you properly trained, as quickly as possible. I still feel responsible—"

"It wasn't your fault, Aunt Maia," Alex interrupted. "We both know that my lack of training is all down to my scheming mother. Can we not discuss this again?" She took the ghost's hand and led her out of the temple onto the wide, marble-floored portico. They passed the half-dozen massive stone columns supporting the portico's high roof, then proceeded down the steps onto the temple's forecourt. The two women walked hand in hand across the courtyard until they reached the low stone wall that surrounded the temple complex.

Alex sat on the wall, then tugged at her aunt's chill hand until the ghost settled down next to her on the wall's flat surface. "Let's just sit for a while and enjoy the cool evening air for a bit," she murmured. Wiping sticky strands of hair off her sweaty forehead, she absently tucked them back into the loose bun fastened at the nape of her neck. "This New England transplant is having trouble handling the San Antonio heat—even at night!"

Sadness and regret reflected in Maia's eyes as she gazed at her niece. "That's just it, though, Alex. You're not really a New Englander, are you?" The ghost patted Alex's hand gently. "Your roots go deep into the southern soil surrounding this Crossroads, my dear. And your mother should never have hidden you so far away. My jealous sister denied you your Keeper heritage and kept the supernatural world from you—and you from it."

Maia squeezed Alex's hand, then released it and rose; her ghostly form floating restlessly back and forth across the courtyard. "Your mother—my sister Helen—is not a good person, Alex. Even as a child, that much was obvious." She sighed deeply and shook her head. "Unfortunately, our mother encouraged Helen's belief that Hecate would choose her as the next Keeper, when the time came. After all, Hecate has almost always chosen the oldest daughter of the current Keeper to train as the next Keeper. And Helen may be my twin, but she *is* older than me, if only by a few minutes."

Maia gazed absently at Alex, remembered grief and pain in her eyes. "When we were twelve, and Hecate chose me as the Keeper apprentice, instead of my sister? Well, it wasn't a pretty scene, let me tell you. And the seed of discontent and entitlement she has always carried took root and grew over the years. And what evil fruit it bore."

The ghost shook off her dark memories, then pursed her lips and gave Alex an apologetic grimace. "I know Helen is your mother, dear, but—"

"She may be my biological mother, Aunt Maia, but she's not my heart mother—you are," Alex protested. "You're the one who took care of me when my mother lost custody, and you're the one who raised me from a toddler until she ... uh,took me away from you once I hit puberty. Once my mother realized I might be useful to her in her quest to wrest the Keeper role from you—and me— she kidnapped me. There's no other word for it, and you know it." Alex shook her head and stifled a heartfelt groan. She'd been avoiding this conversation with Maia since her return to the Crossroads several months earlier, but she knew it was past due. Her aunt still felt guilty that she'd been out of the country when Alex's non-custodial mother had swooped into San Antonio and kidnapped her daughter just after Alex's twelfth birthday. Helen had told Alex that Maia had died, and that meant she had to come live with her in Connecticut, because there was no one else to care for her.

Grief-stricken, Alex had thought she had no choice. She had packed her things and left San Antonio with her mother, journeying from the pleasant warmth of a San Antonio winter to a snowy, freezing one in Connecticut. She had mourned her aunt's death deeply but had wondered about things at the same time. *Why hadn't she and her mother stayed in San Antonio? After all, with her twin sister dead, surely Helen would have inherited the estate?*

Memories from her past stirred Alex's still-smoldering anger. Her hands clenched, chafing against the wall's gritty stone surface. Helen had not tolerated questions from her grieving child. Her mother's icy anger when she had asked questions had scared Alex, but she had kept asking. For a while. Until one day she could no longer remember the questions—or the need for answers. Alex had recently discovered that her mother had paid a small fortune to an extremely powerful witch to shroud her daughter's memories. For years afterwards, whenever Alex's thoughts strayed to her aunt or her former life at the Crossroads, blinding headaches and nightmares had ensued.

Over the years, Alex had finally stopped trying to remember.

She had grown up, graduated university with a mother-approved degree in European history, and accepted a job managing her mother's high-end antique's business ... until several months ago, when a phone call from out of the blue had shaken Alex's world. The caller had revealed that Maia had been alive all these years and had only recently died. He had also told Alex that she was the sole heir to her aunt's estate. Oh, and could she please come to San Antonio to plan the funeral? Dutifully, Alex had booked a flight to San Antonio to plan her long-lost aunt's funeral. Not long after her arrival, she had discovered the full extent of her mother's treachery. Alex's life had been a tumult of recovered memories and inherited responsibilities ever since.

"I really hate her, you know, Aunt Maia." Unheeded tears slipped down Alex's cheeks as she gazed up at the night sky. The moon played hide-and-seek among the clouds, but the stars shone brightly. "She took me from you and denied me knowledge of the supernatural world and my role in it. All because she was—is a jealous bitch."

Maia's eyes softened in sympathy. She sat beside Alex and gave her a side hug. By mutual agreement, they didn't take the painful conversation any further. They both knew that Helen's reasons for kidnapping Alex had been darker than mere jealousy. Helen had planned to hide her daughter until her magic manifested, then drain her power and use it to steal Alex's Keeper heritage. Unfortunately for Helen, the black magic witch's memory spell had worked too well, and Alex's magic had lain dormant long into adulthood.

Alex closed her eyes and heaved a sigh. She was sure her mother would try again. "She's probably still holed up in her lair in Connecticut, plotting another attempt to kill me and take over my Keeper role," Alex said glumly.

Maia nodded in reluctant agreement. "She will try again—but this time, we'll be ready for her." Fierceness filled her aunt's voice and lit her eyes. "She will *not* take any more time from us, my dear. Instead, we'll take it from her."

Both women fell silent. The unspoken thought that they might have no choice but to kill Helen to stop her lay heavy in the chilly night air. The two sat together peacefully until a familiar magic stirred in the temple across the courtyard, charging the night air. Both the old Keeper and the new realized that unexpected visitors would soon arrive through their Crossroads.

3

UNEXPECTED VISITORS

"Hellooo. Hello? Is anyone here?" A deep, vibrant female voice rumbled through the night air from the temple's still-open doors.

A sharp, angry voice replied to the first. "Some Crossroads Keeper our newfound cousin is, Clotho. She isn't even here to greet her long-lost family!"

Alex stood, then frowned and threw Maia a confused glance.

Cousins? Long-lost family? As far as Alex knew, she had none. Her mother's only sibling, her aunt Maia, had had no children. She vaguely recalled her mother telling her that her father was an only child whose parents had died in his teens.

Maia's chill hand on her back pulled Alex from her reverie The ghost urged her towards the temple, murmuring, "Perhaps we'd better see who has arrived, dear."

Reluctantly, Alex allowed her aunt to steer her toward the temple steps. "Okaaaay, but whoever it is must have the wrong Crossroads. I don't have any cousins ... do I?" She whispered urgently.

Maia's gaze slid away from Alex's enquiring one. "Well, not on your maternal side, dear. However..." Her words trailed off into the night air. Instead, she silently urged Alex up the temple's steps.

As they reached the portico, the noise made by the new arrivals inside the temple became louder.

"Who do you think—" Alex cut off her whispered query as the voices drew closer. Soon, whoever had arrived via the Crossroads would reach the temple's open doors.

Instinctively, Alex called her Keeper staff. When the heavy wooden rod solidified in her hand, she poured a powerful burst of her own magic into it. The staff eagerly responded, its own divine blue magic writhing around the staff's crystal tip, dancing in concert with swirls of her ruby red necromantic magic.

Footsteps from within the temple grew closer. Alex positioned herself with her back to one of the massive stone pillars that paraded along the temple's portico. One thing she had learned over the past several months since her reintroduction into the supernatural world was that there were a whole lot of beings in it who would try to kill you, if given the chance.

So far, she'd been lucky; her friends and heart family had helped protect her, but that wouldn't always be the case. After all, once the goddess Hecate had bound her as priestess and Keeper to the Crossroads just a few months ago, protecting the Crossroads had become Alex's oath-bound duty. And she was working incredibly hard to fulfill her new role, despite her inexperience.

Shifting shadows on the portico's marble tiles preceded the new arrivals as they reached the temple's enormous double doors.

Alex tensed, unsure of what was coming but feeling strangely that whatever—or whoever—it was, it would change her life completely yet again. At her side, her aunt's ghost shimmered as she also drew on her power. Maia's ghost had regained some of her Keeper magic since being reunited with the piece of her soul Morpheus had kidnapped and imprisoned in the Underworld. No one knew why, since ghosts rarely retained or regained any magic from their former lives. However, neither Maia nor Alex were asking any questions since Maia's newly returned Keeper magic helped her protect the Crossroads, while Alex completed her training.

Maia leaned close and whispered. "Larry and Conor will soon be on their way. They are just wrapping up a sticky situation in Sylvan City."

"Don't need 'em. We got this," Alex murmured, hoping like hell she was right.

A third voice, this one high-pitched and breathy, wafted through the temple doors. "I hear voices outside, sisters. Perhaps we should see if there is a large welcoming party waiting for us. I do hope not, though, as I don't like surprises."

A harsh female voice replied, "Well, Lachesis, I'd say the surprise is that our dear Keeper cousin isn't here to greet us. And just where that damned Barghest Crossroads Guardian is, I'd like to know." An irritated growl cut through the night air. "At the very least, that mangey Hellhound should be here to protect the temple. I always knew Hecate ran a loose ship at her Crossroads, but her standards seem to have slipped in the millennium or so since we last saw her."

Alex heard a sharp intake of breath on her left and realized the woman's words had rattled her aunt. She knew that breathing was unnecessary for a ghost. However, she suspected that habits of a lifetime died hard.

When the new arrivals exited the temple, Alex's eyes widened in surprise. A trio of Greek goddesses, each very different in appearance, yet somehow bearing a similar, strong power signature, had paused just outside the door. Instinctively, Alex moved forward, blocking her aunt from their view. A derisive snort at Alex's back informed her that her aunt was not best pleased with her niece's attempt to protect her. Maia *was* dead already, after all.

Ignoring her aunt's irritation, Alex bowed her head slightly at the three goddesses sand introduced herself. "Hail and Welcome, divine ladies. I'm Alexandria, Priestess of Hecate and Keeper of this fine Crossroads. How can I be of assistance to you this lovely evening?" Alex knew her tone and words trod a fine line—they fulfilled her obligations as host, while letting the trio of goddesses currently eyeing her appraisingly know that she wouldn't take any shit from them.

The sturdily built goddess on the left, her plump form draped in the traditional robes of an ancient Greek matron, grinned at Alex in delight. "See, sisters, I told you our cousin would surely be here to greet us." The stout woman eyed Alex's Keeper staff, which glowed with writhing red and blue magical flames, with almost motherly pride. "And just look at that beautiful red death magic dancing around her staff. Grandfather Chronos, the old goat, was right—she's definitely family."

Shock arrowed through Alex at the goddess's words. *Death magic?* She knew her mythology; Chronos was the Primordial god of time, which she supposed included both life and death. This goddess had just called Chronos grandfather—and referred to Alex as family? Oh, no. Nope. Just N-O-P-E.

"Um, I think you have me confused with someone else, ladies," Alex said politely. "I'm just a Crossroads Keeper, from a long line of Keepers. My aunt was a Keeper, as was her mother, and on down the family line." Alex tried not to think of her late father, whose dark necromantic magic coursed through her veins—and which currently flamed, violently red, around her staff.

The smallest of the goddesses studied Alex intently. Her head cocked, birdlike, then she nodded decisively. "You're right, Clotho, this girl is definitely family—even if she's not ready to admit it. Yet."

The tallest goddess crossed her stick-like arms over her sunken chest and gave everyone a well-practiced sneer. Stains that looked suspiciously like blood dotted the tattered robes that hung loosely around the goddess's thin form. Her long, thin neck seemed barely able to support her head, which was all angry angles and prominent planes. "Oh, the girl definitely realizes she's a relation of ours, Lachesis," she said, her voice grating like nails on a chalkboard. She narrowed her eyes and peered at Alex knowingly. "She's not thrilled about it, though, are you, Cousin Alex? Either you're not very bright—a distinct possibility, I admit—or you *do* have some brains behind that pretty face and are beginning to realize there may be a thing or two you don't know about your late, and apparently unlamented, father and his side of your family tree."

The haughty goddess smiled maliciously at Maia, who had stationed herself at Alex's side, her ghostly form vibrating with suppressed emotions. "This one knows, though, don't you? I'd bet you know more about Alex's paternal family than you've shared with her. Think she'll forgive you for not telling her? Because we're certainly going to tell her."

Alex schooled her face into neutrality and then placed a supportive arm around her aunt. "I don't care what my aunt has told me, or not, about my father's side of the family. I have absolutely no interest in them—or they in me, I'm sure."

She shivered with remembered pain as memories of her father's many betrayals flickered to life in her mind. He had been an evil man, both in life and in death. Ambitious and amoral, her father, Talon, had spent his life intent on using his rare, powerful necromantic magic to conquer the supernatural world. His most recent attempt, which had originated in the Underworld after his physical death, had almost been successful. Alex's mind shied away from the last image she had of her father as he writhed in agony on the floor of Hades's castle. She had used the necromantic magic she had inherited from him to end his afterlife—and destroy his soul. Of course, her father had been trying to kill her at the time, so there was that.

"I try not to think about my father," Alex said, her voice devoid of emotion.

The matronly goddess, who had first spoken, smiled at Alex, her eyes filled with gentle sympathy. "I can understand that, dear. Your father was considered a black sheep—even in our dark family."

"The girl doesn't have to think about him, Clotho," the tiny bird-like goddess said, giving her sister a distracted glance, then focusing her bird-like gaze on Alex. "But she has to face up to what she did. After all, Alex ended her father's soul without our permission." The goddess tittered and tilted her head. "Patricide isn't pretty, my dear. And for every action, there must be a reaction."

Alex lost both her patience and her temper. "Listen, you old bats," she ground out. "I've had about enough of your cryptic words and insults. Either you stop beating around the bush and tell me what you're doing here, or you're outta here—cousins or not." She brandished her still-glowing Keeper staff. "And I can make that happen."

Maia's warning hand on her back tempered Alex's anger slightly, but she didn't lower her staff. It was probably not wise to threaten a trio of Greek goddesses, family or not, she mused wryly, but what the hell.

The tall, thin, and very rude goddess clapped slowly, her lips curved in an approving smile that just missed her ice-blue eyes. "Bravo, child. So, there's a backbone in there, after all." Suddenly, an enormous pair of gleaming silver scissors appeared in the goddess's claw-like hand. They made a terrifying sound as the goddess rapidly snipped them together. "However, it looks like I'm right about her lack of intelligence. Who would be so stupid as to threaten the three of us—even if they are family?"

Alex's heart sank to her toes, and she fought to keep her chagrin off her face. Only Maia's comforting arm around her waist prevented her from backing up, as if by putting distance between herself and the trio of powerful goddesses, she could refute the painful truth of their words.

The stout, motherly goddess flicked Alex a kind glance, then gently placed a restraining hand on her tall sister's wildly waving arm. "Now, now. Stop that snipping and put those scissors away, Atropos. I'm sure Cousin Alex didn't mean to insult us."

After a final irate snip, accompanied by a maddened snarl, the scarecrow-like goddess finally lowered the scissors. Her black eyes blazed with anger—and more than a hint of madness—as she glared sharply at Alex. Her cousin.

Alex stared silently at the three goddesses, then swore silently.

Well, fuckit, she brooded. *Here comes another supernatural surprise barreling out of nowhere to upend my life.* Several short months ago, she had been living a safe, if unexciting, life in New England as a human. She had been wholly unaware of the supernatural world and her place in it. Then, she'd suddenly been thrust into a heart family and community she had been spelled to forget and had rediscovered her Keeper heritage. Reluctantly at first, she had committed herself to a life of duty and service to the goddess Hecate and the supernatural Crossroads, which now claimed her as its Keeper. Wasn't that *enough* of a life change? It seemed not.

"You three are the Fates, correct?" Alex asked it as a question, but she already knew it was a fact. This trio of Greek goddesses simply couldn't be anyone else. "Let me see if I have my mythology —er—divine history, correct." She pointed at the heavyset goddess. "I expect you're Clotho, the Weaver of the tapestry of life."

When the stout goddess smiled kindly and nodded in agreement, Alex turned her attention to the smallest of the divine trio, who was currently busy pleating her voluminous robe into extremely even lines. "You must be Lachesis, the Measurer of the span of each life, yes?" She asked the seemingly nervous goddess.

With a swift tilt of her head, the diminutive goddess threw Alex a distracted glance. "That would be correct, cousin." She returned her attention to neatening the already precise folds of her robe, murmuring, "I like to measure things. Lives ... robes ... all sorts of things."

The tall, thin goddess gave her sister an impatient, if affectionate, glance. "Yes, Keeper. My sister is a touch obsessive about the exact length of things. In modern parlance, I think you'd call her little quirk not quite normal." She patted her tiny sister's arm and added, "She's crazy, but she's family."

The goddess then turned her penetrating gaze to Alex and bared her teeth in a savage grin. "And, by a process of elimination, that means you know who I am." A different pair of scissors, these hand-forged, black with age, and stained with what looked sickeningly like dried blood, appeared in the skeletal goddess's gnarled hand.

Speaking of crazy, Alex mused, *this goddess takes the prize.* Out loud, she said, "That makes you Atropos, the Cutter. Your divine scissors of Fate cut the threads of each life once its allotted time has come."

"And sometimes before," Atropos retorted meaningfully. She gave a final sharp snip of her blood-covered scissors before banishing them to the ether. Flickering torchlight highlighted the goddess's angular head; the thin skin stretched over her face revealed the sharp planes of the skull underneath.

"Now, Atropos, we've talked about that." Clotho's calm voice counseled her snip-happy sister. "You can't go around ending lives willy-nilly, just because someone pisses you off. We all have to agree—"

"Agree, my ass..."

"We've been over this a million times..."

The three divine sisters lapsed into what appeared to be a familiar argument about which of them had the ultimate authority over Fate and the existence of all living things.

ALEX CONSIDERED BREAKING UP THE GODDESS' argument, but the thought of having Atropos's deadly scissors waved in her face again gave her pause. Instead, she whispered to her aunt. "Uh, maybe we should just leave them to it."

Maia shook her head firmly, but gave her niece a sympathetic smile. "You are the Keeper of this Crossroads, my dear. Keeping order here is your responsibility. We simply can't have a trio of goddesses arguing like a bunch of angry fishwives on the temple portico. It's not seemly. What if other guests arrive through the temple's ley line? Remember, as Hecate's representative, it's your job to maintain the dignity and decorum of the temple and the Crossroads it contains, as well as welcome newcomers." Eyeing the angrily arguing goddesses warily, she added, "Oh, and Keepers must keep the peace at all times, Alex. Have I not mentioned that before?"

Dismally, Alex wondered how many more duties she would discover were now her responsibility in this supernatural world she had been thrown into. If the Fates and their claim of kinship with her were any sign, she had only scratched the surface of the many obligations her new life encompassed.

As Alex reluctantly prepared to referee the fight amongst the bickering goddesses, fate (with a small 'f') intervened. Two furry bodies, one massive and one much smaller, suddenly barreled through the temple doors. Apparently, Conor, in his Barghest Hellhound form, and Larry, in his usual adorable pink-eared poodle body, had arrived to save the day. Instead, they almost ended it.

The furry duo realized too late that there were visitors standing just outside the temple entrance. Paws scrabbling on the portico's slick marble, neither could halt their momentum. Instead, they bowled right into the trio of still-arguing goddesses. Alex's furry rescuers and her newfound cousins collapsed onto the portico's hard marble floor in a tangle of fur, robes, snarls, and swears. Eventually, the flailing group separated themselves and regained their feet, then stood several feet apart, glaring at each other.

Conor growled, then smoothly transitioned back into his human form, his nude body slick with sweat, his powerful muscles shining in the torchlight. He stood proudly, eyes narrowed, as the three goddesses gawked at his nakedness.

Despite the dire situation, heat suffused Alex's girl parts at the sight of Conor's magnificent human form. Conor flicked her a sideways grin and murmured, "Like what you see, sweets?"

Before she could reply, Larry grinned toothily and posed next to Conor's leg, before giving Alex an amused side-eye and mind-speaking a question. *"I don't understand why our female visitors aren't looking at me. I don't have any clothes on, either."*

Alex frowned at her furry Familiar and issued a mind-spoken warning. *"Stop messing about, bud. You're embarrassing me. You're supposed to me my magical partner, so a little decorum wouldn't go amiss."*

Larry just smiled and posed some more, his laughing eyes mocking his magical partner's scolding.

Deciding to deal with her recalcitrant Familiar later, Alex rolled her eyes and addressed the next issue on her agenda. She pulled off her cotton blouse, leaving her in a thin tank top, and threw the shirt at Conor. "Cover yourself up, please. There was no need for your hasty shift. Neither the Crossroads nor I have any pressing need for your protection." She gestured at the trio of goddesses, who were still gazing avidly at Conor's naked form. "These nice ladies are my cousins. The Fates. They've come for a surprise visit."

Conor almost dropped the blouse before he could tighten it around his waist; only his quick reflexes kept the material covering his manly bits in place. He shot Alex a wide-eyed look. "Uh, these visitors are your cousins? The Fates? The Greek goddesses—those Fates?"

Atropos moved briskly forward and stood directly in front of Conor and Larry. Her stick-like neck stretched out as she gave Conor a menacing glare. "Yes, those Fates, you muscle-bound idiot. Which other ones are there?"

The brusque goddess spun to face her sisters and threw up her hands. "See? What did I tell you? Hecate's standards have slipped even further than we feared, sisters. She's got a numbskull Hellhound Barghest shifter for a Crossroads Guardian and this—this magical poodle thing supposedly protecting our Keeper cousin." Atropos smirked derisively at Maia. "Oh, and it appears her mentor is the ghost of a former Keeper who couldn't keep herself from getting dead. It's a damn good thing we showed up when we did."

Atropos's derogatory comments about her heart family infuriated Alex. *She* could complain about them all she wanted, but they were her chosen family. No one else—not even a goddess —had that right.

"Now listen, you three," she spat. "I don't care *who the hell* you are. You will *not* disrespect my family and friends—or me. I'm the Crossroads Keeper here. That makes me the direct representative of the goddess Hecate while performing my Keeper duties. All of which means you three ladies must listen to me. Got it?" Alex considered for a moment, then couldn't help adding, "Oh, and Hecate's standards are just fine, thanks very much. If anyone's standards have slipped, it's yours. Your behavior tonight has been atrocious."

As Alex spoke, Maia's arm tightened around Alex's waist in silent warning. *Damn, she really couldn't keep her mouth shut no matter how much she tried,* she mused. While she didn't regret her chiding words, she hoped they weren't the last thing she ever said. Especially since Atropos had those deadly scissors in her hand again and a furious expression on her skull—er, face. The other two Fates didn't look best pleased, either. *Sigh.*

"Might want to fall back on traditional hospitality, Alex. It could possibly save all our lives tonight." Larry's mind-spoken words, thankfully unheard by the goddesses, echoed sharply in her mind.

Alex gave Larry a tiny nod, then shook off her aunt's restraining arm and paced forward until she stood directly in front of the trio of irate goddesses. With a massive effort, she softened her tone and addressed them. "Now that we've got that all cleared up. Perhaps we can start again, cousins?"

Giving the smallest of head bows she thought she could reasonably get away with, Alex invoked the traditional Crossroads welcome. "Merry Meet, travelers. Welcome to the San Antonio Crossroads, gateway to the magical community of Sylvan City. On behalf of the goddess Hecate, I offer you food and lodging during your stay with us."

For a tense moment, the fates (small 'f') of everyone present hung in the balance. Alex could hear Conor's angry muttering behind her. She sent a silent thank you to her aunt when she started a casual conversation with the furious Barghest shifter. Hopefully, Maia could keep Conor from going all Hellhound Barghest on the trio of goddesses. Talk about an international—even worse—an inter-realm incident. *Well, crap.*

Just as Alex despaired of a positive outcome, two of the goddesses snorted a laugh. Even Atropos cracked a small smile and casually dismissed her scissors to the ether. Alex crossed her arms and schooled her face to stillness, affecting a polite indifference, but breathed a silent sigh of relief.

Clotho, still chuckling, approached Alex and threw her arms around her shoulders, squeezing her in a tight, motherly embrace. "My dear child, you have the family temper, I see. As well as the tendency to speak first and consider the consequences later—or not at all. Good for you, Alex. And welcome to the family."

Shocked into inaction, Alex merely nodded her head, which was currently crushed into the generous bosom of the heavyset Weaver of Life. Once Clotho released Alex, Lachesis approached, smiled up at Alex, and held out her small hand. Alex grasped the delicate, claw-like hand gently, afraid she would break it if she squeezed too hard.

Atropos merely nodded approvingly at Alex and said, "You'll do, girl. You've got spunk." The Cutter of life cords exchanged a silent glance with her sisters. "I say we accept our cousin's offer of hospitality. I do hope the rooms here are up to our standards, though. Let's go, ladies." With that, the tall goddess strode down the temple steps and across the courtyard, before unerringly choosing the correct path through the gardens to the main house.

As Atropos's ragged white robes disappeared into the darkness, everyone breathed a collective sigh of relief, even her sister goddesses.

Maia stepped in then, issuing room assignments to the remaining goddesses and instructions for Conor and Larry. Apparently, the trio had brought a metric crap-ton of luggage through the ley lines, all of which they had piled haphazardly near the temple's altar.

When Alex fell into bed in the early hours of the morning after settling the goddesses into their rooms, she dropped quickly off to sleep. Just before she fell over the edge into dreamland, she heard Larry's voice in her tired mind.

"Oh boy. This is going to be fun. Did you hear Maia invite your newfound divine cousins to tomorrow's poker game? Queen Elizabeth and the other ghosts will not be pleased."

Alex breathed a weary sigh, then ran a hand down Larry's furry side. "Sufficient unto the day is the evil thereof, bud. Time to get some sleep."

4

WHAT LARRY KNEW

Alex woke up to bright sunshine streaming in her window, warming her face. She squinted and pulled the covers over her head. In her exhaustion, she must have forgotten to close the curtains the previous evening. What with the unexpected arrival of a trio of demanding goddesses, along with their startling claims of a familial relationship with her, she hadn't crawled into bed until after midnight. Then brooding on her newfound divine relations had kept her awake until the early hours.

With a tired groan, she threw back the covers, averting her eyes from the bright sunlight. She levered herself off the bed and staggered toward the bathroom.

"I've already been out, no thanks to you, sleepyhead," Larry informed her reproachfully from his seat on the chair by the desk.

Her canine Familiar's sarcastic comment made Alex pause and redirect her steps toward his position. Larry jumped off the chair and pranced out of reach. "Hey! Before you beat me up, have a look at the desk. I had Henri fix you a late breakfast. And Conor provided room service."

Horrified, Alex put a hand to her snarled hair and gazed down at her ancient cartoon character nightshirt in disbelief. "Oh, gods, Conor saw me like this?"

Larry smirked up at her. "Yep. You had even drooled a little in your sleep. The schlep just smiled and kissed you on the head. He's got it bad for you." With quick movements, Larry dodged the slipper Alex threw his way.

"Oh, shut up, fur-ball." Shaking her head in disgust, she resumed her interrupted trek to the bathroom. "And don't touch my food!"

"Wouldn't dream of it. I know how grouchy you get when you're hungry. Besides, it's almost lunchtime, anyway. Your aunt always puts on a decent spread for the Friday poker lunches." Larry licked his chops in anticipation.

Alex's appetite fled when she remembered the upcoming poker game—and the trio of annoying goddesses her aunt had invited to the party. She closed the bathroom door with a snap as Larry snickered at her dismay.

ALEX PICKED DESULTORILY at her breakfast tray. Despite having no appetite, she knew she should eat something. She didn't want to face her newfound divine cousins on an empty stomach. Doubt crept in, and she muttered, "But are they really my cousins? How does that even work? That would mean..."

"That would mean your late and not-so-great father, Talon, is their uncle. And that the Fates share a mutual divine grandfather with him, I presume," Larry replied, giving Alex a guarded look.

She narrowed her eyes at her nervous-looking Familiar. "But *are* you presuming—or do you know? And if you know, you better damn well start spilling the beans. After you apologize for keeping this humongous piece of news from me, you fuzzy little a-hole."

Larry had the grace to drop his gaze. "I knew some of it before —you know—when we met at the animal shelter. The Department of Eternal Animal Familiars gives us a pretty thorough briefing when we're given a new assignment. The rest I learned from Conor and your aunt Maia after we arrived in San Antonio."

Alex stirred her now gloppy and cold oatmeal listlessly. "You're telling me there's even more information about the supernatural world that everyone's *still* keeping from me. Since I arrived in San Antonio, I feel like the knowledge blows just keep coming. First, I'm thrown into a supernatural world that my mother kept hidden from me since childhood. Within days of my arrival, the goddess Hecate appoints me as her priestess and binds me as Keeper to this damned Crossroads. Then I meet my dead aunt, my very much alive Hellhound Guardian, and my Uncle Vinnie—the vampire ... all about the same time I discover that the talking dog I adopted from the shelter last year—that's you, you mutt, isn't just an anomaly, but is actually my assigned magical Familiar."

"Hey, take that back! I'm not a mutt!" Larry snarled. "I'm a purebred poodle on the outside, and a big, tough junkyard dog on the inside, as you well know. And even if I were a mutt, so what?! You prejudiced against mutts or something?"

Her magical partner's indignant response made Alex smile, if reluctantly. "That's all you got out of my rant? That I called you a mutt?" She narrowed her eyes at him. "And don't think you can avoid answering my questions with your false outrage. You know I love all dogs. That's why I was volunteering at the animal shelter where we met." Her eyes widened as it hit her. "Wait a minute— you were a 'plant', weren't you? How likely is it I'd meet my magical Familiar at the animal shelter where I volunteer?" She palmed her forehead and shook her head. "Goddess, I'm soooo stupid. I should have realized that before now."

Larry cocked his head and studied Alex thoughtfully. "I'm not gonna comment on your intelligence, or lack thereof, oh partner of mine. *Of course*, DEAF planted me at that shelter so we could meet. *Duh.*" He rolled his almond-shaped eyes. "And knock off your woe-is-me crap. You'd have withered away from boredom or frozen to death from the cold if you'd stayed living as a human up there in New England and remained ignorant of the supernatural world and your place in it, chickee. So don't give me that crap!"

Alex patted the air soothingly and nodded. "Yeah, yeah. You're right, Larry. I'm glad to be here. I'm happy the memory spell broke and that I've been able to reestablish a relationship with my aunt —even if she's a ghost—and gotten close again with Conor, and Uncle Vinnie, and, well, everyone else." She threw her other slipper at Larry, and only his quick reflexes prevented it from smacking him on the rear. "And I'm even glad that DEAF assigned you as my Familiar. Even if you are a total jerk most of the time."

"That's not fair. I'm a jerk ALL of the time. And you have to admit I'm darn good at it," Larry snarked.

Hands on her hips, Alex glared at the sassy canine. "That's enough avoidance, dog-face. Spill the beans. What do you know about the Fates and my relationship with them? And who here knew what you didn't know and told you the rest, with none of you telling me?"

Admitting defeat, Larry settled on the bed and spilled the beans. "You know how you thought your father and the goddess Nyx were probably lovers, and that's why they were working together on their plans to attack the Crossroads and bring Nyx's chaos magic to Earth?"

"Yeeessss." Alex drew out her answer, unsure of where this story was going.

"Well, Nyx and your father weren't lovers," Larry assured her. He cocked his head. "At least, I don't think so—not that incest is unheard of in divine families. What I've been told is that they're brother and sister. Their mutual father is Chronos—you know, the Primordial god of Time—that god. Your grandfather." Larry lowered his head to the bed and squinted, preparing for Alex's explosive reaction.

Eerily calm, Alex replied, "And nobody thought to tell me that my paternal grandfather is a freaking god—one of the big ones, too?" She threw up her hands. "THE big one. Father of Time, for god's sake. If I've got this right, father of Nyx, as well as my father,

Talon—and who knows who else." Alex puzzled out the last bit of Larry's information. "So, Nyx,—that evil goddess in cahoots with my late father in the whole Underworld Revenant coup we barely defeated last month,—is my aunt? Yuck. And the Fates are her children, so that makes them—"

"Yep, the Fates are definitely your cousins," Larry replied, eyeing Alex warily. "Or something like that." He snickered and added, "Those Greek gods are all related, in one way or another—and often more than one."

Alex stood and paced the room. "How much did you know, Larry? Who told you the rest? Is there more? There's more, isn't there?" She plopped onto the bed next to Larry, her intent gaze meeting his sheepish one. "Spill, bud. Now."

Larry quailed under her irritated glare. "Okay, okay. Chill, Alex. I always knew you had divine relatives, but not which gods you're related to. Not until I got here and had a chat with Conor and your aunt. They—we planned on telling you eventually, but we wanted to give you some time to settle in, learn your Keeper duties, recover from the battle in the Underworld..."

"Recover from destroying my father's soul, you mean?" Alex snipped.

"Well, that too."

"Oh, we are all soooo going to have a huge argument about this, and everyone is going to spill ALL the beans. But it'll have to wait." Alex glanced at the clock and winced. "I've only got twenty minutes to get ready for that damned poker party. With my cousins, the Fates, in attendance this time. Well, fuck."

5

EVERYONE BUT ME

After the eventful—and very nearly deadly—poker game, the three Fates retreated to their rooms, chattering about their upcoming shopping trip to Sylvan City. To distract everyone after the tense poker game ended, Maia had suggested Conor escort the goddesses into the city the next day so they could buy some more modern clothing. At least something from the last century or so, especially if they wanted to play tourist and check out San Antonio's sights and amenities. The goddess' crisp, white, full-length togas just wouldn't cut it.

Once the Fates left the room, everyone at the table, ghost and supernatural alike, breathed a mutual sigh of relief. They had all played poker with the Fates—and lived to tell the tale.

The royal tones of England's first Queen Elizabeth broke the silence. "How long are they staying, Alex? I know you're the Cross-roads Keeper, plus they're your family, so you must extend hospitality, but those awful women had better not be planning a long visit." The ancient ghost gave Alex a thin-lipped smile. "You *will* move them along shortly, correct? Those of us who call this Cross-roads home cannot have our very existence threatened at every turn by that psychotic cousin of yours with her bloody scissors of Fate. That is not at all acceptable, Keeper."

Alex stifled a sigh. Liz only called her 'Keeper' when she was royally pissed. Over the past few months, she had formed a tentative relationship with the prickly royal ghost and thought they had gotten past their initial mutual antagonism. "As their host, it would be the height of incivility to ask my cousins how long they plan to stay. Liz. Surely, when you were Queen, you had to host people you didn't want in your home, er, castle?" She couldn't help herself and snarked a final comment. "I don't think the traditional rules of hospitality have changed *that* much in five hundred years, have they?"

The royal ghost narrowed her eyes at Alex, but thankfully ignored her sarcasm. "In my time, if a guest displeased me too much, I'd merely throw them in the Tower or have my guards separate their heads from their bodies. At least after death, my guests were assured of an afterlife. If Atropos uses her wretched scissors on me—or any of the other ghosts here—our very souls will disappear. So yes, I want those harpies gone. Do you hear me, child?" The queen raised her brows quizzically, fully expecting complete acquiescence to her royal command.

Before Alex could open her mouth and get herself in even more trouble by telling off the ghostly termagant, Conor interjected. "Well, Liz, technically, the Fates aren't harpies. Harpies are—"

"I know what harpies are, you impudent man," the queen replied snippily. Fortunately, Liz let Conor distract her, joining in a lively discussion with him and the other ghosts about harpies and other not-so-mythical creatures.

Alex breathed a sigh of relief. Conor had saved the day. But she was still furious with him and the rest of her heart family for withholding information about her divine ancestry. Oh, they were all going to have such a talk at that evening's Keeper training session. She slipped out of the room while everyone was still deep into Conor's supernatural creature conversation and headed back to her room. An afternoon nap sounded fantastic. She was exhausted after the life-threatening poker game she—and everyone else present—had just survived.

Later that evening, after darkness fell, Alex headed to the old barn for yet another Keeper training session. She tried to suppress her simmering anger, knowing it would interfere with her training. Pausing outside the barn door, she breathed deeply and tried to center herself, then entered the barn to find out what type of training she could fail spectacularly at that evening. *Sigh.*

THE LEATHER on Alex's battle gear squeaked as she dodged another blow from Conor's massive paw. "Do we *have* to practice with you in Barghest form?" She gasped breathlessly. "I sincerely doubt I'll be fighting a Hellhound Barghest anytime soon."

Conor's laughing voice filled her mind as his massive, shaggy form circled her, seeking a weakness in her defense. *"You never know, sweets. Besides, I can tell you're mad at me. Consider this your opportunity to fight a Hellhound and live to tell the tale."*

"I want to fight you with words, not swords or my Keeper staff, you idiot," Alex shot back with a stamp of her foot, momentarily dropping her guard in her pique.

Conor took the opening and launched himself at her, the bulk of his massive Hellhound Barghest body carrying them both to the ground and sending Alex's sword clattering harmlessly away. His muzzle crinkled in a grin, revealing a mouthful of lethal canine teeth. "I win."

Alex had held onto her Keeper staff when she fell. She held it up behind Conor's back, gripped it tightly, and poured her magic into it, preparing to give Conor a magical shock he wouldn't soon forget. Her aunt's polite cough from the far side of the arena where they fought made Alex think twice.

"Alex, dear, perhaps we should have the discussion you're after while everyone is still conscious?" Maia stated. She switched her amused gaze to Conor. "Please get off her and shift back into your human form before Alex knocks you out with the massive amount of magic she's just poured into her staff. I'm sure you realize you're only delaying the inevitable argument by toying with her, Conor."

Alex reluctantly released the magic from her Keeper staff and lowered it to the arena's scuffed dirt surface. She didn't break eye contact with Conor, though. She *would not lose* their staring contest. Conor returned her glare then growled low in his throat, his jowls curled in frustration. Then, a spark of mischief bloomed in his luminescent amber eyes, and he opened his jaws wide. Alex realized what he was going to do a split second before Conor's massive canine tongue licked her face from chin to brow. Before she could respond, he jumped nimbly off her and seamlessly shifted into his human form, grinning as he eyed her drool-covered face.

"Eew! That's disgusting!" Alex gasped as she swiped futilely at her wet face as she sat up. A ghostly hand appeared at her side, a large, white handkerchief in its grip. She accepted her aunt's offering and dried her face as she rose to her feet. "Thanks, Aunt Maia."

"You're welcome, dear. Now, how about we have this argument you're so eager for, so we can get it out of the way and go back to training?" Maia's smile held both kindness and steel.

"I want Uncle Vinnie here for this conversation as well. And Larry." Alex replied, peering around the large arena for her furry Familiar, but not seeing him. "He's probably off with his goblin pal … causing trouble, no doubt."

"I like to be comfortable when I'm having a spirited discussion. Why don't we all go sit on the patio set near the fountain?" Maia instructed as she drifted toward the barn's open door, giving Alex and Conor no choice but to follow her. "I've sent word to Vinnie and Larry. They're already waiting for us in the garden. It's such a lovely evening to sit outside."

Alex eyed Conor and shrugged, then they both trailed after the strong-willed ghost into the garden.

~

As she approached the pond with its gushing fountain, Alex spied Larry and his goblin friend, Grenoble, sitting on the wide stone ledge surrounding the water feature. Both were peering over the side into the lily pad covered water. Alex's heart warmed as she recalled the first time she had seen the two together at the pond. They had been having a rowdy game of 'who can pee on the most frogs from the wall?' Alex had scolded them both but promised not to reveal their shenanigans to her aunt, who would have been furious at their misbehavior.

Alex shook her head, banishing the fond memories. Even though they were her chosen heart family, these people, uh, supernaturals, had been lying to her since she arrived. She was *so* done with having information about the supernatural world hidden or withheld from her. She wanted the whole truth this time. Her gaze scanned the gathering, who were now seated comfortably on Maia's cushioned garden furniture. "Alright, everyone, secret time is over. I want the truth—all of it. Don't you think, after what my mother did to me—kidnapping me, then paying a witch to suppress my memories for years, that I deserve more from you lot?"

After a moment of sheepish silence, everyone responded at once, various assurances and denials washing over Alex, until she held her hand up for quiet. "No excuses," she scolded. "You all know things about me I don't and have kept them from me for months." Her angry gaze raked over her assembled heart family. "This is your one chance to be completely honest with me. I need to know the truth so I can process it all and not keep getting blindsided at every turn. A lack of knowledge about the supernatural world and my heritage is more dangerous to me than knowing everything you're all holding back, surely?"

Alex gave the chagrined group a narrow-eyed glare, then sat across from them, on the pond's edge. She put some distance between herself and Larry, since she was still mad at him. "Well? One at a time, please."

After an uncomfortable period of fraught silence while Alex's heart family exchanged questioning glances with each other, Maia finally cleared her throat and stood. Obviously, the group had elected her as their spokesperson.

"Alex, dear, we understand your anger, and your fear that we have been withholding information from you to your detriment, as your mother did. However, that has never been our intention. We all love you so much, Alex. After your mother took you away, we spent the next fifteen years searching for you, to no avail."

The ghost heaved a dejected sigh. "It wasn't until my mur—death almost a year ago that the blood magic the witch your mother hired weakened enough for us to find you. And if I had known when you were first kidnapped that dying would have accomplished that, I'd have made it happen years ago." Maia choked out her last words. The ghost paused and composed herself and then gave Alex a warm smile. "My dear, everything we have done—even that which we have withheld—is because we love you. Perhaps we have misjudged you, though. Larry has assured me repeatedly you are strong enough to know everything we know, so please don't blame Larry for our reticence."

Alex threw a startled glance at her Familiar.

Larry's serious, almost pleading gaze met hers squarely. "I've been telling them from the get-go they should tell you everything. Unfortunately, I couldn't do that, since DEAF bound me to silence when they gave me this assignment. I was told that I had to wait until you found out about the supernatural world and your role in it through other means. I took that to include information about your divine, uh, connections." The little poodle padded along the wall to where Alex sat, then put his paw on her leg. "Sorry, kiddo. I've been in your corner from the start. You know that."

Alex picked up Larry's paw and shook it. "Okay, I forgive you, fur-face." She turned her gaze to the rest of the group. "As for the rest of you. I understand you love me and have been doing what you think is best for me. But I'm here to tell you—what's best for me is the truth. Always."

Conor and Vinnie exchanged a loaded look, then Vinnie nodded once before meeting Alex's enquiring gaze. The vampire's dark eyes gleamed against his ivory pale skin, while his tentative smile revealed his long, razor-sharp fangs. He shifted uncomfortably; emotion was not something Vinnie's generation showed readily. Feelings were considered a weakness—especially in the head of a major New York crime family.

"I certainly understand your feelings, Alex," Vinnie said. He gestured toward the others. "Maia, Conor, and I have had more than a couple conversations over the past few months about how —and when to break certain things to you. I'm sorry you had to find out about some of them like this."

"So, there is more, then?" Alex queried. She gave her honorary uncle a hard look. "Tell me the rest, Uncle Vinnie."

A gravelly voice interrupted the tense standoff between Alex and her adopted uncle. Grenoble, Larry's goblin friend, fixed Alex with his enormous, round eyes. He stood on the pond wall, making him appear taller than his squat three-foot height. "Since everyone seems so hesitant to tell you, I'll do it. But first, understand this, Keeper. Those gathered here today are your allies, not your enemies. It would be well for you to remember this and treat them well." The goblin growled low. "Or I might take back my promise to Larry not to make a tasty meal out of you."

Alex shivered, recalling her aunt's warning the first time she met Grenoble at the very first poker game she attended upon her arrival at the estate. 'Goblins are obligate carnivores, dear, and they prefer their meat raw—and fresh. And they're not too picky about what creature their meat comes from, either.'

Maia's warning to Alex had been about preventing Larry from palling around with Grenoble. However, once Alex realized Larry's true magical power level, which was off the charts, she stopped fearing that the fierce goblin would snack on his new doggy friend. She wasn't so sure about herself, though, and had been heartily glad when Larry had extracted a promise from Grenoble not to harm her.

"I appreciate the warning, Grenoble," Alex informed him. "And I understand completely. What can you tell me?"

The little goblin sat, stretching out his short legs along the stone wall. Then, in blunt words, he told her what she wanted to know. "You have recently discovered that the Primordial god, Chronos, is your paternal grandfather, yes? As you know, the goddess Nyx is Chronos's daughter, which therefore means she's your aunt. Nyx is mother to the Fates, which makes them your cousins. Have you followed me so far?"

Alex nodded her agreement.

"Here's what you may not know," Grenoble continued. "The Fates have three children of their own. Collectively, their children are called the Oneiroi. These three gods have power over the unconscious, including sleep and even nightmares, like the powerful, dangerous ones you were having after your arrival." The goblin hesitated, then heaved a sigh and added, "This means that Morpheus, the Oneiroi that worked in concert with Nyx and your father during their attempt to conquer this Crossroads, is part of your family, too. Morpheus and his two brothers are your nephews, to be precise."

Alex gasped, the memory of Morpheus's efforts to pull her aunt's soul into the Underworld flooding her mind. She fought off the remembered darkness but couldn't help recalling the look on the handsome god's face when she had fought him in the Underworld. He had told her then they would meet again—and that she would not survive their next encounter.

"Great, so Nyx isn't the only family member who wants me dead," she muttered dejectedly.

Grenoble grinned at her, showing off his pointy green teeth. "From what I know of gods and their descendants, trying to kill each other is almost a family requirement. Anyway, based on the research your aunt has done, there are various other gods and their descendants in your paternal family tree. Too many to mention, I'm afraid. You'll just have to deal with your divine relatives as they arise."

"Or as they try to kill me, you mean," Alex grumbled.

"Yep," Grenoble replied with an amused chuckle. "I imagine you could safely say that anyone trying to kill you—or kidnap you—wants to steal your powers, and is almost certainly a relative of yours."

"Well, shit. Just—fucking fuck." Alex grumbled, rubbing her forehead wearily.

"Language, dear," Maia reminded her in gentle reproach.

"Sorry, sorry," Alex replied automatically. Then she straightened and fixed her aunt with a defiant glare. "You know what? No, I'm not sorry. If any situation deserves a hearty 'fuck', it's this one. Besides, you know very well I learned my foul language from Uncle Vinnie as a child." Alex transferred her gaze to her adopted uncle and smiled slyly at the shocked vampire she had just thrown under the proverbial bus.

Before Maia could take Vinnie to task for the foul mouth he had brought with him from his former life as a mobster, which had unfortunately rubbed off on Maia's young, impressionable niece, Conor spoke up. "Um, there's a bit more you don't know, Alex. In fact, no one else here is aware of this information either, as I've just learned it myself. You know I went to Connecticut last week to spy, er, check up on what your mother is up to, right?"

Everyone, including Alex, nodded and eyed Conor warily.

Conor shifted in his chair and cleared his throat. "First, just to relieve everyone's anxiety, it appears Helen—Alex's mother—isn't up to anything more nefarious right now than possibly dealing in stolen antiquities. She hasn't hired another manager to replace Alex. Instead, she's running her antique importing business and staffing the shop all by herself. However, Helen has recently met with some shady characters." Conor huffed in frustration. "Without breaking cover, I couldn't determine if those meetings were related to stolen antiquities or to something more nefarious. Bottom line is that I don't think she's given up her quest to wrest the Keeper position from Alex, so we'll have to keep an eye on her from now on."

He hesitated and gave Alex a look full of empathy, knowing his next words would devastate her. "I did a little digging while I was there and discovered the name of the witch that helped your mother by creating the blood charm used to cloud your memory and hide both of you from our searches over the years. The witch's name was Grindle, and I'm afraid she is—was—your paternal grandmother."

Alex's mind blanked for a second. She recalled the elderly counselor who had lent a sympathetic ear during the months after her move to Connecticut, when she'd been having trouble coping with her aunt's death. Alex had always been thankful to her mother for that one small mercy. Several months ago, when Conor told her the therapist had likely been a witch her mother paid to suppress her memories using magic, she had been so angry. But she had not thought to wonder why such a powerful witch would endanger herself by performing illegal black magic that could earn her the death penalty if the Supernatural Council discovered her efforts.

"What you're saying is that the witch who helped my mother by binding my memories and hiding us both was actually my paternal grandmother—my mother's mother-in-law. That makes a sick kind of sense. But I don't see what was in it for her?" She asked with a helpless shrug. "After all, a witch caught practicing black magic earns a death sentence, right?"

Conor nodded. "Correct. From what I could work out—and it took a lot of digging and a few bribes—your mother paid Grindle a large amount of money, so that's one big reason your grand-mother took the risk." He shrugged one shoulder. "I can only guess at others."

"Which are?" Alex prompted. Then it hit her. "Oh wait. Knowing my father and his insatiable desire for power, I'll bet my mother promised Grindle a cushy position at the Crossroads once I came into my power—and after she killed me for it." She huffed and rolled her eyes. "What the hell! Is *everyone* in my family out to kill me?!"

"Not everyone, Alex," Maia murmured. "Those of us here tonight love you and have only ever wanted the best for you."

Her aunt's soft words helped soothe Alex's anger, and her defensive posture loosened. "I know, Aunt Maia. You guys have done nothing but try to find me after my mother kidnapped me and then help me once I returned to the Crossroads." She issued a sheepish apology. "And yes, you were all right. The information you've shared tonight is a lot. Even more than finding out about the supernatural world and my Keeper heritage. My apologies. You were right to give me some time to process all that before throwing my divine heritage at me. After all, who suspected my cousins, the Fates, would show up at the Crossroads for a family reunion?"

"I did." Larry's bald statement dropped like a stone into the conversation. "I figured Chronos wouldn't wait too long to send someone from the family to check out his long-lost granddaughter —especially after said granddaughter destroyed her father's soul. That's why I've been pressing these yahoos more than ever to tell you. We can try our best to protect you, but you need to know the truth, so you can protect yourself."

Alex blanched. "You mean, my cousins are here to, uh, take me out for killing my father—Chronos's son—even though I did it in self-defense?"

"Nah." Larry shook his head, pink ears flapping against his shoulders. "If your cousins wanted you dead, you'd already be history. No offense, but no one beats the Fates."

"What *do* they want, then?" Alex mused aloud.

"We can answer that if you'd like, Alex." Clotho's deep, rumbly voice shocked the group, who turned to eye the new arrivals suspiciously.

The motherly goddess of Fate smiled at Alex. "We didn't mean to eavesdrop, child. The three of us were just taking a turn around the garden before bed. When we realized this conversation involved us, we couldn't help but listen. I—we thought you might like to hear the truth, from the horse's mouth, so to speak."

"Oh, but we did so mean to eavesdrop, sister. Don't sugarcoat things, sister," Atropos interjected.

Atropos's caustic rejoinder sounded more like the actual truth to Alex. She hid a grin at her rudest cousin's brutal honesty and said, "Pull up a chair, cousins, and join the party." She gestured toward several empty lawn chairs with a casual hand. What did it matter if a few more erstwhile family members joined the discussion? This wily divine trio might have information only the gods would know. They might even be willing to share a minuscule portion of it.

The smallest goddess flitted forward, appearing directly in front of Alex as if out of thin air. Startled, Alex leaned back and almost fell into the pond. Only Larry's teeth on her leather vest prevented a watery splash.

Lachesis whispered into Alex's ear. "We would like to speak with you alone, cousin, if you don't mind. There are things you need to know about our family that are not for outsiders to hear."

Alex studied the birdlike goddess and considered. She could say no. She would feel safer if her heart family stayed close while she spoke with her divine one, but she knew any safety they offered was an illusion. If the Fates wanted you dead, you would be. Simple as that. Suppressing a resigned sigh, she asked her heart family to give her some time alone with her divine cousins.

6

DIVINE DISCUSSION

"I'm staying, and that's all there is to it.*"* Larry crouched on the fountain wall, his small, trembling body pressed against Alex. *"I'm your Familiar, your magical partner and, most of all, your friend."*

Alex's heart warmed. Goddess, she loved this furry little pain in the ass. *"It's okay, Larry. My ... uh, cousins just want to talk."*

"Yeah, that's what they say. But you and I both know you can't help speaking your mind, no matter the consequences. If I'm here, maybe I can keep you outta trouble." Larry eyed Alex doubtfully. *"Or at least, keep you—and me—alive."*

The duo had been mind-speaking to keep their conversation from the waiting goddesses. When Clotho spoke, however, it became clear they had no secrets from the Fates. "You may stay, Familiar Larry. I commend your bravery and loyalty to our cousin." The stout goddess chuckled. "Although I'm not sure either is enough to keep her out of trouble."

Larry nodded. "Thank you, Clotho. I agree Alex is a force all her own, but I try my best with her."

Clotho smiled at the pink-eared poodle approvingly. "We appreciate your efforts on behalf of our cousin, Larry."

The three goddesses reclined on the comfortable garden furniture closest to Alex, who maintained her spot on the stone wall surrounding the pond. Lachesis settled into her padded chair, her small hand stroking the seat cushion thoughtfully. "These chairs are really comfortable. Maybe we could get some for one of the garden patios at our mansion on Mount Olympus, sisters." She pursed her lips and studied the cushion's striped pattern. "Of course, we'd have to get different cushions. These stripes aren't all the same width. That would drive me crazy."

"Crazier," Atropos murmured, then raised her voice. "Yes, sister, that sounds like a good idea. It appears shopping has improved mightily in the several centuries since we last visited Earth. We'll have to take advantage of that while we're here."

Alex figured she should make an effort at small talk, even though she knew at least one of her divine cousins would probably threaten her life during their conversation. A picture of Atropos's ancient, bloody scissors of Fate flashed through her mind, and she shivered involuntarily. She blurted, "I hear Conor is taking you all into Sylvan City to shop tomorrow morning, so that'll be nice, right?"

Uncharacteristically, Clotho was the goddess who cut the small talk short. She nodded to acknowledge Alex's words and said, "I'm sure the shopping will be great. We three plan to do a lot of it while we're here." She flicked a meaningful glance at her sisters and added, "Sisters, how about we dive into the conversation with our cousin that we came here to have?"

All three goddesses nodded in silent agreement, then leaned forward, their intense and more than slightly scary gazes fixed on Alex.

Alex petted Larry gently, his soft, warm fur giving her some comfort as she prepared for the talk of her life with the Fates. "Uh, from what you've told me so far, I gather that you three are my cousins, on my paternal side of the family. Larry has filled me in some more, as has the rest of my—er, heart family."

She stumbled over her words, knowing that long-lost members of her biological family sat facing her. "I understand that the goddess

Nyx is your mother, and that my father, Talon, is her brother. Nyx and Talon share the same father, Chronos. So yes, that all makes us cousins. From what I hear about the divine side of my family, there's a lot of us. Relatives, that is. Including that bastard Morpheus." Alex winced and stopped that line of conversation when she realized that Morpheus's mother was one of the trio sitting across from her. "Um, sooooo, cousins, what exactly do you want to talk about?" Alex asked, bracing herself for the fraught conversation she knew was coming.

One goddess snickered, although Alex wasn't sure which. After a tense moment, Clotho shared a glance with her sisters, then sat forward in her chair and fixed her gaze on Alex. "First, as we've mentioned before, my dear, we wanted to meet our cousin and congratulate her on her new role in the supernatural community. Being a Crossroads Keeper is a big deal." The goddess shrugged one shoulder and added, "Not as big as your divine lineage and relation to us, of course. Even so, it's a start."

"Keep calm, Alex. Remember, no one is better at backhanded compliments that don't quite disguise a putdown than family. And you've got a doozy of a family, girlfriend," Larry warned, his voice urgent in her mind. He stuck his head under Alex's hand, trying to distract her with a request for more pets.

Life with her cold, manipulative mother had given Alex lots of experience in dealing with difficult family members. *Doesn't make it any easier, though,* she reflected ruefully. She nodded politely at the goddesses and said, "Thank you for your congratulations on my appointment as Keeper." Unable to resist a small dig, she added, "Hecate has been very gracious and helpful in helping me adjust to my new role. She and I may not be related. However, as her priestess and chosen Keeper, I like to think of her as a mother figure."

"Mothers can be more trouble than they are worth." Bitterness laced Clotho's words. "With a mother like ours—or yours—it's a wonder we all turned out relatively normal."

Larry snickered. "Pot. Kettle."

Alex gripped his fur and tugged a warning. "I take it you three don't get along with your mother?" That would be a good thing, Alex mused, considering that the last time she saw Nyx, the furious goddess was struggling to escape the inexorable grip of the army of undead Alex had commanded to return to her to her prison at the far reaches of the Underworld.

As far as Alex knew, her late father's undead Regenerants remained loyal to her, as their new necromantic mistress, and were currently fulfilling her last command: keep Nyx in her undead Regenerant body to control her divine powers and make sure she stayed out of trouble and remained under house arrest in her no doubt luxurious mansion prison at the hind-end of the Underworld.

Atropos's harsh voice cut through the night air. "No, our mother is definitely not someone we associate with any longer. The woman is a total psychopath. Always has been. We also know that she has corrupted at least one of our children as well." Sadness flickered across her thin face, then her features hardened. "Nyx and Morpheus deserve each other."

Her icy words both warmed and chilled Alex. At least her cousins weren't here to exact revenge on behalf of their power-hungry mother. Atropos's explanation helped explain her psychopathy, though—even if she couldn't see it and her sisters remained determined to ignore it.

"Um, so, if your visit isn't about your moth—uh, Nyx, or your misbehaving kids, then..." Alex let the words hang, hoping the goddesses would get to the point. She was so damned tired of having to drag the truth out of everyone.

Clotho shifted in her seat, nodding in understanding as if she had heard Alex's thoughts. Maybe she had. Alex suppressed a shiver at the thought.

"I understand your concern, dear, but you've nothing to fear from any of us." Clotho could not disguise the quick glance she flicked at Atropos. "Well, from most of us."

"At least she's honest." Larry's snarky, mind-spoken quip helped settle Alex's nerves.

Atropos lost patience with the pace of the conversation and interrupted Clotho. "Listen, Alex. We're here because our mutual grandfather, Chronos, asked us to come. As you can imagine, he has quite a few descendants. Since going into semi-retirement a few millennia ago—after that whole mess with the Olympians— he rarely pays much attention to family matters ... or much of anything, really. He only comes to Earth once every generation or so to, ah, scratch an itch."

Clotho gave her sister a warning glance and took up the conversational reins again. "When you suddenly came into your death magic powers a few months ago, Alex, Chronos felt it." The goddess looked at her sisters for confirmation, then turned her warm gaze back to Alex. "We three felt your unique power signature as well. Chronos immediately realized you had inherited his powerful death magic and asked us to make sure you knew how to use it appropriately, since we're the only other descendants of his to inherit his death magic."

Alex snorted. "You mean Chronos realized I had inherited necromantic powers from my father—who *was* trying to kill me at the time, mind you—and then used said power to end his immortal soul?" A niggling worry emerged. "Um, so how exactly does Chronos feel about my father's death? Talon is—was his son, while I'm only his granddaughter, I mean."

Clotho reassured her. "Oh, our mutual grandfather is perfectly alright with you using your death magic to end your father's soul, dear." The goddess gave Atropos an enigmatic look and added, "In fact, he's been asking us to get around to cutting Talon's soul cord for quite a while now."

The goddesses started bickering among themselves, reviving what was obviously an old argument with no end in sight.

"I told you we should have done it when grandfather first asked."

"But, sister, we were having so much fun at that lovely war in—"

"And then we were busy redecorating the mansion."

Alex realized the goddess's animated discussion could go on all night. It was well after midnight, and she was so tired she didn't even feel scared anymore. "Ladies, can we please get back to the reason you're here? You said that Chronos wants you to train me in how to control my, um, death magic. I promise you I have absolutely no intention of using necromancy to raise any dead bodies, so maybe we can call it good?"

The goddesses stopped arguing and turned amused gazes on Alex.

Clotho gave Alex a sympathetic smile. "You really don't understand, do you, child? Necromancy is only a tiny part of your inherited magical powers, Alex. Your father was a powerful necromantic mage, that's true. But that's really all Talon could do—raise a dead body or three. And he never used his powers for good." She shook her head, her eyes dark with memory. "Always wanting to take over the world, that one."

Alex wondered what actual good could come from inserting souls into dead bodies and reanimating them, but she didn't dare ask. "So, you're saying I've inherited than just necromantic powers?" Dread formed a worried lump in her gut. "Exactly what does this death magic you keep saying I have encompass?"

"Anything we three can do, you can do, too," Atropos stated baldly, giving Alex a narrow-eyed glare. "Which doesn't make me all too happy, as cutting life and soul threads is *my* job. In fact, it was my job to end your father, but you got there first." The skeletal goddess rolled her eyes. "However, since you're my cousin, I'll forgive you. This time."

The enormity of Atropos's words hit Alex. Heart pounding in fear, nausea swept through her. "You mean I can kill people with this death magic?"

Atropos sighed and shook her head. "Perhaps my initial low

assessment of your intelligence was accurate. How do you think you ended your father's soul? You did it with death magic, you fool. Necromancers like your father can't do that. They can merely reanimate dead human bodies by binding a soul within, and then command that soul to do their bidding. That's about it as far as necromancy goes."

"Oh." Alex's head spun and her worldview shifted. "So, you're telling me I used death magic, not necromancy, to destroy my father's soul, and that doing so alerted Chronos of my existence?"

"Yes," the three Fates chorused.

"What does Chronos want you to train me to do?" Alex swallowed, her throat tight and dry. "Look, I'm not really interested in helping you guys with the whole life and death thing, if that's okay." She shook her head vehemently and held up her hands. "That gig is all yours. Really. Besides, I'm not a goddess—right? And you really don't need a fourth. Please say no."

Clotho smiled at her gently, her eyes twinkling with amusement. "No, dear, we don't need your help. We've been handling the tapestry of life—and death—almost since time began. As to your other question, no, you're not a full goddess, since your grandmother was merely a supernatural. However, the death magic you inherited from your grandfather, Chronos, makes you a demigoddess, at the very least." Clotho eyed Alex with a surprising amount of respect. "Death magic is a Primordial power, dear. Such a power has never before manifested outside of those with one-hundred percent divine blood. That makes you unique."

"Uh, I don't think this sort of being unique is a good thing, Alex." Larry's worried words slipped into Alex's racing mind.

Alex flicked Larry a glance and nodded mutely, then studied the trio of goddesses facing her warily. "Soooo, you're saying I'm a demi-goddess? Is that something I can abdicate from or renounce, like being a queen?" She shook her head firmly and gazed earnestly at the divine trio seated across from her. "How about I just promise never to use my death magic again? Like ever." She wanted no part of any Primordial god's magic—ancestor or not—especially not one involving power over life and death.

Larry snickered and the goddesses roared with laughter.

"She wants to abdicate!" Chuckled Lachesis.

"She thinks she can just turn her back on her Primordial powers!" Snapped Atropos indignantly.

Only Clotho seemed to understand Alex's concerns. The motherly goddess murmured, "I'm so sorry, child."

Alex raked everyone with a narrow-eyed glare. "Alrighty, then. Enough with the hilarity. From your reactions, I'm guessing I can't just walk away from this death magic thing. Instead, perhaps we can agree that I've got enough on my plate right now with mastering my Crossroads Keeper duties? I'll be happy to train with you all in the future once I've got a handle on my Keeper magic." Alex planned to make damn sure that date was way, way in the future. A couple of decades at least. "How about we make this visit a 'get to know you' one, and discuss my death magic training another time?"

The Fates exchanged considering glances. As the minutes stretched on, Alex realized the trio were having a mind conversation. After several long, tense moments, the divine sisters seemed to come to an agreement.

Clotho turned to face Alex and said, "Alright, my dear. We agree you must honor your commitment to Hecate and learn your Keeper duties well, as ley line intersections such as this Crossroads are critical to the free movement of gods, as well as supernaturals and ghosts. For that reason, we'll limit this visit to a family reunion only. We'll just tell Chronos we've met you and made you aware of your unique Primordial power."

Three pairs of intense eyes pinned Alex in place as Clotho warned, "But you must promise us you won't try to use your death magic again without our training. You could have taken out half the Underworld with the amount of death magic you used to destroy your father's soul, my dear."

Alex's eyes widened, and she gripped Larry's fur so tightly he yelped. "Hey, loosen up a little, Alex. That hurts!"

"Sorry, buddy," she muttered, releasing her death grip on her poor Familiar's fur and stroking her hand softly down his body in mute apology.

Meeting Clotho's enquiring gaze, Alex nodded her agreement. "I promise to be more careful. And I swear to you that I have no intention of using death magic again anytime soon. I just—I didn't know."

Now that she had extracted Alex's promise not to use her death magic until they had properly trained her, Clotho relaxed and smiled kindly at her. "Of course, you didn't know about your death magic, dear. Until a few months ago, neither did we—or your grandfather, for that matter."

Atropos snorted in disgust. "And he's the Primordial god of Time, so he damn well should have known, the moron."

Alex eyed the sky warily, fearing bolts of lightning would strike soon because of Atropos's disrespectful words. "Uh, maybe we should watch who we insult," she protested softly.

Larry started laughing again and the three divine sisters joined him. Lachesis, usually the quietest of the goddesses, stopped laughing long enough to correct Alex's misconception. "That's Zeus you're thinking of, cousin. Our mutual grandfather doesn't stoop to mere lightning. Chronos could smite us all dead with a thought—if he had a mind to."

"Oh, that makes me feel *so* much better," Alex retorted. Then she saw the humor in her fears, real as they were, and started laughing, if a little hysterically.

7

OPPOSITES ATTRACT

Alex and Larry strolled down the garden path toward their room. Their meeting with the Fates had broken up shortly after everyone had finished laughing at Alex's expense. Before heading back to their rooms, the goddesses had asked Alex for shopping recommendations for their upcoming trips into San Antonio and Sylvan City, and Alex had been happy to oblige. Anything to avoid discussing demi-goddesses and death magic.

Just before they reached the path leading to their room, Larry took a sharp left. "I'm outta here. The kitchen isn't far, and it's definitely time for a midnight snack," he called over his shoulder as he loped away into the darkness.

"Don't ask me if I'm hungry or anything. Just take off, why don't you?" Alex murmured absently as she turned onto the short path leading back to her room.

"He knew I was waiting for you, sweets. Probably wanted to give us some privacy."

Conor's deep voice startled Alex. Suppressing a sigh, she stopped short and gazed at the very attractive man—er, Hellhound Barghest. He lounged on the steps leading up to her room, blocking her route to the comfortable bed she'd been craving for hours. She was really not in the mood for another deep conversation tonight, yet her heart still skipped a beat at the sight of Conor's leanly muscled form. She shut those errant thoughts right down. Barghests could smell sexual attraction—an embarrassment and distraction Alex absolutely did not need right now.

"Hi Conor. What do you want?" Alex asked shortly, not having the energy to feign politeness. She admitted to herself that Conor's casual sexiness also contributed to her grumpy tone.

Conor merely raised a brow, then rose smoothly to his feet, put his hands in his pockets, and gazed off into the garden, his face inscrutable. If she didn't know better, Alex would think her shifter Guardian was feeling uncomfortable. *Nah. Never happen.* He was always so self-assured, forthright, and downright irritatingly self-confident. He was also a smartass. A cute one, though, she had to admit.

He flicked a glance at Alex and cleared his throat. "I, uh, just wanted to make sure you got back to your room safely, that's all. The conversation with your psycho—killer cousins could have turned deadly. I'm glad to see it didn't."

Alex narrowed her eyes at Conor; she could swear a blush stained the irritating man's sharply defined cheeks. Attempting to keep her tone neutral, she replied, "Thanks for your concern. I had a pleasant chat with my cousins, thanks—and they're not *all* psychos." *Okay, pleasant was a stretch,* she mused. *And Atropos was definitely psycho enough for all three of the Fates.* "I even gave 'em some tips on shops they should visit when you take them into town tomorrow morning—I mean, later today." It was very late; morning wasn't more than a few hours away.

When Conor merely nodded, but didn't move, she huffed a sigh and murmured, "If there's nothing else?" When he didn't reply, Alex awkwardly approached so she could slide past him and head up the stairs—to bed, at last. Between her exhaustion and her hormones, the confusion between her tired mind and heated body was just too much to deal with right now. "Good night, Conor. See you in the morning."

Conor's next words came out in a rush. "I just wanted to remind you we have a date to train on ley line magic tomorrow afternoon. I mean, not a date. A training session. You know—definitely not a date."

Now that she was closer to him, Alex had a clearer view of Conor's face. He *was* blushing. "That's not what you really wanted to say, was it?" She asked softly.

"No."

"Okay then."

With a lightning-quick movement, Conor caught Alex around the waist, crushed her body to his and captured her lips in a scorching kiss. Her fatigue vanished in a haze of desire; she wrapped her arms around his shoulders and leaned into the embrace, her lips parting for his searching tongue.

A harsh command abraded the night air. "Take it upstairs, you two." Queen Elizabeth's ghost floated down the walkway toward them, her thin lips pursed in disapproval. "I'd like to enjoy my midnight stroll without being subjected to such a rude display of carnality."

Alex turned her head to face the queen, but stayed in Conor's embrace. "You're just jealous, Liz." She purred with a lazy smile.

The ancient royal sniffed in disdain. "Of what? You? Don't be daft, girl. I could have Conor—if I wanted him. In my day, *all* the men wanted to sleep with me."

"Behave, Liz." Conor's voice held a stern warning. "And no, you couldn't have me—even if you weren't a ghost. We've talked about this before. Friend zone only. Remember?"

"You'll never know what you're missing." The queen's lips curved in a baiting smile. "Ghosts can go all night."

Alex's eyes rounded, and she spluttered a laugh. "Liz! I can't believe you just said that." She reluctantly separated herself from Conor's embrace and gave the diminutive ghost a narrow-eyed stare. "That's slutty. And catty. I expected better of you, Your Highness. After all, you're always lecturing *me* about *my* behavior." *Oops, here I go again, insulting a queen*, Alex thought, with a touch of wonder at her never-ending ability to speak without thinking.

Before Alex could apologize to the now-frowning ghostly royal, Conor backed her up. "Alex has a fair point, Liz. What's up with you tonight?"

The ghost transferred her glare from Alex to Conor. After a tense moment, she grinned at him. "Merely testing Alex's mettle, Conor, my dear. Making sure she knows what she has in you." With that parting shot, the ancient queen raised her chin and resumed her stately float down the walkway.

Bemused, they both watched the departing ghost until she disappeared from view.

Hiding a smile, Alex couldn't help baiting Conor. "What exactly *do* I have in you, Conor? What the heck was that kiss all about? I thought we agreed to take things slow—like really slow, at least until I'm fully trained. Isn't there some rule about there being a power imbalance if teachers and students get involved in a relationship?"

Conor shuffled his feet, his eyes fixed on the graveled path, then he raised blazing amber eyes to meet Alex's. "There's definitely a major power imbalance between us, sweets, but it's not me that has more power and magic—it's you, by far. You *must* know that. But I'm still interested and would like to build a relationship with you in the future. A romantic one—well, you know."

The strength, honesty, and truth of Conor's words floored Alex. She had spent the last several months tamping down her growing attraction to the sexy Hellhound Barghest shifter. While Conor had made no secret of his sexual attraction to her, often joking that, as a shifter with acute senses, he could smell her desire for him, they had agreed to keep things light. Teacher and student. Friends only. At least she thought they had an agreement. The battle in the Underworld several months ago had almost ended in disaster because of Alex's lack of training; she had realized then that she couldn't put the Crossroads at risk by diverting her attention from learning her Keeper job properly.

"But I thought we agreed—" Alex stuttered.

"I never agreed to anything," Conor drawled. He shook his head, his warm eyes intent on hers. "You told me you wanted to concentrate on your training, so I've kept us on that task. Until now. Plus, I knew you had a lot to process after the Underworld battle."

"The Underworld battle during which I killed my father, you mean?" Alex retorted, rolling her eyes at him. "Why the heck does everyone keep bringing that up? It was self-defense. I realize that. There may still be a few things I have to work out about it, but I'll get there." She shrugged one shoulder defensively, knowing her words didn't quite match her conflicted feelings.

"You mean, like the fact that you used Primordial death magic to destroy your father's very soul?" Conor inquired softly.

"You heard my conversation with the Fates, then," Alex replied with a sigh, her weariness returning in force. "Your extra-special Hellhound Barghest hearing came in handy during my conversation with my cousins tonight, I take it. Where were you hiding?"

"At the edge of the gardens, on the path to the Crossroads. Vinnie was with me. We were prepared to intervene if things got, uh, dicey."

"Oh, and get yourselves killed?" Alex interrupted, her ire rising. She glared at him and growled, "Don't you dare do that! Either of you. Not on my behalf. The Fates are my cousins; they're my problem, not yours." More softly, she added, "Plus, if anything happens to me, you'll both need to take over at the Crossroads. Again."

Alex's eyes widened when she realized what she was asking of Conor, and she gazed at him in horror. "Oh, fuck, how could I forget? If I die, and the Crossroads goes without a Keeper for too long, its magic will become unstable again. As the Crossroads Guardian, your life is bound to the magic of the ley lines here. An unstable Crossroads would soon drain your magic dry. You'd get stuck in your Hellhound Barghest form, lose your sanity and—"

Conor's expression was grim. "And eventually, I'd lose my

life, as someone would have to put me down. Never fear, Vinnie's already agreed to take care of that minor matter if it ever arises." He forced a smile. "But you're here now, Alex. A properly bonded Keeper and very much alive. Let's keep it that way. Please."

An unpleasant thought struck Alex. Could Conor be seeking a relationship with her to ensure she stayed on as the Crossroads Keeper? After all, she had threatened more than once to leave and return to her 'normal' life in the human world.

"I'd *never* stoop to that," Conor spat.

Alex felt Conor's anger and dismay to her very soul. *Damn it! Their magical connection had allowed him to sense the path her thoughts had taken.*

"I'm sorry. I didn't mean..." Alex stammered an apology.

Conor crossed his arms and glared at her. "Oh yes, you did. You suspected—at least for a moment—I might have ulterior motives for pursuing a relationship with you." He softened his gaze and shook his head. "Look, sweets, I understand your ex-fiancé hurt you badly when you found out he had been cheating on you."

"Ya think?!" Alex retorted. "I found the scumbag in a lip lock with my damn mother, for the gods' sake. That's enough to turn anyone off dating for the foreseeable future." She remembered the awful scene clearly. Arriving early for her shift at the antique shop she managed for her mother, she had heard whispers and soft laughter. Upon entering the back office, she had found her mother and her fiancé in a passionate embrace. Alex's fiancé had spotted her first and jumped away from Helen, hurriedly wiping a hand across his lipstick-covered mouth. What had hurt even worse than her fiancé's betrayal was the small, smug smile on her mother's face. Alex had thrown the shop keys on the floor, muttered curtly that she quit, and fled the shop. Despite her mother's many angry voicemails since, Alex had never returned, nor had she spoken with the woman since.

"It's been almost a year since that happened, Alex," Conor

said, running a hand through his shoulder-length black hair in frustration. "And I'm not your ex-fiancée."

Despite his efforts to control it, Alex heard the hurt in Conor's voice. *Damn it.* She really hadn't meant to hurt him. She had just— well, she'd been avoiding acting on their mutual attraction to protect her heart. And because she was an idiot. Here she was, self-sabotaging what could be a great relationship with an amazing and handsome man—er, Hellhound Barghest, just because she didn't want to get hurt, again.

"You think I'm amazing?" Conor murmured, amber eyes gleaming with sly amusement. "And handsome?"

Alex gasped in shock, her face flaming with embarrassment. "I thought you said you couldn't read my mind through our magical connection. That you just get a general idea of my mood and feelings."

"Alex, your face is an open book to me. I don't need to read your mind to know what you're thinking." Conor smiled mischievously and sniffed the air. "Or feeling. Hellhound Barghest here, remember?"

"You're avoiding the question," Alex pointed out. "And I'm darn sure that my face didn't say 'I think Conor is amazing and hand-some', so you must have read my mind." She glared at Conor, hands on hips, but the irritating man's smug grin didn't waver.

"I told you he could read your mind when you don't have your mental shields up—which is most of the time, Alex." Larry's sly words slid into Alex's mind just before the little poodle appeared, trotting merrily down the path towards them. *"Haven't you guys worked out your relationship problems yet? I took a ton of time over my midnight snack and had a lovely chat with Henri and Grenoble while I was at it to give you guys some space. And yet, here you both are, still talking at cross purposes."*

Larry glanced between them in disgust and spoke out loud. "Look, you two, I'm tired and I wanna go to bed. And I know you're exhausted, Alex. So how about I sort out your mutual dilemma for you?" Giving Conor a grumpy glare, Larry asked him, "You want to ask Alex on an official date, right? A date, date, not a 'let's be friends' dinner, but the real deal. Candlelight, hand-holding, and maybe a smooch or two. That's why you're here tonight. Yes?" Larry's enquiring eyes met Conor's narrowed ones.

After a brief staring contest, Conor dropped his gaze. "Yeah, that's one reason I waited here tonight."

"Okay, now we've got that established." Larry turned his gaze to Alex. "And you would like to go out with this goofy guy, right? We both know you've had the hots for him since you first spotted him at the arrivals lounge at the airport. But you've been doing your best to delay or sabotage things because you're afraid of getting hurt. Again. Am I right?"

Alex didn't bother with a staring contest because Larry, the freaking obnoxious little furball, was absolutely right. She rolled her eyes and admitted the truth. "Yes, I'd like to go out with Conor and, uh, see where things go."

"Good. Now that's settled," Larry stated with a firm nod. He padded by the embarrassed pair and trotted up the stairs, before turning his head and grinning at them over his shoulder. "You guys have a reservation at Vinnie's restaurant for tomorrow night." Squinting up at the moon, he added, "Well, now that morning's not far off, make that tonight. Seven o'clock. Romantic table in the corner, candles, the whole thing. It's a date. Be there or be square." The little poodle yawned widely. "I'm going to bed. Are you coming, Alex?"

Conor and Alex exchanged exasperated and slightly embarrassed glances.

After several moments of awkward silence, Conor recovered first. He gave Alex a cheeky grin and said, "So, it's a date, then, sweets." Before she could reply, he turned on his heel and strode away.

Alex huffed a laugh and spoke to his retreating form. "Yep, it's a date, you dufus." Then she trudged up the stairs after her perfectly obnoxious Familiar. It was way past time for bed.

8

GIFTS FROM BEYOND THE GRAVE

Even though exhausted, Alex had trouble getting to sleep. She dozed off just as the pink rays of dawn lit the sky outside her bedroom window and then slept until almost noon, her restless sleep punctuated by dark dreams of death and violence. The dreams were nothing new. They had been plaguing her since the battle in the Underworld. Despite what she had told Conor, Alex knew she had unresolved emotions about her father's betrayal and his soul's ultimate death at her hands.

She woke slowly, eventually sitting up and rubbing her eyes with a sigh. At least last night's dreams were just run-of-the-mill nightmares, not the god-induced night horrors dangerous enough to kill she had experienced after her arrival. Her not-so-loving cousin, Morpheus, had plagued her with the night horrors in the run-up to the decisive battle in the Underworld several months ago. At his grandmother, Nyx's, bidding, the god had used his divine power over sleep to incapacitate or kill those defending the Crossroads. Instead, Alex and her team had won the Underworld battle and returned Nyx to her prison at the edge of the Under-world. Morpheus had escaped, but Alex knew the rebel god would be back to exact his revenge on her one day. He had told her so.

"You okay?" Larry asked before crawling across the quilt and shoving his head under Alex's hand for pets. "Your thoughts are pretty dark this morning. I think you need some food."

Alex gave her magical partner a reluctant grin as she stroked his soft fur. "I'm fine, dude. You think food fixes everything, don't you?"

"Doesn't it?" Larry asked with a grin, his long pink tongue hanging out between sharp canines. "I'm pretty sure pancakes can cure just about anything."

"You already had pancakes for breakfast?" Alex eyed Larry with concern. "Henri needs to stop feeding you so much sugar. It's not good for dogs."

"I've told you a million times, I'm an eternal magical Familiar," he protested. "I can eat as much or as little as I like. Sugar. Carbs. Meat. All of it. And I don't gain weight, have high cholesterol, or get cavities. It's frikkin' amazing!"

Larry's sly eyes told Alex that his statement was not quite the whole truth.

"You're honestly telling me that your physical body doesn't need proper nutrition to function well?" She cocked her head and eyed the little poodle in consideration. "So, you could eat anything —or even nothing at all, and you'd be just fine, right? How about we stop feeding you, then? Or just give you cheap kibble and nothing else. Either option would save me a bunch of money, since you eat like a horse." Alex smothered a smile and waited for Larry's response. She knew she had backed him into a conversational corner.

Larry gave Alex his wide-eyed innocent look. "Um, well, I didn't actually *say* that my physical body doesn't need any proper nutrition, did I?" His ears drooped. "It's just that—oh hell. You win this round. I'll try to eat better—most of the time. But I'm not giving up my nightly kitchen raids. Snacks are a critical part of my philosophy regarding living a happy life." He nodded firmly and then shook his head, his pink ears flapping wildly.

Alex burst out laughing at the little dog's antics. Life with the sassy, snarky—and magical—canine she called Larry the Kibble

Guy was certainly never boring. "Okay, that sounds fair, bud. Healthier eating, at least most of the time. Plus, midnight snacks to keep your happiness meter pegged."

"Deal." Larry placed his paw in Alex's hand, and they shook on it.

~

CONOR SENT Alex word that they would have to reschedule their afternoon ley-line training session. Apparently, the Fates had been keeping him busy with their mega shopping spree—and they still weren't finished. After cleaning out the shops in Sylvan City, the divine trio had prevailed upon Conor to ferry them to a late lunch at the San Antonio Botanical Gardens and then on to the River-walk to hit a few shops there.

Alex sighed with relief at the news. She wasn't looking forward to the ley-line training and had put it off several times with the explanation that she didn't feel ready to tackle the leys on her own. The truth was more mundane. She found ley line travel disorienting, even *with* a guide. Once immersed in a ley, she lost all sense of time and space and felt trapped in a noisy, howling maelstrom. Plus, she was almost always violently nauseous after-wards. Not a good look for a Crossroads Keeper, but there you go. Mastering the leys was one aspect of her training she would happily put off as long as possible.

Instead, after a delicious lunch prepared by the indomitable Henri, Alex spent the afternoon alternately panicking about her upcoming date with Conor and wishing she had gone shopping with her cousins, as her wardrobe was woefully inadequate. Cross-roads Keeper fighting leathers? Check. Aunt Maia had stocked her up on those. Casual clothes? Check. She had tons of those. But her dress-up wardrobe was incredibly sparse. Once she had committed to moving back to San Antonio permanently, she had cleared out her apartment in Connecticut and donated most of her furniture and clothes to charity. Most of her New England clothes would have been way too warm for the steamy southern Texas weather, anyway. She hadn't really had the time for shopping sprees since her arrival.

~

Just as she gave up and reached for the little black dress she'd worn for the few formal occasions she had attended in the past that required such attire, a heavy thud sounded outside the front door.

Moments later, Larry's disembodied head appeared, framed by the doggie door Conor had recently installed. "Hey! Open the door. I can't fit this ginormous box through this damned doggie door."

Frowning in confusion, Alex opened the door and peered down at her Familiar. An enormous—expensively wrapped—gift box sat by his side, dwarfing Larry's small poodle body.

Larry grinned up at her and said, "Maia is busy in Sylvan City this afternoon. She's got a Town Council committee meeting. That woman is holding onto her Council membership with both ghostly hands. She tells me she's working harder now than before she died." He rolled his eyes and pointed his muzzle at the massive box beside him. "Anyway, your aunt stopped in at her favorite boutique before her meeting and picked out a few things for you. She says to try them on and send anything you don't like back. Her treat."

"What is she, psychic?" Alex muttered, eyeing the large gift box apprehensively. "How the heck did she know I'd be contemplating the sorry state of my wardrobe this afternoon? Wait! Don't answer that. You told her about my date, didn't you?" She gave her Familiar narrow-eyed look. "Also, since when does my late aunt have money to spend? She's a ghost. That's how her attorney boyfriend got me to travel down here in the first place ... so he could explain the—very impressive—extent of the estate I inherited from her."

Larry nudged the box. "You gonna bring this thing in or let it bake outside in the sun?" He cocked his head questioningly. "Don't you want to see what lovely things the money you inherited has purchased for you?"

A bittersweet, yet amused smile crossed Alex's face. "What you're saying is that 'her treat' means Maia paid using the money I inherited from her. *Of course* she did." She sighed and nodded. "I wish—"

"You wish you could have gone shopping with your aunt when she was still alive, but you missed all that because of that bitch of a mother of yours," Larry replied gently. "Well, the next best thing is here, waiting on the porch. Just like me. Waiting on the porch..."

Alex's eyes widened when she realized her Familiar wanted to see what was in the massive gift box as much as she did. "Why, you little toad. Are you a closet shopaholic? Maybe I should take you shopping for some new blingy collars."

"Now, wait just a doggone minute," Larry replied as he backed away, shaking his head in horror. "First of all, I'm soooo not a toad. Luckily, that's one form I've never had to take in any of my Familiar incarnations, thank the gods. Second, we've discussed my collar preferences before. You promised—no bling, remember? Or I'll crap in your shoes." He shot past her and jumped on the bed then gave her a reproachful look.

Snickering at Larry's protestations, Alex retrieved the large gift box from the porch and placed it on the bed next to her grumpy Familiar. "I remember, fur-face. No bling. And you'd better keep your promise, too. No crapping in my shoes—or anyone else's, for that matter." She grinned and asked, "What is it you would like to shop for, then?"

"You."

Larry's simple statement warmed Alex's heart. She reached out and stroked her Familiar's soft topknot. "Oh, Larry. You are so sweet."

"Uh, no, I'm not. Massive junkyard dog on the inside, remember? I can't help this obnoxious poodle body DEAF lumbered me with." Larry sneezed in disgust. "It's just that your wardrobe—dayum girl, does it need a makeover! Sometimes, I'm embarrassed to be seen with you."

Alex didn't argue. Larry was right. She had been living in shorts and tank tops or Keeper combat leathers since her arrival. Pulling the box closer, she murmured, "Let's see what Aunt Maia's idea of my style is, shall we?"

Inside the box, she found an array of lovely—and very expensive-looking clothes. Alex had never been a fashionista, but she knew quality when she saw it. Maybe it was a good thing her aunt had left her a rather extraordinary fortune. There was not a single article of expensive clothing in the gift box that she didn't love. Her heart contracted with gratitude and love for her aunt—and for the rest of her heart family.

Alex spent the rest of the afternoon trying everything on and laughing at Larry's snarky style and fashion commentary, most of which was positive—and hilarious.

9

———

FIRST DATE

"Have a good evening, Alex! Don't do anything I wouldn't do," Larry barked with a wag of his tail and a huge grin. "I won't wait up for you. But please let me know if you'll be bringing Conor back to the room so I can make myself scarce."

"Larry! It's a first date, you numbskull." Alex's face burned in embarrassment at her Familiar's teasing words. "Conor and I will have a nice evening, then say good night. Maybe one kiss. Maybe. And that's it." She tried to convince herself she didn't want more than that with Conor. She had to admit that she absolutely did—but not yet. This thing between them felt real, but she also had to work professionally with the man every day for the foreseeable future. So, she was going to make damn sure before—

"Good idea," Larry agreed, making himself comfortable on the bed. "You both should take things slow. Just some kissy face. Maybe with tongue."

"Stay out of my mind, fur-face."

"Sure thing, partner."

Alex snapped the door shut on Larry's grinning face, straightened her elegant new dress, admired her comfortable new sandals, and headed out on her first date in what seemed like forever. She had insisted on meeting Conor at the restaurant for several reasons. For one thing, it would feel more like a date if they didn't arrive together. Plus, she really wanted to drive the brand new, cherry-red sports car she had treated herself to after the whole Underworld fiasco. She'd been so busy with Keeper training over the past several months that she never had enough time to drive it.

When Alex arrived at the restaurant, her Uncle Vinnie welcomed her and led her to a semi-private table set in a private alcove, screened by lush greenery. From the merry twinkle in her adopted uncle's dark eyes, Alex realized everyone must know this dinner with Conor was a real date. *Sigh.*

"You look stunning, sweets."

Conor's compliment came from behind Alex, and she twirled around to face him, face reddening at the warmth in his words. "Uh, thanks. Aunt Maia did some shopping for me this morning. She has great taste in clothes."

"It's not the clothes, Alex," Conor replied, his amber eyes filled with heat. "You'd look great in anything, or noth—" he paused and flicked a nervous glance at Vinnie, desire and dismay battling for dominance on his darkly handsome face.

"You'd better not finish that thought, you mangy hound dog," Vinnie growled. "I strongly suggest being on your best behavior tonight is your ... ah, healthiest option, Conor."

"Uncle Vinnie!" Alex exclaimed, aghast—if slightly tickled—at her vampire uncle's protectiveness. "Please don't threaten Conor."

Conor just grinned easily. The vampire's pointed threat had given him time to recover his composure. "It's okay, sweets. Vinnie's all hot air, and he knows better than to tangle with me. I'd flatten his vampire ass."

After giving his soon-to-be-ex friend a final narrow-eyed glare, Vinnie left the two of them in peace and waved a server over as he walked away.

Conor gestured to the table. "Shall we sit?"

"Sure," Alex murmured as she settled into the chair Conor held out for her.

After placing their drinks and dinner orders, the two eyed each other uncertainly.

"So, what now?" She murmured, nervously smoothing the cloth napkin in her lap.

"Now, we do the date thing," Conor replied as he picked up his wineglass.

"Okay."

"Great."

"Oh, for all the gods' sake, will you two just talk to each other like normal supernaturals who have the hots for each other?" The annoying words came from over their heads. "You don't bite, either of you. That's Vinnie's thing, right?" Maniacal laughter echoed from the room's high ceiling.

Alex glanced up and spotted Crazy Sam hanging from the exposed rafter directly over their table. The nineteenth-century ghost wore his usual: full cowboy gear—right down to silver spurs, chaps, and bolo tie.

The ghost waved his tattered cowboy hat and grinned down at them. "I won haunting rights for Vinnie's restaurant at last week's poker game." He whooped before launching himself off the beam and swooping around the dining room, flicking hats, tugging napkins, and tipping an almost empty wine glass over before returning to his roost directly over Alex and Conor's table. "Course, none of us ghosts won haunting rights at this week's game, since your crazy cousin cheated her butt off, so I thought I'd use last week's prize and drop by for a quick haunt." The dead cowboy crossed his arms and swung upside-down from the rafter, eyeing Alex meaningfully.

She heaved a defeated breath and said, "Okay, I get the message, Sam. I'll make sure my divine cousins don't horn in on your poker game again. Can we have some peace now? You've got haunting rights tonight, so ... go haunt." She shooed the ghost away, waving vaguely at the other diners scattered around the large restaurant.

"Alright, I'll leave you two yahoos in peace." The ghost grinned widely, then winked at Alex. "We're all rooting for you!"

After Crazy Sam flew off to enjoy his haunting rights, Conor and Alex grinned at each other, amused by the ghost's antics. Sam's interruption had served its purpose, and they slipped into casual conversation, enjoying their dinner and each other's company.

"Can I get you anything else?" The efficient but unobtrusive server asked as he removed their dessert plates and refilled their coffee cups.

"Just the bill, please," Conor replied.

"Oh, there's no bill tonight, sir. Mr. Vincent said, it's his treat. Including the tip." The server smiled and slipped away.

"That damned vampire. I'm gonna pay him back every penny," Conor growled.

"Why you?" Alex inquired innocently. "I enjoyed tonight's meal, too. I could just as easily say I'm going to pay Vinnie back. After all, he's *my* uncle." She suppressed a grin and observed Conor's consternation with glee.

He opened his mouth to reply, then snapped it shut. "There's nothing I can say that won't get me in trouble, is there?"

"Nope, there isn't." After letting Conor stew for a minute, Alex grinned and let him off the hook. "I can't really talk. After all, my aunt treated me today, too, when a whole new wardrobe showed up at my door this afternoon. How about we let Vinnie treat this time? Next time, we'll go somewhere else, away from prying eyes and paying relatives."

Conor relaxed and nodded his agreement. "Sounds good."

After that, they sipped their coffee and chatted desultorily, both loath to call it a night.

Then, a goddess with a problem interrupted their date.

Alex often wondered afterwards if they had left quickly, instead of lingering over coffee, would the ensuing events have occurred? Probably. Definitely, in fact. However, after what happened next, lingering over dinner would likely be a nerve-wracking experience for quite a while.

"MA'AM! Ma'am? You can't go back there. I'm afraid we're closed for the evening." The server's protestations grew louder when the woman completely ignored him. The poor guy jogged beside the intruder, still protesting, as she strode across the almost empty dining room.

Alex's eyes widened when she recognized the beautiful goddess steaming toward them. The goddess Persephone, her elegant attire in disarray, soon reached their table, then pulled out a chair and sank into it. Her normally immaculate hairdo was a mess, hair sticking out at all angles, and tears streaked the woman's lovely face.

A stab of envy touched Alex at the goddess's smooth skin and clear eyes, despite the tears glistening on her cheeks. Alex knew she did not cry 'pretty'. Blotchy skin and bloodshot eyes always accompanied her luckily infrequent bouts of tears. No ugly crying for this goddess, she mused, then wondered why Persephone was crashing their date—and was so obviously distraught. Whatever the issue, it wouldn't be anything good.

Conor leaned forward and offered Persephone his napkin, which she took and dabbed under her brimming eyes. Alex exchanged a confused glance with Conor, then realized he was deferring to her in dealing with their unplanned dinner guest.

Sincerely hoping the goddess's tears were merely the result of another fight with her husband, Hades, Alex suppressed a sigh and waded in. "Um, hi Persephone. I can see you're upset. How can we help?"

10

PERSEPHONE'S PROBLEM

The distraught goddess sniffed mightily and then wiped her nose with Conor's hapless napkin. "Listen, I—uh, I've got a big problem," she blurted. "I may have made a mistake, and I need your help to fix it." Persephone gazed at Alex, hope and despair battling in her brilliant blue eyes. "Um, the thing is, I suspect war is about to break out in the Fae realm—and it *may* be kind of my fault."

Conor and Alex shared an alarmed glance. *Holy shit. What the heck had Persephone been up to?*

Trying hard not to panic or lose her patience with the flighty goddess, Alex asked her, "Why don't you explain what happened, Persephone, and why you think you may have started a war in the Fae realm?"

The goddess crushed Conor's much-abused napkin in her hand, then shifted uncomfortably and glanced away before replying. "Um, well, I've ... well, I've kind of been having an affair with Cair, and he wants me to help him—"

"Do you mean Prince Cair, the son of King Donal? Heir to the Fae throne—that Cair?" Conor interrupted. He put his coffee cup down slowly and released it gently, as if afraid his crushing grip might shatter the delicate china. His intense, questioning gaze remained fixed on the anxious goddess.

Persephone pursed her lips and nodded once. "Yes, that Cair." She wrung Conor's soggy napkin between her long, slender fingers and turned a pleading gaze on Alex. "It's just—he's soooo hot. And I've always loved a man with a sexy accent and a tight butt. And when we—you know—he calls me a goddess." The goddess smiled and sighed softly.

Alex fought not to roll her eyes. Talk about too much information. "Persephone, dear, you *are* a goddess. So, this guy calling you one isn't anything but a simple fact."

Persephone's dreamy gaze met Alex's. "But when he calls me that, it sends me—"

"No. Just nope." Alex held up a hand. "We really don't need to know what it does to you, either in bed or out."

Conor snickered, and Alex purposefully avoided his amused gaze. She'd lose her composure if she met his eyes, and this really wasn't a laughing matter. "Just tell us what your affair with this prince of a guy has to do with starting a war, Persephone," she asked.

"I THINK we can answer that, dear."

Startled, Alex glanced up. Her Aunt Maia hovered next to their table, her ghostly figure appearing almost completely solid in the restaurant's dim lighting. Her long-term—and very much still alive—beau, Alan, stood at her side, his arm protectively around Maia's waist.

Alex knew Alan had some Fae blood, so the stark fear in his eyes worried her. If anyone would know the consequences of a Greek goddess sleeping with a conniving Fae prince, it would be Alan.

Conor and Alan brought over chairs for the new arrivals. Once everyone had scooted over, made room, and sat, silence descended around the now-crowded table. Everyone fixed their gaze on the wayward goddess and waited.

Persephone protested. "What?! Why is everyone staring at me like that?" She threw her hands in the air. "How was I to know this would happen?"

"You know the rules, Persephone," Alan replied. Anger and worry creased his distinguished face. "You should never mess with supernatural beings outside your own pantheon—or you'll have to answer to their gods." He sounded just like the attorney he was.

Persephone opened her mouth to protest, then snapped it shut. After a tense pause, she dipped her head in acknowledgement. "Yes, of course I know the rules." But she couldn't resist a last protest. "But it's not like I was hurting him or anything. In fact—"

Alex cleared her throat. Loudly. The goddess flounced back in her chair, her beautiful features drawn into a pout.

Conor covered a smile and turned to the attorney. "Alan, having as much Fae blood as you do, I'm assuming you keep up with what's happening in the Fae realm. I know that the fairy mounds have been closed for ages and that only a very limited number of Fae from Underhill are allowed to access the Fae realm's few Crossroads, but I'm willing to bet you've got your finger on the pulse of what's going on there. Can you shed some light on this matter?" Left unspoken was the fact that it had so far been impossible to get any clarity from the fickle goddess.

Alan closed his eyes briefly, then sighed and nodded.

For the first time, Alex noticed the man's handsome features were not quite human. She couldn't put her finger on it, but it was obvious from his appearance that her aunt's boyfriend had more than a little Fae blood running through his veins. She recalled her fraught first meeting with Alan after her arrival. The attorney's early morning phone call a few days previously, informing her that her aunt had died, had shattered her world.

After that, Alex's initial dealings with Alan had been in his role as her aunt's attorney and the executor of her estate. She had since discovered that Alan and her aunt had been an item for years—and that he didn't want their relationship to end with Maia's death. The unlikely couple remained close—the ghost of a Crossroads Keeper and a mixed-blood Fae. Alex shrugged. Who was she to judge? The two of them seemed happy together.

Alan smiled at Alex, his eyes twinkling with merriment, as if he could sense her thoughts. Blushing, she realized she wasn't too sure that he couldn't. *Damn it. Can everyone in the supernatural world read my mind?* She mused. She'd have to get Conor to teach her how to raise her mental shields. He'd offered regularly, but she had put it off, just as she had put off ley travel training. She'd have to get her butt in gear and learn both if a war in the Fae realm really was imminent. *Well, crapola.*

The clink of a fork on delicate glass snapped Alex's attention back to the present. Alan pushed his chair back so he could see and be seen by everyone at the table, then he nodded at Conor. "You're right, Guardian. While most travel between the two realms was closed many centuries ago, there are ... byways. Word gets out —and in, pretty regularly."

After an enigmatic glance at the table's resident goddess, Alan explained. "It seems Persephone has gotten herself caught up in a looming battle for the Fae throne. It has long been rumored that Prince Cair aspires to replace his father on the Fae realm's throne sooner rather than later. However, the Fae live a very long time, and Fae royalty even longer. King Donal has ruled the Fae realm for over five hundred years. Barring meeting with an unfortunate accident, he could easily rule for another five hundred."

"And Prince Cair is tired of waiting his turn," Alex murmured, worry congealing in her full stomach. *I shouldn't have had that last piece of cake,* she mused. *Oh well.*

"That's one rumor, yes." Alan replied, pursing his lips thoughtfully. "Although there is another royal offspring who has an equal, if not greater, claim to the Fae throne than Cair. Her name is Princess Aine, and she is Cair's sister and King Donal's eldest child. However, based on unfounded accusations by Cair, King

Donal exiled Princess Aine from the Fae realm a long time ago. From what I hear, Cair told the king that his sister was plotting a coup, and the old fool believed it, at least enough to exile his daughter. It appears Cair has just made his next move, and Persephone here has gotten herself caught up in that ambitious Fae prince's scheme."

The half-Fae attorney sat back in his chair and shrugged philosophically. "Not that a change of leadership in the Fae realm would be a bad thing, mind you. King Donal has never been a wise or kind ruler. When his wife died, her moderating influence was removed, and I fear he's no longer even an honest one."

Maia's gusty sigh sounded loud in the stunned silence surrounding the table after Alan's revelations. Alex knew her aunt often forgot that she didn't need to breathe. Or maybe she didn't forget but just liked to be reminded of her former life, before her untimely death.

When no one seemed inclined to speak, Alex took up the conversational mantle. "To sum up, Prince Cair started an affair with a horny goddess," she pointed at the offending goddess, "to get her to use her divine powers and help him win a war for the Fae throne?"

A chorus of quiet nods and affirmations circled the table. One pained protest from the goddess in question acted as a counterpoint to the group's general agreement.

Persephone twisted the sodden tissue in her grip and eyed Alex inquiringly. "Well? What are you going to do about it, Alex?"

"Who, me?" Alex sputtered. She threw her hands in the air and eyed the goddess with growing irritation. "What exactly do you want *me* to do about it, Persephone? I'm just a mere Crossroads Keeper, remember? How in the hell does this mess you've created involve me?"

The lovely goddess narrowed her eyes and gave Alex a haughty glare. "I helped you save your Crossroads a few months back, remember, Keeper? Who got the battle party safely into the Underworld and convinced Charon to help us cross the River

Styx? When we got to the castle, who made Hades tell his men to fight at our sides instead of against us? Me. That's who." A sly smile graced Persephone's full lips. "You owe me, Alex."

Alex had to admit that Persephone had indeed been a big help in the battle to save the Crossroads. Her stomach sank as horror dawned. Maybe she *did* owe the goddess a favor. But this? How the hell was she supposed to prevent a civil war in the Fae realm?

"Oh, and you also need to get Danu off my back," Persephone murmured. "That bitch has been sending me threatening messages for the past month." The goddess added the request almost as an afterthought while she casually studied her long, hot-pink nails. "Those Celtic goddesses are always so freaking sensitive. And boy, do they love a good war."

Alex slammed her hand on the table. "Dammit Persephone! What the hell made you think it was a good idea to have an affair with a traitorous prince whose bloodthirsty patron goddess might just take it as a personal affront? And don't tell me about how good the sex was, because I don't wanna hear it." Alex reined in her anger with a weary sigh. Her mouth often ran away with itself, and she darn well knew that spouting off to a goddess was particularly unwise.

After a tense moment, Persephone let the insult slip, merely quirking one eyebrow. "The sex was better than good, Keeper."

Alex covered her ears. "I said, don't tell me."

11

A FAVOR DUE

After almost an hour of protests and arguments, Persephone issued an ultimatum and stalked out of the restaurant. She had made it crystal clear that she felt Alex owed her—and that she expected results. According to the goddess, having Alex sort out the goddess's love life, avert a war for the Fae throne, and appease an ancient, bloodthirsty Celtic goddess would make them even. Almost.

The one remaining server relocked the door after Persephone swept out of the building, then drifted over to ask if anyone wanted more coffee. Visibly upset, the man stammered an apology. "I'm really sorry about that. Normally, the boss helps with the gatekeeping. If he were here, that woman would never have made it past the front desk but he left for New York right after welcoming you this evening, ma'am. His grandnephew is getting married in a few days."

Alex smiled at the man's obvious consternation. She was sure the server knew his boss regarded Alex as his niece, and, therefore, a VIP. Plus, Conor and Vinnie were good friends, even though they often pretended otherwise. The poor guy appeared petrified that word would get back to her Uncle Vinnie about their evening being so rudely interrupted while they dined in his domain.

Vinnie may be a softie with her, but Alex knew he ran a tight ship at the restaurant. Plus, being a former mob boss and current vampire, her heart uncle had a tough-guy reputation to maintain.

"Don't worry, Fred, our lips are sealed," Alex assured the flustered server with a smile. "Especially if you bring us each a pint of that lovely Mexican beer you have on tap. I know you're closed, but if you can bear with us a little longer, we'll soon be out of your hair."

The obvious relief on the server's face gave Alex a twinge of conscience. She would have to have a word with her uncle and ask him to tone down the hard-ass act, at least with loyal employees like Fred.

As Fred hurried away to get their drinks, Maia echoed Alex's thoughts. "Poor man appears petrified of Vinnie. I'll have a word with him about that when he gets back." The ghost shook her head in resignation. "He's lucky to have such a professional and loyal staff. If he doesn't treat them well, they'll leave him for a boss who will."

Alan placed his hand over Maia's chill one. "I agree with you, dear. Speaking of eateries that might be looking for staff, I hear Cassie is planning to expand her new cafe's hours already. Ever since she and her business partner opened their cafe and bakery last month, business has been booming. Sylvan City has needed a good coffee shop and bakery for ages."

"Ooooh, I love their croissants," Alex said.

"Their rye bread is my favorite," added Conor.

The two couples engaged in small talk until the server returned with their beers. Alex stifled a smile when the man placed a full, frothy glass in front of her aunt. Ghosts couldn't drink any more than they could breathe, but the thought was nice.

Conor drained the last of his beer, then placed the glass carefully in the center of his beer mat. Thoughtfully, he turned the wet glass on the mat, as if debating his next words. He glanced at Alan as if for confirmation, then said, "The situation in the Fae realm might explain a few things, though."

Alex had had enough of everyone's hesitation to discuss the divine elephant in the room. "Exactly what things does it explain? And exactly how am I supposed to sort out Persephone's mess?"

"We," Conor replied.

"We?" Alex frowned at him in confusion.

"Yes, we," Conor repeated with a grin. He toasted her with his empty glass. "Those of us around this table, plus the rest of the supernatural posse, are at your service, Keeper, remember? You don't have to tackle Persephone's problem on your own."

Alex's heart warmed. She knew Conor's words were meant to remind her she was not alone anymore and that her heart family and friends were always available to help her. He knew Alex's lonely teenage years with her distant mother had made her very self-sufficient and reluctant to trust or accept help from others.

When Alex had rediscovered her Keeper heritage upon her return to San Antonio, the Crossroads had been under threat and her aunt was recently dead. Murdered. She had had no choice then but to accept help. And her heart family and friends had really come through for her during the fight to protect the Crossroads. They had won that battle. Together.

Alex winced, realizing her old habits had been creeping in lately. That was why she'd been delaying important training and avoiding events that required socializing with her new supernatural community. *Sigh.* Suddenly, she sympathized with her ghostly aunt's unnecessary breathing. Old habits sure were hard to break.

Maia's gentle voice broke into Alex's dismal musings. "Conor is right, my dear. We really are all here to help you."

"But why should sorting out Persephone's mess be my—our responsibility?" Alex protested. She worked hard to keep the whine out of her voice, but suspected she she hadn't succeeded.

"Because you *do* owe her, Alex," Maia explained. "Without Persephone's help, the battle in the Underworld might very well have had a much different result." The ghost pursed her lips and shrugged. "Then none of us would be here to argue about this. Plus, I'm sure word has gotten around by now that the Fates are your cousins and that you're a newly discovered demi-goddess. Your semi-divine status kind of makes helping solve divine difficulties your responsibility."

Alex drained the last of her beer, then stared into the bottom of her glass. Nope. No answers there. "I understand that Persephone helped us in the Underworld, and agree that I might owe her something. Dinner out? A new toga or two? But for her to expect me to solve her boyfriend woes, avert a Fae war, and appease an angry Celtic goddess? That's a bit much, don't you think?"

Then her aunt's last words registered in Alex's tired, muzzy brain, bringing her instantly alert. "Wait—what?! Since when does my being a demi-goddess—and I still have my doubts about that, mind you, make me responsible for sorting out disputes amongst the gods? What. The. Freaking. Hell."

Conor placed his hand on Alex's shoulder and squeezed. When she met his eyes, she saw a mix of sympathy and pity. She rolled her eyes and sighed in resignation, suddenly positive another supernatural responsibility was barreling her way.

"What do I need to know about being a demi-goddess that's worse than having the Fates for cousins?" Alex asked, meeting Conor's gaze with determination and a spark of anger. "And don't you dare pity me, asshole."

Conor sat back in his chair, hands up defensively. "Sorry. Sorry."

Alan banged his empty glass on the table to interrupt the brewing argument. "Alright everyone. Simmer down. Alex, let me explain, since it appears your aunt just threw you a curveball, and Conor is intent on making things worse."

Alex speared Conor with one last narrow-eyed glare, then turned an enquiring gaze on Alan the Peacemaker. And hopefully, the Explainer. "I'm calm now. Super calm. Now, spill." *I could have put that a bit more politely,* she reflected, *but oh well. She was all out of polite for the evening.*

Alan's eyes widened at Alex's abrupt tone, a smile lurking in their depths and revealing itself in the curve of his lips. "You are so much like your aunt, my dear," he murmured. Then, the distinguished older man's shoulders straightened, and a professional expression smoothed his handsome features. He now appeared every inch the attorney about to argue a case. "Some explanation is probably due before I get to your specific case. As you have likely surmised, Alex, demi-gods are supernaturals who have inherited an especially potent amount of their divine ancestor's magical power. Typically, a supernatural with a divine ancestor merely receives a small boost to his or her natural magical abilities. For instance, a siren with Venus's blood in their veins can cause not just humans, but also supernaturals, and even minor gods, to fall in love with her—or him."

The attorney shifted forward in his chair, his gaze intent on Alex's. "However, once every half millennium or so, a demi-god is born. This supernatural being inherits an especially large amount of magical power from their divine ancestor. If that ancestor is a Primordial god, well, the magic they inherit can really pack a punch." He paused, his fingers tightening around the empty beer glass in his hand. "However, only once has a demi-god ever inherited a full Primordial power."

"And that's me, I presume, based on your hesitation." Alex nodded in reluctant agreement. "You're not really telling me anything new, though. My three new cousins told me all this last night. They say I've inherited Chronos's—my grandfather's—Primordial death magic. Listen, I've already told them I have no plans to use my death magic." She flinched when a vision rose of her father screaming, twisting in agony, then dissolving in a pile of ash. "Well, I won't use it again anyway, so everyone can just relax."

She frowned and got back on topic. "What does my being a demi-goddess have to do with me having a responsibility to help wayward goddesses sort out their, uh, affairs?"

Everyone at the table exchanged wary side eyes, taking care not to meet Alex's questioning gaze.

"Oh, and one other thing," Alex asked, recalling Conor's earlier comment. "Conor, what did you mean when you said, 'that may explain things?' I take it that's yet another issue I should know about, but don't." She crossed her arms and tapped her foot against the table leg. "Come on, hit me with it."

Reluctantly, Conor met Alex's inquiring gaze. "I think it can wait until the morning, sweets. Besides, it may have nothing to do with Persephone's issue."

"But you think it does. I can tell by your expression," Alex insisted. Eventually, Conor relented and told her what he had meant by his cryptic comment. With a sinking heart, Alex soon realized that she would *have* to get involved, whether or not she liked it.

She had just recovered from their last battle and was still learning the extent of her Keeper duties. The weight of new knowledge and ever more responsibilities crashed through Alex's wall of denial. She rose and pushed her chair back so hard it fell over, then rushed out of the restaurant with a mumbled apology. "I need some air. I'm gonna walk back to the house. Alone."

SMALL POOLS of brightness from the landscape lights guided Alex's steps as she ambled down the graveled path. Her breath had finally slowed after her precipitous flight. She had jogged down the road away from the restaurant until reaching the back gate that led onto the estate. Once on the grounds, her steps led her inexorably towards the Crossroads and the now-familiar sight of the temple, its pale stone reflecting luminously in the moonlight.

She sensed Conor had followed her from the restaurant. She had heard him keep pace behind her as she ran, but at least he had respected her request to be alone and maintained a generous distance. He veered off once Alex reached the Crossroads and she no longer sensed his presence. A howl from the woods at the far side of the estate informed her that Conor had shifted into his Barghest Hellhound form and was now patrolling the grounds, doing his Guardian thing.

Alex sank down on the temple steps and rested her head against the smooth column at her back. The coolness of the stone calmed her, and she let her eyes close as she considered the tumultuous events of the evening.

Despite herself, Alex snickered. Some first date that had been.

Before she'd so precipitously run out on everyone, Conor had explained his earlier comment and how it related to their current issue. The reason he and Larry had taken so long to arrive at the Crossroads the night her cousins had arrived was that they had been busy breaking up a brawl between two Fae factions in Sylvan City. None of those involved had been willing to explain the reasons behind their fight, instead merely sloping off in sullen silence. That was also not the first fight among the normally well-mannered Fae residents of the city in recent weeks.

Conor was right, Alex admitted to herself. The recent discord amongst the Sylvan City Fae almost certainly had its roots in the unrest Persephone's affair with Prince Cair was causing in the Fae realm. The Fae king's loyalists in Sylvan City were fighting with his treacherous son's supporters.

Alex pressed her cheek against the cool column, the incised carvings on its surface rough against her skin. As Keeper of the San Antonio Crossroads, she was well aware that the adjacent supernatural enclave of Sylvan City was also her responsibility. Since the unrest Persephone and her idiot prince had started was spilling over into Alex's demesne, she had no choice but to get involved.

It also seemed clear from her aunt's comments that the gods expected their demi-god progeny to help sort out disagreements between their fully divine family members. Yet another brick in the wall of responsibility that had grown up around Alex since her return to San Antonio and immersion in the supernatural world.

She briefly considered using the portal within the column to travel to the In-Between for a fireside chat with Hecate but decided against it. She wanted some quiet time to figure things out on her own, and the deserted temple in the center of the Crossroads at midnight was as good a place as any to do that. *Then* she would seek help from her goddess, as well as her heart family and friends. She really had no choice. *Sigh.*

12

DID YOU KNOW?

Alex opened the door slowly and tiptoed into her room. She peered over at the bed, expecting to see a sleeping Larry. Instead, he lay flat out on the covers with his head between his front paws, alert eyes trained on her.

"I heard your first date was a bust," Larry said. "You got gate-crashed by a goddess and were also told some stuff you really didn't want to hear." Larry's serious and sympathetic expression belied his blunt greeting.

"Word sure travels fast around here," Alex muttered as she collapsed on the bed next to her Familiar, her hand automatically reaching out to stroke the soft fur on his back.

Larry rolled over and reached out a paw, a silent entreaty for Alex to transfer her attention to rubbing his belly. "Grenoble and I were monitoring the Crossroads this evening. When you showed up by yourself looking all forlorn, I went in search of Conor. He filled me in once he was done with howling his frustrations at the sky."

Despite herself, Alex smiled. "I thought I heard a smaller canine voice accompanying him. Didn't sound nearly as fierce as Conor's Hellhound howl, though."

Larry snorted in disgust, then rolled over onto his stomach, ending the belly rub session early. "I can't help it if I'm stuck in this damn poodle body. Inside, I'm still a massive junkyard dog with a bad attitude."

"I'll grant you the bad attitude, dude." She rubbed Larry's nose, her eyes warmed by a wicked twinkle. "And you may have been a 'real' junkyard dog in your last Familiar incarnation, but in this one, you're just a cute, fluffy, pouffy—"

"Fuck you," he snorted, then sneezed hard, coating Alex's hand in a layer of doggy drool.

Alex rubbed her wet hand on the covers and shook her head in admonishment. "As Aunt Maia would say, 'Language, dear.'"

Once reassured by their usual snarky banter, the duo moved on to more serious matters.

"Did you know when you met me? About my being a demi-goddess?" Alex asked, eying Larry intently, seeking the truth in either his words or actions.

"Um, I knew you had divine blood," Larry admitted, lowering his head onto the bed with a sigh. "DEAF told me that Chronos was your grandfather during my Familiar briefing. The powers that be keep track of those things, you know. Wouldn't want any divine descendants going off radar." He flicked a glance at the silent woman at his side to gauge her reaction, then continued. "What neither I nor DEAF knew was exactly how much divine magic you inherited from your divine ancestor."

"So DEAF thought I had merely inherited run-of-the-mill necromantic magic from my father, Chronos's son, correct?" Alex's neutral tone gave nothing away.

"Yeeees, that's what they told me. DEAF knew that necromantic magic was Chronos's biological 'gift' to your father, since it's frequently inherited down the Chronos family line," Larry explained with a shrug. "They thought that's all you had, too. New necromancers are rare these days though, because, uh, Chronos doesn't get out much anymore, not since his wife laid down the law a couple centuries ago." He snickered. "Word is, she told him she'd tie his pee-pee in a permanent knot if he didn't keep it in his pants."

Alex grinned. Sounded like Persephone and Hades weren't the only divine couple who had ongoing issues with fidelity. "What is it with the gods? They all act like a bunch of horny teenagers."

Larry cocked his head. "Remember, Alex, the gods don't operate by the same moral code that humans—or even most supernaturals—do. The gods may look and sound like us, but they are an ancient, unique race. Many millennia of existence have magnified their cultural differences at the same time that it has mitigated their ability to act in a manner that we can understand."

"You can say that again," Alex murmured. "So, you're saying that the gods play by their own rules, always, but sometimes deign to interact with the supernatural beings and humans they created —but again, on their terms."

"That about sums it up," Larry replied with a yawn. "Don't try to understand the gods' behavior, Alex, or it'll drive you to drink. We can only try to roll with their punches—"

"And clean up their hot messes," Alex retorted. Her eyes drooped tiredly; she had had enough of divine discussions for the evening. "Time for sleep, bud. I'm exhausted."

"Sounds like a plan," Larry replied. He snuggled into the pillow on his side of the bed and curled up. "Get the light, will you?"

COUNCIL COLLUSION

Alex swung her Keeper staff at her attacker. The solid wood of the staff cracked against the tall Fae's skull, and he dropped to the ground, unmoving. She had put little magic into the blow, so she knew the idiot was alive, just unconscious.

"Behind you!" Conor's warning saved Alex from a nasty sword slash.

Just in time, she pivoted on one foot, swinging her staff as she turned. The muscle-bound Fae at her back snarled, then screamed when his sword struck her glowing staff. Alex had put more magic into this blow, as she considered it unsporting for her assailant to attack from the rear. The Fae cursed, dropped his sword, and fell to his knees, clutching his still-smoking hand to his chest. Alex's blue Keeper magic still danced with her red necromantic magic, flickering along the man's discarded sword where it lay on the dirt.

"That'll teach you to attack from behind, asshole. I thought Fae honor required a frontal assault." Alex growled, eyeing the injured fighter in disappointment. "Looks like the traitorous prince you fight for has delegated his dishonorable actions to his followers. For shame." She resisted wagging her finger at the chagrined Fae, but only just.

"That's the last one, Alex," Conor said. "Let's round this lot up and haul them to the Sylvan City jail. We can take any we want to question in depth to the estate's dungeon later." He tied a gleaming black magical null rope around the unconscious Fae's wrists.

Alex nodded, then created her own null rope and did the same with Mr. Smoky Hand. She silently thanked Conor for teaching her how to channel her Keeper magic to create the glittering black ropes of binding magic. These suckers sure came in handy.

Once they dropped their Fae cargo off with Manny, the Yeti in charge of the city jail, Alex and Conor hurried to the City Council meeting, which was where they were headed before having to sort out yet another scuffle between the supporters of the Fae king and those of his traitorous son, Prince Cair.

"You're late." The satyr standing at the podium admonished the latecomers. Alex winced when the satyr stamped his hooves on the floor in irritation. If he kept that up, he'd crack the Council chamber's lovely marble floor.

Before Alex could apologize for their tardiness, Maia addressed the angry Councilor. She sat to the satyr's left, her hands folded neatly, hovering over the long, curved table behind which the assembled Council members sat. "Adrus, I'm sure you heard the fighting outside, just as we all did. You know as well as I do that Alex and Conor were rather busy defending the city's peace until a few minutes ago."

Maia studied Alex worriedly, then flicked a glance at Conor. "Are you both okay?"

"Yes, Aunt Maia. We're both fine," Alex assured her aunt. She grimaced and added, "But the same cannot be said for the half a dozen Fae who turned their weapons on us when we intervened in their fight. They are all now nursing their injuries in the town jail, under Manny's tender ministrations."

Several snickers sounded from the audience arrayed on benches in front of the Council. Most of the Council members worked to contain their own grins as well. Everyone knew Manny ran a tight ship at the jail. Yetis were notoriously tough characters. His Fae prisoners would not enjoy their stay. At all.

Adrus snorted and banged his gavel on the podium. "Quiet in the chamber! I will not have members of the public or my Council members disrespecting this sacred civic space."

Once everyone had simmered down to Adrus's satisfaction, he banged his gavel on the podium again. "I call this emergency meeting of the Sylvan City Council to order." The satyr's head dipped sharply, his curling horns just missing the crystal vase resting on top of the podium. The vase held a single massive rose, its ivory petals spread wide, and its face curved toward the speaker.

Alex realized someone had spelled the rose to amplify the speaker's voice throughout the vast room. In fact, a similar vase and flower sat in front of each Council member. The sight of the magic-microphone flowers saddened her. She recalled her first introduction to them, when she spoke into one while conducting the service at her aunt's funeral several months ago. Shaking off her morbid thoughts, Alex addressed her aunt's ghost—still very much present in the world and handling her Council duties with ease.

"Aunt Maia, thank you for clarifying the reason for our late arrival," she said, before turning her gaze to the irate satyr chairing the meeting. "Um, Your Honor, apologies for the delay. And thank you for, uh, requesting a report on the Fae unrest troubling the city."

At her side, Conor's shoulders shook with suppressed laughter. Fortunately, his face remained stoic and respectful. Just to be on the safe side, Alex dug her elbow into his side and whispered a warning. "Knock it off, you dingus."

She knew Conor's amusement resulted from her choice of words when she addressed the Council's chairperson. The Council had not requested their presence today—they had demanded it. When Maia explained the Council's summons to them over breakfast that morning, she had put as nice a spin on their request as possible, but Alex recognized an order when she heard one.

Seemingly satisfied, the satyr nodded at them and resumed his chair. While his handsome face bore no trace of his earlier anger, his eyes still glittered with an emotion Alex couldn't name. It unsettled her.

Adrus said, "Let the record show the Council excuses the Crossroads Keeper and her Guardian from the normal Council penalties for tardiness. Just this once." He smoothed a hand over his curled horns, then clapped his hands abruptly. "Well, now that you're here. Let's get on with the report." Giving Alex a narrow-eyed glare, he demanded answers. "Keeper, what are you doing to stop the Fae from fighting on the streets of Sylvan City? We can't have Fae realm politics spilling over into our city. Remember, Crossroads cities such as this are under the protection of their oath-bound Crossroads Keeper. That's you, Alex." The satyr didn't bother to hide his derisive sneer. "Explain your plans for resolving this situation."

Alex blanked her face and fought back a snarky reply. Conor's supportive hand on her back helped her avoid replying in anger. "I realize that Sylvan City is under my protection, Your Honor. My team and I have been working hard to contain the fighting among the city's Fae residents. We believe the fights are being instigated by Prince Cair's men, several of whom have recently infiltrated the local Fae community." Alex hesitated, hating to admit failure. "Unfortunately, we haven't been able to capture any of them, despite our best efforts. They slip in and out of the city without using our Crossroads, which I've locked down tight. No Fae are traveling the leys to or from the San Antonio Crossroads right now without my express permission—"

A female Council member interrupted Alex's speech. "You still haven't answered the question, Keeper. What exactly *are* your plans to resolve this issue?" The woman's short stature and yellow skin identified her as a river troll.

For a moment, Alex's thoughts spun. Her mind's eye filled with the vision of another river troll—one who had given her life for this community during the battle in the Underworld. She had held Greta in her arms as she died. With her last breath, the gruff river troll had extracted a promise from Alex to protect the city and its Crossroads. With effort, Alex suppressed her dark memories and dragged her mind back to the meeting. She couldn't defend her actions or explain her plans unless she had her head in the game.

Composing herself, she replied, "Well, we have a posse meeting scheduled for this evening. Our plan is to have posse members on duty around the clock to act as peacekeepers and intermediaries until we solve the Fae infighting. As for the prince's men and our efforts to locate them—" Alex paused. She had no clue how to go about finding them. Despite their best efforts over the past week, neither she nor Conor had discovered how the Underhill Fae were getting in and out of the Fae realm undetected and without using the Crossroads. She had requested information from several local Fae, but they had no clue, either—or so they said.

Familiar footsteps sounded behind Alex; she turned her head and heaved an internal sigh of relief at the sight of Tyre and his two companions. Hopefully, they had news. The Indigo Fae bowed his head in greeting, then spoke into her mind. *"Keeper, I have the answers the Council seeks. However, I have also come to suspect there's a Council member in the prince's pay. It might be unwise to share the extent of my knowledge with the full Council."*

"Do you know who it is?" Alex mind-spoke her query.

Tyre hesitated, his deep unease communicating itself into her mind as easily as words.

"So, that's a no, then," she answered her own question, while staring intently at the Indigo Fae warrior who had been her aunt's close friend and ally. Upon Maia's death, Tyre and his warriors had

transferred their allegiance to Alex, although their ultimate commitment was to Hecate, to whom a previous Fae king had bound them many centuries ago. As a Priestess of Hecate, Alex and Tyre served the same divine mistress.

"I have my suspicions about which Council member is corrupt, but —" Tyre shrugged slightly, his gaze intent on hers.

Alex made a split-second decision. She turned to face the Council, noting their restlessness at Tyre's interruption. Her gaze slid across the faces arrayed along the curved table above her, wondering which of them was in the prince's pocket.

"Please excuse the interruption, esteemed Council members," she said calmly. "Tyre and his men have been investigating the incursions from the Fae realm on my behalf. They have discovered some information; however, because of its sensitive nature, it would be best not to reveal it in open chambers." She gestured at the public seating, which was filled with an avid audience. "Conor and I, along with the posse, will discuss this information at tonight's posse meeting." Alex's heart pounded as she prepared to practice a small deception. She had never been good at lying. With a small nod towards her aunt, she continued. "Since one of your trusted Council members will be present at tonight's meeting, she will be privy to this sensitive information. Council Member Maia can then share it, in private, with the rest of the Council at your next meeting." She held her breath and awaited a reply, hoping her ruse worked.

The Council members rose and huddled together, murmuring softly among themselves. Adrus's angry voice rose several times, but the satyr appeared to be on the losing end of the argument. Hopefully. Finally, their deliberations ended, and the Council members retook their seats.

Alex shot a furtive glance at her aunt to see if she could garner any information, but Maia's neutral expression gave nothing away. However, she was the one who stood to inform them of the Council's decision. When Alex met her aunt's gaze, she saw a faint glimmer of approval and triumph in her eyes.

Maia's neutral voice and firm delivery didn't reveal her feelings when she addressed the room. "The Council has deliberated and voted on your request, Keeper Alex. Most of us agree it would be unwise of you to provide such sensitive information in a public setting. The Council has delegated to me the responsibility of getting the information from you at tonight's posse meeting and to provide it to the Council in a closed-door session at a later date."

Alex nodded gratefully. She knew her aunt had been a force to be reckoned with on the Council during her lifetime. Her physical death had apparently not diminished her influence in the least.

The frustrated satyr banged his gavel sharply on the podium, his displeasure clear. "This Council meeting is hereby ended. Record Keeper, please make a note of the requirement that Council Member Maia report back to the Council with her niece's information at the earliest opportunity."

A squat Brownie, perched precariously on a stool to one side of the raised platform, nodded and scribbled furiously in his notebook.

"Good job, Alex," Conor whispered in her ear as he escorted her quickly out of the council chambers. "But let's not stick around in case the traitor on the Council figures out the truth about why you didn't want to share Tyre's findings. I'm assuming there's corruption on the Council. No surprise there. And you're a terrible liar, by the way."

Tyre chuckled softly at Conor's words. He and his men had fanned out around their group in a protective triad, following closely as they exited the building. "We'll escort you back to the Crossroads, Alex, just to be on the safe side." The Indigo Fae gave her a wry grin. "Plus, we wouldn't mind enjoying one of Henri's excellent meals before tonight's posse meeting."

Alex smiled at the Indigo Fae warrior. "Thanks, Tyre. Of course, you're all invited to dinner. The more the merrier." Then she remembered her cousins, the Fates, who would also be present at her aunt's dinner table that evening. "Um, how about we all grab pizza at Vinnie's restaurant instead?"

"Coward." Conor's amused voice echoed in Alex's mind.

Tyre's abrupt bark of laughter informed Alex that Conor had shared his accusation with the Indigo Fae.

"I'm not a coward," Alex protested. "I just don't want Tyre and his buddies to have to deal with my troublesome—and rather deadly—cousins over dinner tonight. After all, Tyre and his men are probably tired from their investigations. And there's nothing like a good pizza to fill up a weary warrior."

The group of friends bickered amicably as they made their way to the ley line just outside the city. Once they reached the Crossroads, by mutual agreement, they headed directly to the best pizza this side of New York City.

14

A ROYAL INVITATION

"SILENCE!" Hecate's shout echoed from the rafters of the barn's massive arena. The supernaturals seated on the risers around the walls immediately ceased their excited chatter and turned their sheepish gazes to the annoyed goddess.

"I'll have no more discussion on this issue," Hecate growled. She cast a quelling glance around the arena, then fixed Alex with a penetrating glare. "As my priestess and the Keeper of this Crossroads, it is your duty to keep the peace at the Crossroads and the city it supports. Just because the matter at hand originated outside this realm does not make the results manifesting here on Earth any less real." The goddess gestured pointedly at the supernaturals seated around the arena. "It's not as if you don't have any help, Alex. I've activated the posse, and they are here to support your efforts. Fix this mess."

You mean fix the mess caused by one of your own, Alex fumed silently at the angry goddess's demands. After all, there wouldn't *be* a war brewing in the Fae realm, or fighting in the streets of Sylvan City if Persephone hadn't fooled around and found out her Fae prince lover planned to involve her in his coup attempt.

Instead of voicing her frustration, Alex merely nodded at the goddess in acquiescence. She was learning to hold her tongue.

Sometimes. "Yes, ma'am. I understand. That's why we're having this meeting tonight, so we can plan our course of attack." Alex winced inwardly after she finished her reply. Probably not the best choice of words, considering their goal was to prevent an attack—or, even worse, a civil war in the Fae realm that would undoubtedly spill over onto Earth—and into her Crossroads.

Thankfully, Maia stepped into the conversational gap. The ghost bowed her head respectfully to the irate goddess. "Now that you have kindly established order, Hecate, perhaps we should concentrate on the meeting's agenda? Since the Indigo Fae have information that may help us decide on a course of action, why don't we let them speak first?"

Recognizing his cue, Tyre strode to the long table at the center of the arena, behind which the meeting's ersatz organizers sat or stood. The Fae warrior faced Hecate, who had retaken her seat on the elegant, throne-like chair provided for her. The Fae warrior bowed low, not rising until the goddess acknowledged him.

"Rise, Tyre, and tell us what you have discovered," Hecate commanded wearily.

When Tyre spoke, his deep voice filled the arena effortlessly. "Yes, my goddess. With Alex's permission, my team and I have used the Crossroads to journey into the Fae realm and poke around. We traveled about the realm but kept a low profile and watched and listened."

Worry flickered over Tyre's usually inscrutable features. "It seems the unrest in the Fae realm has been simmering for a while. Over the past several years, King Donal has levied onerous new taxes on his people. He has become less responsive to his realm's needs as well. In fact, there hasn't been a royal court session in over a year, thus denying his subjects the opportunity to appeal their grievances to him. Sadly, last year's harvest was not a good one, yet the king has refused to relieve farmers of their royal food tithe. He has also refused to open the emergency food stores to help feed the population. Hunger has stalked many Fae hearths this past winter. There are even rumors that the food stores are completely empty." The Fae warrior shrugged helplessly. "No one we spoke with knows where the money from the king's extra taxes has gone. It certainly hasn't been used to improve his subject's lives or fill the food stores." He hesitated, then added, "There's even a rumor that the king's newest advisors are controlling him somehow."

Hecate's eyes narrowed as she considered Tyre's words. "What you're saying is that the Fae realm has been ripe for a coup attempt for quite a while. And into that breach has stepped King Donal's ambitious son, Prince Cair." The goddess's expression was thunderous. "That spoiled brat is exploiting his father's heavy-handedness, inattention, and possible corruption to stoke unrest, which it seems has convinced some that he might make a better ruler than his father."

Tyre nodded in agreement. "Yes, ma'am. Most of the Fae I've spoken with agree on the need for a change of ruler. However, given Prince Cair's unpopularity, he hasn't achieved the overwhelming support he needs to pull off a successful coup." The Fae warrior pursed his lips, then reluctantly added, "We suspect that's why the prince has sought divine support for his traitorous plans. By seducing Persephone, he had hoped to lure her into helping him with his bid for the throne."

Hecate laughed aloud. "You're being diplomatic, Tyre. I'm sure the prince didn't have to try very hard to get Persephone to fall into bed with him. That goddess gets around." She snorted and rolled her eyes. "In fact, I'm sure we wouldn't be here today if not for her rash actions several millennia ago, when the wily minx seduced Hades and staged her supposed kidnapping so they could spend some time together—away from the prying eyes of her mother—in the Underworld."

Those present silently agreed but kept their feelings off their faces. Only a goddess could openly criticize another goddess without serious repercussions. However, everyone accepted the truth of Hecate's words. If Demeter had not sought Hecate's help to rescue her daughter from the Underworld all those centuries ago, the Crossroads network would not exist. After all, it was that divine trio, Hecate, Demeter, and Persephone—after her purported rescue—who had worked deep magic together to create crossings between the ley lines, so that no god could ever again hold another against their will. It was mere serendipity that these Crossroads also enabled other supernatural races to travel the same leys. Demons, ghosts, and all manner of supernaturals now used the connected leys to travel easily between and across the realms. That Persephone had been a willing participant in her abduction to the Underworld was a memory conveniently lost to the mists of time.

Atropos startled everyone when she clapped her hands sharply. The audience sighed quietly in relief when the goddess's hands remained scissor-free. "And just where is Persephone this evening?" Atropos growled. "Since her rash actions have caused this ruckus, I think the little hoyden should be here to help organize the cleanup."

Alex suppressed a sigh. When her divine cousins had insisted on attending tonight's posse meeting, she had reluctantly relented, but only after securing their agreement to be seen but not heard. The last thing she needed was a trio of goddesses with Primordial powers and an unhealthy obsession with death interfering in matters. The Fates would make things worse, if only to precipitate another 'lovely' war. Of course, Atropos would be the one to break her promise. The wily goddess probably had her fingers crossed behind her back when she made the promise to be seen and not heard. *Sigh.*

Hecate raised her brows at Atropos's interruption but answered calmly enough. "Persephone is back in the Underworld —lying low if she knows what's good for her. Danu is pissed. After all, the Fae are her people, and Persephone broke the rules by exacerbating an already dangerous political situation." She tapped her fingers on her chair's ornately carved arm. With a rueful grimace, she added, "When I spoke with Danu via mind-speak last night, it was all I could do to convince her not to go stomping down to the Underworld and drag Persephone out by that lovely, long hair of hers."

"Now, that would be a catfight I'd like to witness." Larry's amused, mind-spoken comment disconcerted Alex. Although she agreed with her magical partner, she knew a divine throw-down between two powerful goddesses would only make matters worse. For everyone. In every realm.

She threw Larry a reproving side-eye and whispered, "Let's concentrate on solving the situation, not throwing fire on it, smartass."

"Okay. Still—what a sight that would be," Larry replied with a grin. Beside him, Grenoble rumbled a chuckle.

"Knock it off, you two. This is serious shit." Alex scolded the two reprobates sternly, then turned her attention to her divine, but deadly, cousins. "Atropos, thank you for inquiring about Persephone's whereabouts. It seems she's in the best place possible right now." She cast her gaze around the arena, taking in everyone present, including her cousins. "How about we have no more interruptions during the meeting? We have already set the agenda, and the next speaker is Conor."

Atropos slouched back in her chair, an amused smile playing on her thin lips. "Your message comes across loud and clear, Cousin Alex. We don't want to cause you any problems, so we'll just sit here like good little goddesses and shut up."

"That'll be the day any of those three are good—or little," Larry snarked into Alex's mind. *"Well, except for Lachesis. She's a tiny little thing. Even in my dog form, I was bigger than her in my last Familiar body,"* he added, regret coloring his words.

Alex knew her Familiar had been a large, muscular Rottweiler-Pitt mix in his last incarnation, when he and his former magical partner had guarded a magical scrapyard—and saved the world. Even in his current small, fluffy form, Larry still had the heart of a junkyard dog—and he never failed to remind her of that. *"But now you're a measly poodle, bud, weighing all of what, twenty pounds? And will you please shut up?! I wanna listen to Conor."* Alex mind-spoke her admonition, then turned her attention back to Conor, who was currently addressing the group.

"And I propose we set guards on all the roads into Sylvan City, and lookouts in the trees," Conor said. "We have several Earth-bound Fae volunteers who have agreed to travel to the Fae realm to search for the prince, as long as Alex agrees to open the Cross-roads and let them through." He turned to Maia and asked, "What do you plan to tell Council Member Adrus about our plans? I know he's expecting you to report back to him and the rest of the Council on tonight's meeting."

Maia smiled slyly. "Oh, I can prevaricate with the best of them, Conor. I'll tell them enough to keep Adrus and his cronies happy, but not enough to give our plans away, in case there is a corrupt Council member or two in the King Donal's pocket." She pursed her lips, and added, "Which wouldn't surprise me in the least."

As Conor and Maia went over the posse's plans, Alex tuned out. She and Conor had gone over them at length prior to the meeting. She was fighting to keep her eyes open and at least appear to be paying attention, when a commotion by the open barn door snapped her wide awake.

"Someone's coming!" Larry barked, a golden haze of magic already surrounding his body. "It's a Fae, but not one of ours."

Alex immediately stood, held out her hand, and called her Keeper staff. Before she could sound the alarm, a puffing Henri raced into the arena. Just behind him strode a tall, gold-haired Fae.

"So sorry to interrupt the meeting, Alex, but a messenger has arrived who claims to represent the Fae king." Henri gestured to the man standing at attention next to him. "He insisted on seeing you right away on a matter of royal importance." The flustered chef peered nearsightedly across the arena at Alex. "I hope I did right by bringing him here?"

While Henri spoke, several posse members, including Tyre

and his Indigo Fae warriors, had formed a loose half-circle around the newcomer. Stances casual, but eyes alert, their hands weren't far from their weapons.

Reassured by the posse's quick response, Alex turned her attention to the Fae messenger and found the man's intent gaze trained on her. She recalled her Aunt Maia's oft-repeated words, *'When unsure of your guest, always fall back on courtesy,'* so she addressed the stranger politely. "Hail and Welcome, sir. I understand you have a message for us?"

The tall Fae bowed his head slightly, then raised his gaze to meet Alex's, an expression in his eyes that she couldn't decipher. "My message is for your ears alone, Keeper. It is from King Donal of the Fae realm. If we could speak in private?"

"Oh, no way—just nope! He's not getting you alone, Alex." Larry's worried words rushed into Alex's mind. This time, she was in full agreement with her furry sidekick.

"Everyone present here tonight is either an advisor to me or a protector of this Crossroads," she informed the Fae messenger. "I trust all of them implicitly." *No harm in letting the man know he was vastly outnumbered,* Alex mused. "Whatever you have to say to me you can freely share with all those present."

The Fae messenger's forehead wrinkled, and his eyes narrowed in consideration. After a brief hesitation, he came to a decision and nodded sharply. "As you wish, Keeper." A parchment scroll appeared in the messenger's previously empty hands. As he unrolled it, a dozen trumpets blared, making Alex—and everyone else—jump and wince at the racket.

Alex gripped her Keeper staff tightly, readying a defense for the herd of attackers she expected to charge into the arena any minute. *What the hell? How did this guy get into this realm and onto the estate, anyway?* She wondered. He definitely hadn't come through her Crossroads, that was for darn sure. She had that sucker locked down tight. Currently, no Fae could travel through her Crossroads without her express permission. In advance.

"Don't worry, Alex. There's no one outside. I suspect I know how

this man got here, though, and I'll explain later." Tyre's calm, mind-spoken words reassured Alex, and she tipped her chin to acknowledge his reassurance. The Fae warrior's lips twitched, and he nodded silently at the pompous messenger, who was ceremoniously unrolling the scroll as the obnoxious sound of trumpets faded away. Out loud, the warrior Fae muttered, "King Donal likes his messages to be dramatic, so he has the scrolls spelled to sound a royal trumpet call when opened."

Alex rolled her eyes.

Larry snickered.

Conor snorted.

Even Hecate suppressed a grin.

Obviously not pleased with the general amusement his king's magical fanfare had elicited, the Fae messenger cleared his throat ostentatiously, studied the scroll, then spoke, his voice reverberating through the high-ceilinged arena.

"King Donal, ruler of the Fae kingdom and all its environs, attachments, islands, and protectorates, requests the presence of Alexandria, Priestess of Hecate and Keeper of the San Antonio Crossroads, at his upcoming Beltane Ball, which will take place four nights hence at the king's royal castle. She may bring a standard retinue of guards and servants with her into the Fae realm. The king expects her arrival one day prior to the ball. Appropriate attire is required for all public appearances during the celebration."

The messenger pointed to the ground near Alex's feet and added, "A royal pass granting travel to and within the Fae realm, directions to the king's castle, and additional instructions are enclosed in that scroll."

As the messenger finished speaking, a cream-colored scroll appeared in a glittering cloud of smoke, before dropping to the ground directly in front of Alex. She took a cautious step back, eyeing the scroll in concern, in case the damned thing came to life. Or blew up. In the ensuing tense silence, the pompous Fae messenger turned smartly on his heel and marched out of the arena, a flustered Chef Henri on his heels.

Tyre nodded to Alex and gestured to his warriors. "We'll make sure the messenger makes it safely off the premises, and I'll set a guard so we have no more unexpected visitors this evening." Left unsaid was that Tyre and his men would attempt to discover exactly how the Fae messenger had crossed the realms, considering every Crossroads leading to the Fae realm, including theirs, were locked down tight against Fae intruders.

Once Tyre and his warriors had left, the silence stretched, then pandemonium reigned when everyone began talking at once.

BETWEEN HECATE'S shouted commands and Maia's shrill whistle, the arena eventually quieted, although the Fates continued to whisper quietly amongst themselves about how unexpectedly exciting they were finding things, especially since the trio had expected so little from their duty-bound visit to the Crossroads to meet their long-lost cousin.

As the cousin in question, Alex chose to ignore the gossiping goddesses. Everyone else, including Hecate, did the same. *After all, Alex mused, who was going to tell off the freaking Fates? No one, that's who.*

Maia's chilly, translucent hand gently touched Alex's arm to get her attention, then the ghost whispered a request. "Let me handle the rest of the meeting if you don't mind, dear?"

Alex gestured to the expectant audience. "Sure thing, Aunt Maia! Go for it."

Conor and Larry snickered softly. Obviously, they had heard the exchange—and the relief in Alex's words.

Maia smiled at the audience, but the fiery determination in her eyes and steel in her voice belied her kindly expression. "Okay, everyone, listen up. You heard Hecate. We need to fix the mess that

Persephone has, if not created, at least exacerbated. First, I need some volunteers to mount a permanent guard at the estate's gates."

Several supernaturals and ghosts raised their hands, and Maia acknowledged the volunteers. "Thank you, everyone." She smiled at the translucent form of the ancient English queen. "Liz, since you're the senior member among the volunteers, perhaps you could organize a schedule and advise your new security team? You can use the dining room in the main house for your meeting."

When the volunteers hesitated, Maia and the queen exchanged a silent glance. The normally surly ghost smiled in anticipation and nodded at her friend. "Alright, everyone who volunteered for estate guard duties, follow me!" The hem of the queen's massive dress seemed to trail along the ground as she floated toward the exit. "Chop, chop, my new guardsmen. Let's go!"

Those who had volunteered scurried to follow their appointed leader from the arena, leaving the massive space substantially less crowded.

Maia transferred her attention to the massive squid arrayed against the far wall. "Billy, can you please patrol the Sylvan City lake? Perhaps you could have a word with the river trolls and establish a plan to keep an eye on things around the shoreline."

The giant fifty-foot squid waved a tentacle in agreement. The tiny cowboy hat perched on his head almost fell off when he nodded enthusiastically. "Sure thing, Maia! Between the river trolls and me, we can handle any trouble at the lake." With that, Billy made his way toward the door at speed, his massive tentacles churning deep paths through the hard-packed dirt.

Alex made a note to ensure she had the arena's dirt floor re-leveled. Wouldn't want anyone tripping. Namely, herself. She marveled silently at her aunt's expert handling of the posse members—and how quickly she was clearing the room.

Once Maia finished assigning most of the rest of the posse to various committees and tasks and encouraging them to begin their duties immediately, the vast space soon echoed with emptiness. The ghost gestured the few remaining posse members forward.

"Grab a chair, people, and join us at the head table. We've got a lot to discuss tonight."

Still seated to one side of the table, the Fates sat forward expectantly. *Ah, fuck!* Alex sighed in resignation. She couldn't expect Maia to deal with her divine cousins, but from her aunt's urgent glance, she knew they needed to go. The Fates' idea of 'helping' likely involved a whole lot of blood and killing first and asking questions later. If ever.

As Alex considered how best to ask the Fates to vamoose without offending the powerful trio and being threatened with death by Atropos's deadly scissors of fate, Hecate saved her the trouble.

The goddess's melodious words filtered into Alex's mind. *"I'll entertain your cousins while the rest of you strategize, Alex. You can fill me in when you return from the Fae realm."* Hecate fixed her with a stern eye. *"Be careful, Keeper. The Fae are a dangerously proud people. Sadly, their king is a fool. Oh, and watch out for Danu during your journey. She probably won't harm you, but she's, um, rather unpredictable."*

Alex nodded mutely at Hecate, then silently brooded, *Oh goodie, yet another dangerous goddess who might or might not kill me. And another momentous fireside chat to look forward to when she returned from the Fae realm.* If she returned. She recalled her first visit to the In-Between several months earlier. She had started that visit positive that a recurring childhood nightmare had come to life. By the end of that evening, Hecate had revealed Alex's supernatural heritage, bound her to the Crossroads as its Keeper, and tasked her with saving her new Crossroads from a deadly attack. Idly, Alex wondered how many extra duties the goddess would task her with during their next fireside chat. *Sigh. Some things never change.*

Hecate kept her word to Alex and smiled brightly at her fellow goddesses. "Let's not waste our time here any longer, my divine sisters. I have some wonderful Babylonian wine, along with a sumptuous feast, awaiting us by my hearth in the In-Between." She grinned slyly and added, "I also have an amazing Earthly magic called the internet. It resides in a lighted box and allows you to shop for anything your heart desires, without moving more than a finger or two." The goddess stood and strode toward the barn door, not waiting to see if the Fates followed her. But she had baited her trap well; the three goddesses hurried after her, chattering excitedly amongst themselves about fine wine, food, and magical shopping opportunities.

Those left at the table breathed a collective sigh of relief at Hecate's deft goddess-wrangling talents.

"Aunt Maia, thank you for handling the volunteer assignments. I really appreciate your help," Alex said, fighting to keep resentment out of her tone. While Alex valued her aunt's help, she was the Keeper now. Everyone—including her aunt—kept telling her she needed to grow into the role, take responsibility for things. Hard to do if everyone was always jumping in and handling things for you.

"Chill out, Alex. No point in getting upset when others help you. That's what we're all here for, remember?" Larry cocked his head and threw Alex a warning side-eye along with his mind-spoken warning. *"Your aunt resisted the call of the Underworld after her death so she could remain here at the Crossroads, hoping we would find you someday. She desperately wanted to stay so she could train and help you upon your return. That took a lot of guts—and effort, on her part. She loves you, Alex. We all do."*

Larry's simple statement almost undid Alex. She blinked rapidly to dispel unbidden tears, knowing he was right. She needed to suck it up and stop being so sensitive. Love involved giving and receiving support, both emotional and tangible. While she was getting better at both, occasionally she backslid into her earlier habit of wanting total independence. But that was no longer an option for her.

Conor interrupted Alex's silent self-castigation. "I'm assuming, Aunt Maia, there's a reason you wanted most everyone gone before we had this discussion?"

The ghost's gaze touched everyone in the group before she

spoke. Choosing her words carefully, she said, "I don't think we had a traitor in our midst tonight, but you can never be too careful. After all, the Underhill Fae seem to slip in and out of our realm like there's a supernatural highway between the realms—"

When laughter interrupted Maia's words, she realized their unwitting accuracy and joined in sheepishly. After all, there really *was* a supernatural highway of ley lines between the realms that allowed free travel for gods, ghosts and supernaturals—the Crossroads. And those seated around the table were its protectors.

Some of the tension in the air melted away as everyone laughed.

Finally, Maia patted the air gently. "Alright, everyone, settle down. My apologies for the unintentional humor. But seriously, we really must discover how the Underhill Fae are getting here. We know they aren't using this Crossroads, as we've got it locked down. Plus, Hecate has instructed the two Keepers at the only other Crossroads that intersect with the Fae realm not to allow the Fae to travel for the foreseeable future." She shrugged in helpless confusion. "And we know they aren't driving here..."

Intrigued, Alex interrupted, "*Can* they drive here, though? I thought—"

Conor shot Alex an amused grin. "No, the Fae can't drive here from their realm, sweets." Then he sobered and added, "While you were busy lying to the Council yesterday, Tyre and I mind-chatted a bit. He thinks he knows how the Fae are avoiding the Crossroads and yet can still travel between the realms. If he's right, we've got a major problem."

Alex bristled at Conor's accusation of lying to the Sylvan City Council, but then admitted to herself that's exactly what she had been doing, so she let his comment go. "Okay, spill, Conor. How the heck are these guys popping in and out between the Earth realm and the Fae one without using a Crossroads?"

Tyre's familiar voice sounded from the still-open barn door. "Merry Meet, everyone." When he hesitated near the entrance, Maia waved him in, inviting him to rejoin those gathered around the table. "Come, Tyre, and tell us what you have discovered. I'm assuming that's why you returned?"

The warrior Fae strode to the table, his normally stoic face creased with worry. "I discreetly followed the king's messenger to see if I could discover his method of gaining access to this realm." Tyre sank into an empty chair wearily. "And it is as I feared. The Fae have somehow reopened at least one of the ancient fairy mounds. I saw the king's messenger disappear inside one with my own eyes."

"But I thought fairy mounds were—are a myth," Alex protested. She reached into her long-term memory, dimly recalling her Celtic mythology classes at university. "Weren't the fairy mounds also called hollow hills? In Celtic mythology, they were considered entrances to Underhill—the land of the Fae." She frowned and shook her head. "But of course fairy mounds don't really exist—oh shit."

"Yeah, oh shit, you dingleberry," Larry interjected with a rueful shake of his head. *"You are a priestess of an actual goddess. Your paternal grandfather is the big kahuna of Primordial gods. Around this table sits a motley crew of supernatural and mythological creatures. And you're questioning the existence of freaking fairy mounds?"* Her Familiar's snarky mind-speak made Alex blush in embarrassment. She caught the others seated around the table hiding smiles, so she knew Larry had shared his thoughts with everyone.

Maia eyed Larry reprovingly. "Be kind, Familiar. The supernatural world and its workings are still very new to my niece." She turned her gaze to the Indigo Fae warrior and said, "Please continue, Tyre."

The blue-skinned Fae shifted uncomfortably in his seat—the one Hecate had recently vacated—obviously recalling that a divine butt had been the last to occupy the ornate chair. "First, let me apologize for not discovering the open fairy mound earlier." He turned an apologetic gaze on Alex. "Most of you already know this, but Alex doesn't, so I'll explain. Many centuries ago, the Fae race played havoc here on Earth. They were difficult to punish, as they were impossible to catch, since they would just jump into a fairy mound and disappear into Underhill anytime the authorities got too close. After a while, the other gods got fed up with their antics. They got together and demanded that the goddess Danu, the creator of the Fae race, recall her people to Underhill. They forced her to seal all the fairy mounds and close off these escape hatches forever. After that long-ago time, the locations of the fairy mounds have faded into the mists, even amongst the long-lived Fae. Since then, most of the Fae race has been restricted to the Fae realm, except for those who avoided Danu's roundup. The few Underhill Fae still allowed to travel between the realms must use one of only three Crossroads linking their realm to Earth and the other realms beyond it. Ours is one of those Crossroads, as you know, Alex."

Tyre's tale fascinated Alex. Idly, she wondered what the Fae warrior wasn't saying. *What the heck had the Fae race done to make the gods force Danu to recall and contain most of her people in Underhill and seal the fairy mounds for good?* She would bet the other gods' intervention in her realm's affairs still pissed the Fae goddess off, even all these centuries later.

"Well, *someone* remembered the fairy mounds," Conor stated the obvious. "And it sounds like that someone has reopened some of them—or at least the one between Sylvan City and Underhill. And I doubt they've done this out of the kindness of their heart." Conor's words caused concerned chatter amongst the group. Eventually, everyone agreed that an unsealed fairy mound best explained how the Underhill Fae were traveling undetected between realms without using a Crossroads. The question remaining was who had enough power to open an ancient fairy mound sealed centuries ago by a Primordial goddess—and why did they do it?

After a heated discussion, and not a little angst, the group agreed on a plan.

Tyre had explained that the magical strength needed to reopen a fairy mound likely meant that a god or goddess had been involved. It would take a divine being of incredible power to undo the magic an ancient Primordial goddess had used to seal the mounds. The team agreed that, once they had more information about the who and the why, Alex would inform Hecate of their findings, then leave the matter of the reopened fairy mounds to the gods to wrangle amongst themselves. There was, of course, no doubt that the mounds had to be closed, come what may, or the coming battle for the Fae throne would surely spill over onto Earth, despite their best efforts.

The next part of their strategy involved Alex accepting the king's invitation to the Beltane Ball. It was the best and most direct way to get to the heart of the situation and to determine what they could do to diffuse it and, hopefully, avert a deadly coup.

Alex resisted the group's consensus as long as she could, but not out of fear—or not completely, anyway. She just *really* didn't want to wear a low-cut, barely there Fae ball gown, and she especially didn't want to be seen wearing one. A vision of Conor's heated gaze fixed on her as she showed off her body in a racy Fae gown caused her to reconsider momentarily, then she firmly shut down that train of thought. She fully expected to have Conor's heated gaze on her partially—or preferably fully—unclothed body in the not-too-distant future. In private. Not in the middle of a ballroom filled with Fae nobility.

But since the king obviously expected what he referred to as 'appropriate attire' at his celebration, Alex had no choice in her clothing style for the Beltane ball. She sighed, knowing what she was getting into: she had seen several Fae women wearing the silky, tight, and extremely low-cut garments at formal events in Sylvan City—and they were sooo not her style! *Sigh.*

15

ARE WE THERE YET?

"Listen, fur-face, if you ask 'are we there yet' one more time, I'm gonna let those man-eating bushes behind us have you for dinner," Alex growled as she wiped sweat off her dirty forehead. "You're such a baby."

Larry glared at his magical partner. "It's a legitimate question. We've been walking for days, and I still don't see any sign of the king's castle." He sniffed in derision. "And the bushes back there would love to munch on your human-looking body, but they don't eat dogs, especially not magical ones."

"Maybe they'll make an exception if I ask nicely," Alex retorted. "And it hasn't been days since we left the estate, you goofball. We only arrived in the Fae realm a couple of hours ago. I told you not to come. But noooo, you insisted."

"If I stayed behind, who would keep your ass safe?" Larry barked. "It's my freaking job to protect you, remember?"

"My ass is fine, thank you very much—"

Conor interrupted the brewing argument. "Alex, while I whole-heartedly agree that your ass is fine, we've got company, so now might not be the time—"

The group halted, everyone suddenly on high alert. Tyre and his warriors moved closer, drawing their swords in readiness.

Someone was crashing through the undergrowth on one side of the path, making no attempt to hide their approach. Alex relaxed her grip on her Keeper staff, dialing back the magic she had initially poured into it. No competent bad guy would alert the enemy to their presence in such an inept manner. At least she hoped not.

Eventually, a small, dumpy elderly woman appeared between the trees. She had leaves and sticks tangled in her long gray hair. The ragged green cloak she wore had seen better days—or maybe even centuries. She huffed to a stop upon reaching the path. The old woman's gnarled hands clutched a forked walking stick, around which twined a bright green snake. The serpent eyed Alex and her team critically; its forked tongue flicked in and out, tasting the air.

Alex suppressed a shiver. She could swear a malicious intelligence shone in the snake's obsidian gaze.

"What are you staring at, girl? Don't you know who I am?" The ancient crone's surprisingly powerful voice rumbled through the clearing. She raised her staff, around which the snake twined restlessly, and added, "Oh, and this here is Ed."

The three Indigo Fae, led by Tyre, sheathed their swords, and knelt down, heads bowed. Conor nodded respectfully at the woman, while Larry bowed, his front legs almost touching the ground.

Alex gaped at her suddenly subservient team. What the hell. If one Fae old woman could prostrate them, what chance did they have against the might of the Fae king?

"Alex, bow your head. Slightly. Not too far, since you're a demigoddess. But Danu outranks you—by a whole lot. And this is her realm, remember."

Larry's mind-spoken words woke Alex from her frozen stupor. As their meaning penetrated her dazed mind, she struggled to hide her shock. This elderly, disheveled senior citizen was Danu, the Primordial Celtic goddess of the Fae. *Holy shit.* Quickly, Alex dipped her head respectfully and greeted the goddess. "Um,

Merry Meet, goddess. I'm Alex, Priestess of Hecate and Keeper of—"

"I know who you are, girl," the goddess interrupted, "now lift your pretty chin and look me in the eye." Danu frowned and waved her hand at Alex's still-kneeling team. "Oh, for all the gods' sake, you lot, stand the heck up. I'm not royalty. Just an old, tired goddess who wants to be left alone—and who doesn't care for interference in her realm from any other goddesses, demi-goddesses, Keepers, or anyone else, for that matter." The goddess's eyes narrowed in irritation. "Do I make myself clear?"

"Yes, ma'am," Alex and her team chorused.

When no one moved or spoke, Alex realized she'd have to take the goddess by the proverbial horns. She cleared her throat and addressed Danu. "Um, I understand your concerns, ma'am. But we aren't here to cause any trouble. Really. The thing is that King Donal has invited me to the Beltane Ball." Alex scrabbled in the satchel hanging at her waist. "I have a royal pass."

The goddess's lips pursed in displeasure. "That old goat. Still as horny as ever, I reckon. Bed hopping at Beltane always was Donal's favorite pastime." She cackled. "Oh, he's careful to ensure his royal mages honor me properly at each Sabbat celebration, but that rat-bag hasn't attended a ritual in years." Danu shrugged and admitted, "Not that I've attended one in a fair few decades myself, mind you."

The ancient goddess of the Fae studied Alex intently, her brows raised in consideration. Without unconscious thought, Alex straightened her posture and forced herself to meet Danu's rheumy-eyed gaze. She chided herself silently, *'I'm a demi-goddess, damn it. My grandfather is a Primordial god, and they're top of the proverbial heap, as far as divine beings go.'* A stray thought crystal-ized, and Alex gasped. *Ah crap! Does that mean I'm related to Primordial goddess standing before her? Well, crapola.*

Danu's wrinkled face stretched in an amused grin, and a reluc-tant twinkle lit her hooded eyes. "Took you a while, Keeper. To answer your silent musings, yes, you and I are likely related in some fashion or other. After all, there aren't a lot of us—Primordial gods, I mean. Don't ask me to figure out how we're related, though. Those early millennia, after this whole Earth thing got off the ground and we gained consciousness, are all a bit hazy for me at this point." The divine crone clapped her gnarled hands and cackled in delight. "For all I know, I could even be your many times great grandmother."

Alex heard Larry snicker and sensed Conor and Tyre's amusement through their shared magical connections and cringed inwardly. Would the supernatural revelations never end? She was quickly discovering that familial relationships between the gods and their descendants were rather fluid.

The crone's eyes darkened with malice. "You might be a relation, girl, but I wouldn't hesitate to kill you if I'd a mind to."

Here we go again, Alex mused wryly. She couldn't have a single conversation without one of her newly discovered divine relatives threatening her life, it seemed.

After a tense moment, the goddess sniffed and changed the subject. "Speaking of which, your goddess and I need to have another little chat about her sex-crazed sister goddess. I've already told her once that I will not have that slut, Persephone, interfering in my realm. I've half a mind to let that imbecilic prince get his way and start a war for the throne, just to see the look on Hecate's face."

"Uh, well..." Alex stuttered, then chided herself. *Get it together, woman. Don't let Danu control the conversation.* Her goal during their visit to the Fae realm was merely to gather intelligence, not to provoke the irate goddess into precipitating a war. She took a calming breath and started again. "I agree that whether we have a familial relationship or not is beside the point, ma'am. However, I'm here at the invitation of King Donal to attend the Beltane ball, which is a celebration in *your* honor."

She cleared her throat before continuing. This was where things could get sticky. She'd have to tread a fine line. "Listen, Danu, I understand your grave concerns about Persephone's ill-considered actions, and I share them, as does Hecate. But I'm sure the two of you could work things out if you meet in person and sit down for a really good chat. From experience, I can tell you Hecate has some really great Babylonian wine in her wine cellars. Lots of it."

The ancient goddess hawked and spat on the ground. "That stuff tastes like shit. I've never understood Hecate's fascination with the Babylonians. They were lousy vintners and even crappier warriors." She cocked her head in consideration. "Now, if she's got some decent Phoenician wine in that In-Between place of hers, I might consider a visit."

Alex crossed her fingers behind her back and took a risk. "I'm positive Hecate has a selection of Phoenician wine in her cellars. I shared a glass with her just the other day, and it was delicious." *Liar.* During her first meeting with Hecate, the goddess had poured her a different, but equally ancient, Mediterranean vintage. Alex had choked on the rough, bitter beverage and resolved never to partake again.

Larry gave Alex a quick side-eye. *"I'll get a message to Hecate telling her to raid her wine cellar and bring up a case or three of Danu's favorite tipple. I hear she can really knock 'em back."*

Alex suppressed a relieved sigh at Larry's mind-spoken remarks, but was careful not to smile at his irreverent comment about the ancient Fae goddess's drinking habits.

Danu stroked the head of her serpent gently, her eyes narrowed in consideration. The snake hissed softly, obviously enjoying his mistress's ministrations. After a tense moment, when the fate of Alex's mission—and perhaps her life—hung in the balance, the goddess nodded her head decisively. "It's been a wee while since I've left these woods. I do like my cottage, and my alone time, but perhaps it'll do me good to take a little trip. Tell Hecate I'll call on her in a bit. I'll need to get my chariot out of storage and round up a horse or two. Dammit, perhaps I shouldn't have listened to the gods when they asked me to close the fairy mounds. Those things made travel soooo much easier.

Instead, I'll have to use one of Hecate's newfangled Crossroads, dammit."

The goddess's words trailed off, turning into vague mumbles. "Robes cleaned ... servants ... do something with my hair. Hmmm."

Alex squinted in confusion, afraid to derail the goddess's plans. *Chariot? Horses? Exactly how long had it been since Danu had left her realm and traveled the leys to Earth? It seemed the goddess didn't know someone had reopened at least one of her fairy mounds. The question was—why not?*

Conor rescued Alex from her silent musings when he assured the goddess that she wouldn't need to arrange for road transport. He didn't mention the reopened fairy mound. "If you go to the Crossroads temple at the edge of the far south hills, goddess, you can travel the ley line directly to the In-Between. Just tell the Keeper there that Hecate is expecting you."

"Sounds like a plan, young man." Danu nodded approvingly at Conor, then grinned lasciviously at Alex. "If you haven't bedded this Barghest yet, girl, I'd suggest you get on the ball, so to speak." Cackling with laughter at her ribald joke, the goddess made a rude gesture, then disappeared in a puff of dirty gray smoke.

No one spoke for several minutes. Alex and her team just stood still, basking in relief, and breathing in the still-smoky air.

"Well, shit." Larry summed up their experience with the ancient mother goddess of the Fae. "What a woman—I mean, goddess."

Everyone nodded in silent agreement, then the group resumed their interrupted journey.

The dangerous political tightrope they walked here in the Fae realm had shaken, but held. Hopefully, their meeting with the king would go at least as well as the one with Danu.

Alex smiled wryly. *One could only hope, right? At least no one had died. Yet.*

∼

SEVERAL HOURS LATER, with no end to their journey in sight and after another bout of complaining by Larry, Alex forced a change of subject. Time to get some answers to the confused musings rolling around in her mind.

"Larry, if you'd just shut up for a minute, I've got a couple of questions for you."

Her Familiar grumbled a last complaint, then shook his head, pink ears flapping against his face. "Since you're not listening to my quite legitimate concerns about the length and difficulty of this journey, I guess I can answer a few questions." Larry gave his partner a toothy grin. "But first, I've got a question for you. Are we ther—"

Alex rolled her eyes and groaned in frustration. "Don't you dare ask that damn question again, you furry whiner. No, we are not 'there yet', and you darn well know it. Tyre says we've got another hour or so on this path. Then we should emerge from the Fae wood and see the castle in the distance."

Larry snorted. "In the distance—so it's even further away than the end of the trees."

When Alex's gaze hardened, he hastened to reply. "Okay, okay. What are your questions? I might not know all the answers, but what I don't know, I can probably guess."

"Don't guess, please. Let's concentrate on what you know, bud." Alex paused, gathering her thoughts. "First of all, exactly how old is Danu? She looks ancient."

"Danu is one of the oldest, if not actually the oldest, of the gods," Larry replied, nodding solemnly. "Even amongst the Primordial gods, she's respected as an elder and referred to as Mother Goddess."

Awed, Alex whispered, "So she could very well be my great-grandmother. That would make Chronos her son."

Larry nodded, a twinkle in his chocolate brown eyes. "Yep, she's old enough to be Chronos's mom, and then some. I'd be willing to bet the creatures she used to pull her first chariot weren't horses, but dinosaurs."

Everyone burst out laughing at Larry's irreverent comment.

A stiff breeze sprang up, shivering the leaves on the trees over-head, precipitating a shower of pinecones and other debris, all of which seemed to concentrate its aim at the prancing poodle below.

"Ow! Damn, that hurts!" With little success, Larry ducked and dodged, attempting to avoid the falling missiles.

Alex and the team glanced around nervously. The powerful goddess of the Fae might just enjoy eavesdropping on the intruders in her realm.

"I suggest you keep your comments respectful, Larry, if you want to reach the castle without being covered in bruises—or worse." Alex threw her Familiar a warning glare.

"Yes, ma'am." Larry shook himself thoroughly, leaves and bits of pinecone flying from his fur. He bowed his head and said, "I got the message, Danu. Just the facts from now on, ma'am."

Alex could swear she heard a distant cackle, accompanied by a protracted hiss. Sounded like Ed the Snake wasn't pleased with her smart-mouthed Familiar, either.

Larry pranced to the front of the group, probably eager to resume the journey, and to avoid answering any more questions, Alex reflected wryly. That was too bad, as she had a ton more, but she vowed to ask them through mind-speak from now on. The ancient goddess couldn't possibly overhear that. Hopefully not, anyway. She shrugged in resignation and took the risk.

"Let's keep this conversation to mind-speak from now on, Larry. From what Danu said, it sounds like she doesn't know that someone has reopened a fairy mound. Who could have done that, and why? And why did she close them in the first place?" Alex trudged along beside her Familiar, purposely not paying him any mind. No point in queuing in the goddess to their silent conversation. *"I know the gods got fed up with refereeing disputes between the Fae and the supernaturals on Earth, but just exactly was the issue?"*

Larry cocked his head in consideration. *"Not that the gods treat their own people much better, mind you. But it's just not done to allow your people to go around stealing other gods' humans and supernaturals to take back to your realm as slaves and servants. Fed up with Danu and her people's bad behavior, the gods got together and staged an intervention. The Primordial gods requested Danu control her people—or else. When she told everyone to piss off, the gods put their collective foot down. They forced her to call most of the Fae back to Underhill and made her seal the fairy mounds to keep the Fae troublemakers locked away in their own realm."*

Alex considered Larry's explanation. Sounded like Danu—and her people—had been causing problems almost since time began. Hooo boy, and Persephone had instructed her to 'just fix this mess' like it wasn't a big deal. *Yeah, right.*

Tyre's deep voice rumbled into Alex's mind. *"Forgive the interruption, but allow me to clarify a few things."* The Indigo Fae warrior's gaze met Alex's, his eyes a well of remembered grief and repentance. *"Larry is right—to a point. My Fae ancestors were out of control—but not everything was their fault."*

Alex bit back a reply about people—and gods—being responsible for their own actions and resolved to listen to Tyre's explanation. "Go ahead, then. Fill us in on Fae history."

The Fae warrior's stoic expression as he strode along bore testament to his inner turmoil. Alex had to hurry to keep up with the long-legged Fae. *"Talk to me, Tyre,"* she pleaded.

Tyre rubbed his face, then sighed with a nod. *"In the mists of time, my people, the Fae, had another name. When Danu birthed us, she named us the Tuatha de Danann. The people of the goddess Danu. We don't know our paternal heritage, but it's rumored that our father was also a god, just not a Primordial one."*

Alex's eyes widened in disbelief. *"Wouldn't that make her children—your direct ancestors—gods as well?"* She whistled silently. *"That would explain a lot."*

Waggling his head in a 'yes and no' movement, Tyre pursed his lips. *"If only it were that simple, Alex. Or clear. While a divine father should have meant the original Fae were also divine, it soon became apparent that they weren't gods—at least, not completely. Just mostly.*

While the Tuatha de Danann certainly had the normal divine charac-teristics of extraordinary magical powers, overweening pride, and a disregard for commonly accepted morals and ethics, there were indica-tors their heritage was more complicated than that."

Alex eyed the Fae in confusion. *"How complicated?"*

"The Tuatha weren't immortal, you see. While long-lived, their life spans ended naturally after a millennium or so. And when they coupled with other Tuatha, their offspring did not possess divine natures." The warrior shrugged. *"Thus, the Fae were born."*

Trying to work her way through Tyre's convoluted explanation, Alex thought she might see the issue. *"So, Danu birthed a race of super-charged supernaturals who were pissed they didn't quite make the 'god' category. They acted like a bunch of entitled teenagers and rampaged across Earth, causing the actual gods in charge of that realm to tell Danu to get a handle on her, uh, kids."* She nodded in under-standing. *"At first, Danu wouldn't listen to anyone speaking ill of her offspring. However, once the Primordial gods got involved, they forced Danu into accountability for her people, making her recall the Fae to her realm and lock down the fairy mounds."*

Tyre's lips curved in a reluctant smile. *"You've summed up the Fae situation nicely."*

Alex met the Fae's gaze with empathy. *"This all must have happened ... what, several thousand years ago?"* She smiled and point-edly raked the handsome, broadly muscled warrior with a sexy once-over. *"But you don't look a day over what—a century? None of that ancient history is your fault, you know."* She gave a resigned shrug. *"It doesn't sound like anyone's fault, really."* Except maybe the goddess who birthed a race of amoral—almost, but not quite divine—progeny, she mused wryly. And Danu's irresponsible actions had consequences that had echoed down the generations until now, as a once semi-divine race starved while their corrupt king overfilled his coffers and his treacherous son schemed for the throne.

Conor summed up everyone's thoughts. *"The question is,*

though, where has Danu been for the past century or so? She's dangerously out of touch with what's been happening in her realm."

Worry clouded Larry's gaze. *"And if Danu didn't do it, who the hell reopened that fairy mound—and how did they do it?"*

Alex set her face and increased her tired pace. *"Hopefully, we'll get some answers while we're at this damned Beltane celebration."*

16

NOW WE'RE THERE

Silence blanketed the travelers as they continued their journey through the dense forest, each consumed by their own thoughts.

After what seemed like hours, Tyre stopped suddenly, and Alex stumbled to a stop beside him. He pointed ahead at a patch of blue sky, visible for the first time since they had entered the forest. "See that gnarled oak tree on the left? That's the boundary of the Fae Forest. Beyond that begins King Donal's lands."

Intrigued, Alex asked, "But doesn't the king rule the Fae Forest as well?"

"No one rules the Fae Forest," the Fae warrior whispered, shivering as he eyed the dense greenery surrounding them. "Some say this forest is sentient—another of Danu's living creations. Others say the forest was here first, even before the most ancient goddess of them all."

Alex echoed her companion's shiver. The foreboding sense of existential dread that had followed the travelers from the moment they arrived in the Fae realm and entered the forest made perfect sense now.

They left the cover of the trees and spotted an enormous castle in the distance. Its massive walls sported sharp crenellations and surrounded an inner courtyard filled with an amazing number of turrets and towers. The castle-city sprawled across the rolling foothills of a towering, knife-edged mountain range.

Between the forest and the castle lay a rich, green patchwork of fields, crisscrossed with narrow lanes leading between quaint farmsteads and villages that would not look out of place in Medieval Europe. Smoke rose from multiple chimneys, while horses and carts clopped along the narrow byways.

"If we ever want to get there, we better get a move on," Larry grumbled, padding into the sunlight beyond the trees. "My paws are freaking killing me. I hope that damned castle has modern plumbing. I'm dying for a hot bath."

The team trudged wearily after the complaining canine. Alex didn't disagree with him, though. There damned well better be a bathroom somewhere in that monstrosity of a castle. She was sooo not into chamber pots or outhouses.

Luck was with them. Soon after they entered the rustic landscape, a farmer had offered the team a ride in his cart, agreeing to drop them directly by the castle gates. *Probably not luck*, Alex reflected tiredly as they bounced along in the back of the wooden cart. It likely had more to do with the heavy gold coins Tyre had pressed into the man's work-roughened hand.

The castle grew until the view of it almost eclipsed the enormous mountains soaring at its back. Finally, the plodding horses drew to a stop in the main square in front of the castle gates. The team wearily clambered down from the uncomfortable cart while Tyre thanked the driver with a bow and a quiet word.

Alex eyed the stone-faced sentries guarding the massive archway cut into the castle wall. The tall, slender Fae guards wore elaborate green uniforms similar to those worn by the bands of soldiers they had seen roaming the villages they had passed through. The king obviously ruled his kingdom with an iron fist.

The massive wooden gates swung slowly open as a blast of trumpets blared from within the castle courtyard. Alex jumped and covered her ears at the deafening sound.

"Well, they know we're here. Let's hope this establishment lives up to the hype." Larry's cryptic words slid into Alex's mind.

"What hype?" She asked.

"Modern plumbing and excellent food," Larry replied succinctly. "Oh, and decent dungeons."

"Dungeons?" Alex echoed, brows raised in concern.

Conor aimed a gentle kick at Alex's grinning Familiar. "He's teasing you, Alex. At least about the dungeons. We won't be touring those."

"Hopefully," Alex muttered, crossing her fingers. She had a really bad feeling about this.

ONCE ALEX PRODUCED the scroll containing King Donal's invitation, the guards' dour demeanors lightened. They produced a senior functionary, who hurried to greet them and arranged for them to be escorted to sumptuous suites within the castle.

When the last obsequious servant finally withdrew from their shared room, Larry hopped onto the massive four-poster bed, then scratched at the covers until he had created a comfortable nest. Once settled, he heaved a sigh and reiterated his earlier grievance. "I still don't see why we have to share a room, Alex. After all, this place must have a thousand bedrooms."

Alex yawned and eyed her Familiar through bleary eyes. "I guess dogs—even magical ones—don't rate special treatment in this realm, bud, so you'll have to make do with sharing." She peered into the massive marble shrine that housed their private bathroom and sighed with pleasure at the sight, glad to have at least one of her worries assuaged. The large room featured a full complement of modern bathroom fixtures, plus a bathtub that could comfortably fit three. She turned on the tub's swan-shaped golden faucets and grinned with delight when hot water immediately gushed forth. *Maybe this visit wouldn't be so bad, after all.*

Larry jumped off the bed eagerly when a timid knock sounded on the bedroom door. "I'll get it. Pretty sure it's for me."

Frowning in confusion, Alex peered around the bathroom door so see a trio of squat Brownies entering the room, hauling a massive copper tub filled with steaming water between them. The Brownies heaved it into position in front of the roaring fire, then eyed Larry with shy smiles. A fourth Brownie brought up the rear, the fluffy stack of towels in her arms almost obscuring her vision. The shortest Brownie, whose head barely reached the top of the tub, bobbed a curtsey and spoke, her tone respectful. "Does this meet with your approval, Familiar Larry? Would you like us to stay and help you bathe?"

Larry nodded solemnly at the gathered Brownies. "I greatly appreciate your help in supplying bathing water and towels. I'm quite able to handle the bath part myself, so no need to stay. Please pass my gratitude on to the head housekeeper for me, as well. It's still Yeselle, I believe?" The little poodle met Alex's shocked gaze over the nodding heads of the Fae, an amused gleam in his eyes.

After the door closed behind the gaggle of giggling Brownies, Alex glared at her Familiar in disbelief. "Why didn't you tell me you'd been here before, you butthead? In another Familiar life, I assume? You knew exactly how long the journey here would take, didn't you?" She threw up her hands in frustration. "All that 'are we there yet' whining during the trip here was a complete lie!"

Larry snickered, but didn't reply, instead testing the water in the tub with a tentative paw. Prancing to Alex's side, he presented his neck. "Hey, take my collar off, will you? I wanna get in while the water's still hot." He grinned mischievously up at Alex as she unlatched his braided leather collar. "Any chance you could scrub my back?"

As Alex slipped the collar from Larry's neck, she pinched his side. Hard. "You ordered the water yourself, so you can bathe your-self, buster."

"Ow, that hurt!" Larry yelped and scurried away, then hopped

into the still-steaming tub, settling in with a groan. "Oh, that feels so good! You should go get in your own bath, Alex. You stink."

"Oh, shit!" Alex realized the water in her tub had been running all this time. She raced into the bathroom and heaved a sigh of relief when she saw the water level in the massive tub had barely reached the halfway point. Spying several jars of sparkling bath salts perched on a shelf over the tub, she smiled in delight, but then hesitated before choosing one. *What if they contained Fae magic?* She mused, then shrugged and poured a generous amount into the foaming water. *What the hell.*

After a relaxing soak, during which she just might have dozed off, Alex dried herself with a fluffy towel, then fell into bed beside her already snoring Familiar. *Why hadn't Larry told her he had been to the Fae realm before?* That question still rankled, so she poked him awake.

"Hey, wake up, fur-face! Why didn't you tell me you'd been to the castle before? And why complain the whole way here as if you hadn't?"

Larry rolled over, exposing his tummy for a belly rub, then snorted in resignation when she failed to comply. "You're pissed, Alex. I get it." With a lithe movement, he sat up and met her annoyed gaze with a somber one. "Truth is, Alex, I couldn't tell you. DEAF makes us Familiars take an oath not to reveal details of missions from previous lives to their current magical partners." Cocking his head, he added, "There are a few exceptions, of course, but I don't think our mostly uneventful journey here qualifies."

After a tense staring contest, Alex blew out a breath and nodded. "Okay, I understand, I guess." Her eyes narrowed. "I get that you couldn't tell me about your previous missions to the Fae realm, but why did you complain the entire way here? Surely that wasn't necessary."

Larry gave her a twinkling side-eye. "You know what a poor traveler I am, right? If I hadn't complained, you'd have eventually wondered why not. Besides, our banter took your mind off the journey, didn't it? Well, until we ran into that bit-shit crazy goddess in the woods."

Alex snickered. "You may have a point there, fuzz-but." Her snicker turned into a belly laugh. "It was hilarious when Danu got even with you for badmouthing her by pelting you with all those pinecones and stuff."

After a moment of pique, Larry joined her in laughter. "I'll never speak ill of that old crone while in her woods again."

"Wonder if she can hear you here in the castle?" Alex asked, her voice innocent.

Larry glanced nervously around the room and shifted closer to Alex in the bed. She smiled and closed her eyes, considering them even.

SAVORY SCENTS WOKE Alex the next morning. She opened her eyes at the gentle click of the door closing. Larry jumped on the bed and bestowed a bacon-flavored lick on her cheek.

"Yuck! What'd you do that for?" Alex wiped her wet face on a pillow. "I'm assuming you've already been out for your morning constitutional—and made your way back here via the kitchen."

"I was bursting this morning, Alex," Larry protested. "Despite the wonders of modern indoor plumbing, the castle's bathrooms aren't really set up for dogs and their business, if you know what I mean. I'd much rather leave my morning messages outside on a bush or two." He grinned at her and licked his chops. "And yes, I stopped by the kitchens on my way back to the room, but not just to grab a snack. I had a very informative chat with my old friend, Yeselle, while she plied me with breakfast."

Interest lit Alex's eyes. "Oh? What did she have to say? Wait, let me use that modern plumbing you just mentioned so I can have some of whatever smells so good on the tray the maid just left." Upon her return, Alex settled down to eat her breakfast, then got back to her original question. "Well? What's the scoop, bud?"

Larry gave the room a narrow-eyed once-over, then flared his power. Golden magic wafted from his fur, weaving hazy patterns in the air until it filled the room with a yellow glow. *"Okay, we should be good once my magic 'sets'—which'll take a minute or two. Just to be on the safe side, let's limit our conversation to mind-speak until then."*

Alex's jaw dropped. *"You think they bugged the room?"* She eyed the room's antiquated decor doubtfully. *"The Fae realm doesn't appear very tech savvy, so I highly doubt that."*

"Don't let looks deceive you, Alex. They've got almost as much tech in this realm as we do on Earth. They just choose to hide it under medieval trappings." Larry sneezed, then wiped his face on the covers. *"Plus, they don't even need technology to bug the room, nimrod. Magic, remember?"*

Alex's eyes widened as understanding dawned. "Oh, yeah. I forgot about that."

"You might wanna get dressed. I stopped by Conor's room on the way back here. He and Tyre will be here shortly, so we can have a planning session," Larry told her.

Gazing down at her ratty sleep shirt in horror, Alex abandoned her breakfast and dashed to the bathroom. "Why didn't you tell me sooner?"

"I wanted to see how fast you can run."

Alex slammed the door on her obnoxious Familiar's smirk, then hurriedly dressed and brushed her shoulder-length black hair. She had just finished putting it into a practical ponytail when she heard Conor's voice in the bedroom.

She opened the bathroom door just as Tyre entered behind Conor. Once the bedroom door was firmly closed and locked, everyone found a seat, then eyed each other in silence through the hazy golden mist of Larry's magic.

"Larry thinks the room may be bugged, so he put up a magical barrier," Alex said, fanning the air, making the magic-filled haze dance and swirl.

Both Conor and Tyre nodded in agreement.

"He's right, Alex. All our rooms are probably bugged." Conor lowered his voice. "In fact, it would be wise to guard our words anywhere in the castle."

Alex's stomach tightened with anxiety as she considered their precarious situation. The closest Crossroads was over half a day's trek away. If anything went wrong during their visit, there would be no fast escape route. Things could get ugly, and she had no desire to spend any time in the king's dungeons.

Larry's voice pulled Alex out of her dismal musings. She tuned in to hear her Familiar give a report of his conversation with his housekeeper friend, Yeselle.

The little poodle summed up his findings. "The bottom line is, Yeselle says the king's rule has been getting worse over the past few years. He's never been the best king. Then, several years ago, there was a shakeup on his Council of Advisors. He fired most all the old ones and appointed unknown newcomers—a few who are not even Fae. Things started changing for the worse not long after that. About a year later, he exiled his daughter to Earth and kicked his son out of the castle, sending him to live in a royal hunting lodge at the far reaches of the Fae realm." Larry shook his head in disgust. "It's no wonder Prince Cair is pissed, and the people are restless. As for the princess, no one knows what became of her once she left the realm, but rumors abound that she's preparing an army and will soon return to rescue the realm. Wishful thinking, if you ask me."

Everyone sat in silence for several minutes after Larry finished his report, absorbing the fact that the Fae kingdom's problems involved much more than a traitorous prince with a wayward goddess for an ex-girlfriend.

"Well, fuck." Alex swore vehemently. "Sounds like Persephone merely poked an existing hornet's nest when she slept with the prince."

"Pretty sure the poking went the other way—ow, what'd you do that for?" Larry skittered away from Alex's pinching fingers. "I'm just saying."

"Yes, and we don't need your risqué remarks about who has been poking whom," Alex retorted.

Smothered snickers alerted the quarreling duo that the others were enjoying their banter.

"Sorry, guys." Alex apologized to Conor and Tyre, who both lounged in chairs set on either side of the flickering fireplace. Alex and Larry were both perched on the end of the bed.

"Apologies accepted." Conor's lips curved in amusement. "You two are an absolute riot to watch."

Tyre, usually reserved and serious, snickered and nodded in agreement.

Conor soon sobered. "Well, now that we know the lay of the land, so to speak, we've got our work cut out for us. Larry, have you been able to find out why the king invited Alex to the Beltane ball?"

Larry shook his head in disappointment. "Afraid not. In fact, Yeselle told me the king's advisors didn't inform her of our visit until just before we arrived."

Tyre sat forward, rubbing his forehead, and squinting when the light from the window fell across his face. "I think I might have information about that. My warriors and I refused rooms in the castle and instead stayed in the barracks last night. We joined the soldiers in a local bar for a few glasses of mead, and my head is still pounding." He turned apologetic eyes on Alex. "I hope you don't mind about last night. It would have taken us longer to reach you from there if danger arose, but—"

Alex cut him off, offended by his insinuation that she might need defending. "I'm good, Tyre. I can take care of myself. Sorry about your hangover." *No, she wasn't.* "What did you find out?"

"Apparently, King Donal is worried. His spies have told him there's a coup in the offing, but they haven't been able to confirm who is behind it. The king knows his son isn't happy with his banishment from court, and I get the feeling from the soldiers that they have little respect for the prince. Cair certainly doesn't seem to have their support. From what I hear, money is on the princess as the next Fae ruler. Apparently, even though the king exiled her several years ago, support for her amongst the populace is still very high."

Tyre paused his report, his gaze heavy with concern. "I also got an earful of discontent. The king hasn't paid the soldiers in months, and the people are starving after a hard winter. According to the soldiers I spoke with, the king hasn't opened because they're empty. The consensus is that there *will* be an uprising. Whether it turns into a war, or a full-fledged coup, and who the winner will be are the only things in doubt."

The Indigo Fae shook his head and blew out a breath. "And you're not the only powerful non-Fae invited to tonight's ball—most for the first time. My guess is that the king is attempting to shore up support for his reign, hoping to form alliances that will help him hang on to his throne."

Alex ran her hands through Larry's soft fur, seeking comfort. "So, we've walked into a damn mess. And it's much bigger than just a horny goddess sleeping with an ambitious and handsome Fae prince."

"Yes, I fear so, Keeper." Tyre's shoulders drooped, weariness and worry filling his eyes.

Conor rose and paced the length of the room.

Alex could sense his disquiet through their magical bond. She slapped the bedcovers, determined to attend the king's ball and then get everyone safely back to the Crossroads as soon as possible. They could figure things out once back on Earth.

Smiling with false brightness, she said, "Why don't we all keep our eyes and ears open today, then gather back here before the tonight's ball to share our intelligence?" She turned to Tyre. "I'm assuming you'll be attending the ball as my personal guard?" At Tyre's nod, she addressed Conor. "And you are going as my, er, date?"

Conor grinned at her. "Eager for a second date, are you? After the disaster that was the last one?"

Alex winced in pained remembrance. Their first date had

ended when the goddess Persephone crashed the party, told them about her affair with the Fae prince and Danu's threats, then demanded they 'fix this mess.' She stammered, "Um, no, not really. I mean, it's not that I don't want to go on another date with you, but—"

"No worries, sweets. We can arrange a second date once we clean up Persephone's problem and prevent a Fae war. I never got that goodnight kiss you promised me, remember." Conor's lips curved at Alex's blush. "Tonight, I'll be attending the ball as your Guardian, a position that is recognized in all the realms as a shifter protector assigned to protect a VIP supernatural. Such as you."

"Oh," Alex responded with a sigh. Every time she turned around, more details about her role in the supernatural world emerged. "Thanks for the explanation." Weariness lowered her shoulders. "I didn't get a lot of sleep last night, guys. Mind if I take a mid-morning nap?"

Conor headed towards the door. "Let's go, Tyre. Get some sleep, Alex. It's gonna be a long night tonight."

17

HAVING A BALL

Once Conor and Tyre left, Alex and Larry napped for a while, then enjoyed a late lunch, when one of the Brownies who had brought Larry's bathwater the previous evening delivered a fragrant tray from the kitchens.

"Can't fault the food around here, that's for sure," Alex mumbled, her mouth full.

Larry nodded as he polished off the last of his steak and gave a cryptic reply. "Well, Yeselle owes me a favor or two."

After their meal, a combination of weariness and worry had Alex's eyes closing. "I don't know about you, Larry, but I could use another nap. I'm still exhausted."

Larry jumped onto the bed and settled down. "Sounds like a plan."

When Alex woke, the last of the sun's golden rays slanted into the room, and Larry's spot on the bed was cold.

A gentle knock on the door sounded. "Are you in there, Your Excellency? I really do need to come in now."

Alex realized a prior knock must have woken her. She rubbed her eyes blearily and pushed back the covers. "Yes, I'm here. Please come in."

The door opened, and a tall, thin woman slipped timidly into the room. When she spotted Alex, her eyes widened, and she gave a low curtsy. "Your Excellency. I'm Maisy. Yeselle sent me. I'll be your lady's maid this evening and help you get ready for tonight's ball."

Alex started to refuse the maid's services, then realized she had no clue how to put on the many undergarments and the silky Fae ballgown that she had purchased in Sylvan City. "Um, hi Maisy. I could use your help, thanks. And please call me Alex. I'm not an Excellency." *At least, she didn't think so, but who knew?*

Maisy proved to be a lifesaver. She deftly guided a bemused Alex through several hours of bathing, hairdressing, makeup, and more.

"It's time to get dressed now, Your Excellency." Maisy eyed Alex's lace-edged scarlet underwear critically. "Are you sure you don't have anything with more lace, ma'am? Most Fae women wear full lace undergarments for formal occasions." The maid turned toward the door. "Let me get you some."

"No!" Alex yelped, then lowered her voice, realizing she had shouted at the hapless woman. "No, Maisy, that's okay. These will do. No one's going to see them anyway, so I'll be fine." An image of a certain sexy Hellhound Barghest filled her mind, but she cut off the thought ruthlessly. Conor would not see her underwear tonight—not while in a restless realm on a spy mission, where danger lurked around every corner. *Sigh.* Another time, maybe. Definitely.

Maisy cocked her head, confused. "But it's Beltane tonight. And you'll be so beautiful in your gown." The maid's eyes twinkled. "There will be many Fae who would eagerly accept an invitation from you this evening, Your Excellency."

"An invitation to what? Oh." A fiery blush swept over Alex's face when she remembered the occasion for the ball. Maia had warned her that Fae women celebrated a traditional Beltane by bed-hopping with one or more men—or women—of the woman's choosing. "Um, no, Maisy. That's not gonna happen tonight, thanks. I plan to return to my room solo."

The maid nodded doubtfully as she fingered the silky, sparkling ballgown laid out on the bed. "Yes, Your Excellency. If you say so. But this dress will ensure you have plenty of opportunities—if you change your mind." She reached for the corset next to the dress and turned toward Alex with a sly smile. "Let's make sure you have lots of choices."

Alex allowed the maid to begin the laborious task of dressing her. Ten minutes later, she sighed and fidgeted with the delicate lace lining the corset that barely contained her breasts until a tug at her back almost sent her tumbling to the floor.

"Please don't let go of the bedpost, your Excellency," Maisy instructed as she tugged hard on the corset strings.

Alex renewed her grip on the bedpost, winced, and sucked in a pained breath.

"Excellent!" The maid enthused. "With that grip, we'll get your waist nicely curved and your bosom to the proper height, your Excellency."

If her bosom went any higher, Alex brooded, she'd be able to blow her nose in it. "That's tight enough, Maisy. I still need to breathe tonight. And for the last time, I'm not an 'Excellency'. You can call me Alex, or ma'am, if you prefer."

The willowy maid nodded deferentially as she tied the last knot in the torturous garment. "Yes, Your Exc—ma'am."

Stifling a sigh, Alex let go of the bedpost and turned to face the maid. "I really do appreciate your help tonight, Maisy. I'm just not used to wearing Fae formal attire." She added a silent promise to herself. *And I'll never wear it again if I can help it.*

As the maid tied the last of the silk ribbons that fastened the gown, Alex viewed herself in the full-length mirror. The woman who stared back at her was a complete stranger. Multiple braids strung with pearls wound loosely around her head, their gleaming luster peeking through her thick, black locks. Her skin looked flawless; she had never worn so much makeup in her life. Lined with glittering emerald green and deep black kohl, her green eyes appeared huge. And the dress—what there was of it—clung to her every curve, revealing far more than it covered.

Alex resolved not to bend over during the evening's events. She was pretty sure her boobs would tumble out of their perch at the top of the gown if she did. The corset wrapped tightly around her body surely meant sitting was out of the question. She'd just have to stand all evening and avoid catching anyone's eye, in case they mistook her idle gaze as an invitation. *Sigh.* This spying thing would be much more fun in 'traditional' spy gear. Cotton under-wear and loose black clothing would be much more comfortable than her current attire.

"Oh, ma'am, you look so beautiful," Maisy breathed. The maid stood back and clapped her hands. "Magnificent! Every man in the room—and some ladies, I'm sure—would jump at an invitation from you tonight."

Before Alex could again deny any intention of participating in the evening's more carnal activities, a sharp rap on the door inter-rupted her.

Conor's voice, muffled by the closed door, asked, "Alex, are you almost ready? It's a long walk to the ballroom."

Alex's eyes narrowed at Conor's implication that she might not be ready. She strode to the door and yanked it open. "What? Are you assuming that because I'm a woman, I'll be late getting ready? You know what they say about assumptions." Her rebuke trailed off when she realized Conor wasn't listening.

He stood in the doorway, unmoving, his heated amber gaze ranging over her body, setting a sensuous fire in its path. Alex stifled a smile and tamped down an answering flare of desire. Maybe the past two hours of torture were worth it, after all. She couldn't resist teasing him. "You might want to shut your mouth, Conor. I'm pretty sure I spotted a fly in here earlier."

Conor's jaw snapped shut, and his gaze finally made it to her eyes. The ardent desire she saw there warmed her right to her lacy, and not-covering-enough, underwear. She turned away to hide her deep blush.

"Come on in. I'm ready, but I haven't seen Larry since lunchtime. Should we wait for him, or will he meet us there, do you think?" Alex spoke to distract Conor from the scent of her attraction. He had told her often enough that Barghests had an excellent sense of smell. Usually, he said it with a sexy grin, letting her know he could smell her arousal whenever it occurred. Like right now. *Fuck. How the heck was she going to make it through the evening without at least one wardrobe malfunction?*

Movement at the door caught Alex's eye. Conor swung around, hand on his sword. Both relaxed when they recognized the newcomers. Tyre, flanked by his two warriors, stood in the corridor.

Alex's eyes widened at the Indigo Fae's apparel. Gone were their normal loose white shirts and dark breeches. Instead, they wore scarlet uniforms dotted with tassels, ribbons, and gleaming silver buttons. And they wore them well.

"Wow! You guys look great!" Alex exclaimed, then eyed her deep red ballgown. "We even match." She smothered a grin when a flash of irritation touched her mind. Conor was jealous of her compliments to the Fae warriors. *Hah!*

"You don't look half bad yourself, Conor," Alex assured him, eyeing his elaborate midnight black attire with approval. She got in a last dig. "But you don't match the rest of us."

"Speaking of matching, Yeselle dug up a scarlet collar for me. What do you think?" Larry pranced into the room, the deep burgundy satin and ruby jewels adorning his new collar glittering in the firelight.

Alex snickered. "I thought you hated bejeweled collars, bud. You've always warned me you'd poop in my shoes if I made you wear one."

Larry stuck his nose in the air. "And so I would—if you forced me to wear one. Would *you* wear formal attire for a trip to the coffee shop? No? Well, neither would I. However, a Fae ball requires a certain amount of bling." The little poodle studied himself approvingly in the mirror. "This collar fits the bill nicely."

Flanked by three Indigo Fae warriors, with a Hellhound Barghest Guardian at her side and her furry Familiar prancing along at her feet, Alex began the long walk to the ballroom. She silently thanked the gods that, despite the restrictive, yet risqué, ballgown, at least Fae footwear favored comfort over style. She would keep the low-heeled silk slippers, if nothing else in her current getup.

Prompted by Conor, Alex smiled, shook hands, and nodded during the introductions at the ball. Upon her arrival, the footman had announced her to the room as Her Excellency, Alexandria, Keeper of the San Antonio Crossroads, and Priestess of Hecate. *Maisy was right. I am an Excellency, at least in the Fae realm*, Alex mused.

Tyre had told her the party wouldn't really get started until the king arrived, and that he was notoriously late for most events, so Alex strolled aimlessly around the massive ballroom. Conor and the Indigo Fae formed a tight knot around Alex, allowing the many attendees curious glances but no contact with her.

Someone had spelled the ballroom's ceiling to resemble the night sky; overhead, stars glittered against inky blackness. The massive ballroom's walls featured an ever-changing panoply of scenery, from rugged mountains to pastoral scenes—and even a few bedroom ones. Each scene had one thing in common: Fae of all genders involved in sexual situations, either as couples or in groups.

Alex fought a blush each time the display featured another graphic interlude.

"The orgies a bit much for you?" Conor murmured, teasing her.

"I told you, get out of my head. No mind reading tonight, please." Alex warned, eyeing a grinning Conor over her glass of sparkling water. He had advised her to avoid the punch unless she wanted to wake up with a severe hangover—or worse, in the morning.

"I know you said they spiked the punch with nectar," Alex said. "What's worse than waking up in bed with a hangover?"

Conor's gaze contained humor and heat. "Waking up in someone else's bed with a hangover."

"Oh. Oh!" Alex's eyes widened. "The punch contains an aphrodisiac?"

Before Conor could respond, a tall, elegantly dressed Fae joined their group. A lecherous leer marred his handsome face. "I have drunk no punch tonight, ma'am, and yet I'd bed you in a trice."

The man's feet left the ground as Tyre hauled him up by his silken neckcloth. The Fae's purpling face and swinging feet spurred Alex to intervene to avoid a diplomatic incident. Wouldn't want to explain a dead Fae aristocrat to the king.

"Put him down, Tyre. Let me handle this." Alex studied the struggling man through narrowed eyes as he regained his feet. "You dare insult me, and break the traditions of your own people, you cretin? Women rule the romantic roost this evening, as you well know." Her lips curled in disdain. "And no amount of nectar would make me stoop low enough to issue you an invitation to share my bed. Get out of my sight before I let my guards have you."

Eyes flashing with anger, the Fae raised a threatening hand. Before he could strike, two massive castle guards appeared and yanked him off his feet. The furious man fought their firm grip. "Put me down, you imbeciles. You know well who I am!"

"They know exactly who you are, you fool." A short, stout Fae stepped out from behind the guards. The man's elaborate gold uniform sparkled with jeweled medals, and a simple gold circlet sat on his snow-white hair. Alex realized the king had arrived. The rotund royal turned to face Alex. He clicked his heels and nodded once. "My most sincere apologies, Keeper. My son has no manners, and even less sense."

The king gestured to his guards. "Take Prince Cair back to his room and help him pack. I don't think inviting him this evening was a good idea, after all. Please muster a troop of guards to escort the prince during his journey back to the royal hunting lodge. The northern Fae woods can be dangerous at night."

Alex worked to keep the dismay off her face as the king unceremoniously banished his son from the castle. *Holy shit! She'd just insulted Prince Cair! But why would the king invite him to the ball in the first place? Surely, he knew his son planned a coup. Or did he?*

With pursed lips, the king watched the guards escort his fair-haired and extremely red-faced son from the ballroom. Murmurs of disquiet flowed through the attendees in the guards' wake, their unease clear as the king unceremoniously ejected his royal heir from the ballroom, sending him once again into exile.

"Oh, the king knows damn well his son's got it in for him." Larry's mind-spoken words confirmed Alex's suspicions. *"That's probably why he invited him tonight. Keep your friends close and your enemies closer and all that. Besides, what a piece of theater—show your tight grip on the throne to your not-so-loyal subjects—and to all the guests from other realms—by publicly banishing your heir. Again."* Larry snorted. *"The king's no fool. Be careful, Alex."*

Alex maintained a pleasant smile when the king turned toward her. He smiled in return, but it failed to reach his eyes. Instead, an unpleasant eagerness shone in his gaze. He reached for her hand, then raised it to his lips.

"Keeper Alex. Welcome to the Fae realm. As you may have guessed, I'm King Donal, ruler of this realm. Thank you for accepting the invitation to visit my kingdom. I do hope you are enjoying the ball?" The king leaned closer. "Perhaps we could have a private word this evening, since you're leaving tomorrow morning?"

Suppressing a shiver of distaste, Alex nodded. "Thank you for extending the invitation, Your Majesty. Your kingdom is beautiful, and the ball is lovely. I'd really like to stay and enjoy the festivities tonight. I'd be happy to speak with you privately tomorrow morning, though. However, we plan to leave right after breakfast, since we have such a long journey ahead of us. Perhaps we could speak before that, if it's not too early for you?" *No way was she staying in this realm one second longer than necessary,* Alex vowed to herself.

"Of course, Keeper. I'm an early bird," the king replied with a chuckle. "I'm not as young as I used to be, so I'll be in bed—by myself, well before midnight tonight, while the festivities carry on without me." He eyed Alex slyly. "But you are young, Keeper. It's certainly not me who'll be exhausted, in more ways than one, come sunrise."

"Ugh. Could this guy be any more of a horny Fae stereotype?" Larry mind-spoke to Alex. He sneezed, aiming his muzzle toward the king's velvet shoes. *"What a sleazeball. No wonder the Fae want this idiot gone."*

Alex smothered a laugh at Larry's scathing opinion of the king. When a servant hurried to kneel and wipe the king's shoe free of Larry's wet sneeze, Alex frowned at her Familiar and chided him silently. *"While I agree with you about the king, let's not make more work for his servants."*

Larry lowered his head and licked his lips. *"I'll apologize to the man later. The servant, that is. Not the king."*

Alex frowned down at Larry and then turned her gaze to the king. "I apologize for my Familiar's actions, Your Majesty. He hasn't been feeling himself today. And I look forward to speaking with you in the morning."

With a curt nod, the king accepted her apology. "I'll send an escort for you at first light. No need to wake your guards so early." He turned on his heel and strode through the crowd as fast as his short legs would carry him.

"I'm sleeping in your room tonight, Alex. There's a cot under your bed that'll do for me." Conor's grim expression brooked no argument. "And no way are you meeting with that man without me."

Tyre nodded his agreement. "My guards will remain on watch outside your room tonight, Alex. I'll return before sunrise to accompany you to your audience with King Donal."

"I'm coming too." Larry sneezed again. "I think I'm coming down with something. Travel wreaks havoc with my delicate disposition."

Alex snickered at Larry's complaint. "You're an eternal magical Familiar, fur-face. You don't get colds. Besides, you're always telling me you have the heart of a junkyard dog. Would a rough, tough dog like that complain about a little cold?"

"I can be more than one thing." Larry grinned up at Alex. "On the inside, I'm a junkyard dog. On the outside, I'm a delicate furry flower." He flapped his long pink ears to emphasize his point.

Conor's hand on her arm prevented Alex from replying. "We might want to mingle now that the king has made an appearance. The Fae court would consider it an insult not to do so. Plus, we might learn a thing or two."

Alex spent the rest of the evening engaged in small talk with assorted Fae dignitaries, as well as VIP guests from other realms. The highlight of Alex's night was a proposition by a seductive siren princess from the Oceanic realm. Obviously, the princess planned to take full advantage of the Fae realm's carnal Beltane tradition.

"I'm flattered, Your Highness, but I'm afraid I've already committed to spending the evening with these gentlemen." Alex placed her arm around a surprised Conor and threw a flirty glance at her Indigo Fae guards.

Alex's refusal backfired when the sultry siren eyed the handsome men hungrily. "The more, the merrier."

Conor saved Alex from herself. "While that sounds like an excellent idea to me, Your Highness, I don't think your grandfather would agree. Please say hello to Poseidon from me when you next see him, would you? Tell him Conor the Barghest sends his best wishes."

The pretty princess pouted at Conor in disappointment. "I'll give my grandfather your greetings, Conor," she promised, then smiled and waggled her fingers in farewell. "Oh well, there's plenty more fish in the sea."

Alex and her team sighed in relief when the royal siren sashayed off in search of other, more willing, bed partners.

18

NO PLACE LIKE HOME

Late the following morning, when the luxuriously comfortable royal carriage pulled to a stop near the path leading into the Fae Woods, Alex heaved a quiet sigh of relief. Who would've thought she'd be happy to reenter such a forbidding place, but anything was better than spending more time in creepy King Donal's castle.

She stifled a yawn and accepted Tyre's extended hand to help her down the carriage steps. Her sunrise meeting with the king, after a late night at the ball, had left her short on sleep, but bursting with questions she couldn't ask until the team left behind the last of the castle's Fae guards.

"Thanks for the ride." Alex politely thanked the carriage driver. Unsure if she should also thank the four mounted guards the king had insisted on sending along with the carriage, she opted for courtesy. "We appreciate your team accompanying the coach, Captain Shaw. We've got it from here. Please thank the king again for his, ah, generosity."

The leanly built captain nodded at Alex. "No thanks are necessary, Keeper, at least not yet." He gripped his mount's reins and gazed enigmatically at the dense forest that lay ahead. "The king wishes to ensure you safely reach the Crossroads on the far side of the Fae Forest. Therefore, we'll be accompanying your party through the woods, ma'am."

Before Alex could formulate a reply, Tyre interjected. "Captain Shaw, many thanks to you and King Donal for your kindness. However, we have traversed this forest once already and suffered no harm. We are more than able to do so again. In fact, we'd prefer it."

Larry snorted softly and mind-spoke his complaint to the team. *"Speak for yourselves. I still have the bruises to prove this place— and the creeptastic goddess within—are very dangerous."*

Conor flicked Larry a glance and gave an almost imperceptible shake of his head. *"Our team needs to discuss matters privately before we arrive home. The forest is the best place for that."*

Alex wondered if Conor was right. The ancient goddess who called these woods home had already proven that she heard every word spoken within her stomping grounds. She shivered with unease. It wouldn't surprise her if Danu could even hear words and thoughts not spoken aloud. She wouldn't put anything past the powerful, and extremely irritable, Primordial Mother goddess.

Captain Shay frowned and pursed his lips in indecision. "The king was very specific about our orders."

"I'm sure he was," Tyre replied with an amiable smile. "The king ordered Fae warriors to accompany the Keeper and her team through the forest, correct?" When the captain nodded hesitantly, Tyre gestured toward his own warriors. "Well, she will have them. As Indigo Fae warriors, my men and I fulfill the letter of the king's command."

The captain frowned, worry clear in his gaze.

Determined not to have the company of the dour captain and his men during the next part of their journey, Alex intervened. The ancient, forbidding forest ahead had likely seen its share of treachery over the millennia, and she didn't trust the captain or the king as far as she could throw them. She'd rather take her chances with the forest.

Her eyebrows raised, Alex nodded haughtily at the captain.

"Tyre is right. I really don't need your protection, Captain Shaw. As you can see, I have my own Fae guard." The uneasy Fae flicked a fearful glance at the forest ahead. *Hah! She had him.*

"Captain, I'm sure you know that your goddess, Danu, inhabits these woods. In fact, we met her on our way here, and she was *not* in a good mood. She told us she doesn't like to be disturbed. We lived to tell the tale, as she seemed to expect us, and so let us pass. Does she expect you? If not, I really don't think it'll go well for you in there."

The man looked away, fidgeting with his horse's mane. The warhorse, sensing his rider's unease, snorted and stamped his massive hooves. Alex had left the Fae guard with the unenviable choice of obeying his king or angering his goddess.

Finally, after several tense moments of indecision, the captain wheeled his horse around and gestured curtly to his men. "As you wish, Keeper. We'll leave you to Danu's tender mercies." The guards galloped away without looking back.

"Good job, Alex." Conor smiled approvingly. "You're getting the hang of negotiating—and playing hardball, when necessary. Both are valuable Keeper skills."

Tyre huffed a laugh. "I don't envy the captain when he explains to the king that he abandoned his charges at the edge of the forest. While I doubt they had orders to harm us, I'm sure they were under orders to report every word we said."

Alex studied the woods ahead, which cast long, green shadows along the path. The branches of the ancient trees creaked and swayed, as if eager to embrace them. She shivered. "I don't blame the man one bit, though. These woods give me the creeps."

Larry snorted. "I'm sure Danu encourages, if not causes, the wood's unwelcoming atmosphere. She obviously really, really wants to be left alone."

But was the Fae goddess leaving her people alone at the same time? Alex wondered if the ancient goddess had abandoned her duty of care toward the race she created. Was Danu aware the Fae were starving, their society collapsing under the weight of a corrupt king and the fear of a war for the throne that could only worsen their plight? Did the ancient goddess even care?

Larry padded up the path, eyes intent on the trees ahead. "Come on, guys. The sooner we get through these damned woods, the sooner I can enjoy my comfortable bed back at the estate."

"You mean *my* comfortable bed," Alex snarked.

Conor rolled his eyes at their squabbling and followed Larry toward the woods.

When Alex didn't move, Tyre hesitated and gave her understanding smile. "Your Familiar is right, though, Keeper. Hesitating on the edge of these woods will only make our journey longer."

With a weary sigh, Alex reluctantly walked into the oppressive embrace of the forest. "You're right, Tyre. I know you are. It's just— well, you know." She didn't finish the thought, certain that the three tough Indigo Fae warriors at her side were as uneasy as she was at entering Danu's sacred domain for a second time.

"Are we sure she can't hear us?" Alex asked for the third time. "Maybe we should just wait until we get back to the estate—ouch." She stumbled as she tripped over an exposed root, saved from a nasty fall only by Conor's quick reflexes when he grabbed her arm. "I swear, that root wasn't there a minute ago," she griped.

"Told you this place wants to hurt you." Larry snickered, then sobered. "I already told you, Danu isn't here right now. I'd be able to tell if she was anywhere in the woods. My guess is that she took your advice and is currently sprawled before the Crossroads fire on one of those comfy sofas Hecate has, a glass of Phoenician wine in one hand and a plate of peeled grapes in the other."

"Larry's right, Danu isn't here, but the forest itself has ears." Tyre mind-spoke a warning while warily eyeing the gnarled trees encroaching on both sides of the rough path. *"Although rumor has it that these trees can only 'hear' spoken language. If we limit our conversation to mind-speech, we should be okay."*

Alex merely shrugged, exhausted beyond belief. *"If you say so, Tyre. I'm good with the mind-speak only decree."* She flicked a glance at the man ahead of her. *"Conor, I'm assuming you want to discuss the meeting I had with King Donal?"* Her tense talk with the king seemed like a lifetime ago, even though it had only taken place that morning.

Conor slowed his pace until he walked by Alex's side. He glanced at her, concern clear in his eyes. *"I'd offer to carry you the rest of the way, sweets, but I'm pretty sure that would damage your pride."*

Larry snickered at Conor's gallant offer. *"And your back, Conor. You may be a Hellhound Barghest, but Alex here is no lightweight."*

Alex mustered a smile at Larry's attempt to lighten the atmosphere. *"Thanks for that, Larry."* She peered down at her Familiar, who pranced along at her feet. *"Speaking of which, maybe it's time we both went on a diet. It's half rations for your kibble when we get back, fur-face."*

Eyes rounded with dismay; Larry shook his head vehemently. *"But I already told you, my Familiar magic means I can eat as much as I like and not gain weight."* He crinkled his muzzle in a grin, tongue lolling as he eyed his magical partner critically. *"Speaking of which, you don't look fat in those pants, Alex. At all."* He barked a laugh and skittered away when she aimed a gentle kick at his side.

"All right, you two. Enough avoiding the conversation you both know we need to have," Conor interjected. He gave Alex a searching look and asked, *"Exactly what did the king say to you this morning?"*

Alex considered how much of her conversation with the king to share with her team. Conor, Tyre, and Larry had accompanied her to the early morning royal audience and had refused to leave, despite King Donal's curt command. The king had merely raised his brows and waved a hand. Instantly, a wall of translucent green glass appeared around the small breakfast table at which she and the king sat, leaving Alex's shocked team on the other side.

~

"THEY CAN SEE, but not hear us, Keeper," King Donal had informed Alex with a wicked gleam in his eyes. "Your acolytes cannot communicate with you magically, nor you with them. Hopefully, they'll realize that before they hurt themselves." The stout king had leaned back in his chair and studied Conor dispassionately as he shouted and punched the glass. A bolt of emerald lightning flashed from the glass, throwing Conor across the room, where he landed hard and then skidded into the far wall.

"Conor, stop. Please! I can take care of myself." Alex mind-spoke her command. She patted the air and silently begged her Barghest Guardian and the rest of her uneasy team to stand down.

Conor gained his feet, eyes fixed on the seemingly impenetrable glass wall separating them. He caught her pleading gaze and nodded once in understanding before stepping back, but not before giving the king a warning glare.

King Donal dismissed Conor's ire with a casual shrug, then turned his intense gaze on Alex. "Now that we have some privacy, Keeper, there's a rather delicate matter we need to discuss. I understand the gods have charged you with cleaning up the mess created by my idiot of a son and your horny, and rather gullible, goddess."

Alex tamped down her dismay. The king obviously had an extensive network of spies—or there was a traitor in their midst. Again. Dread filled her, but she kept her face blank and merely nodded. "I take it you are aware your son plans a coup?" She murmured.

A thin smile stretched the king's lips. "My son has dreamed of overthrowing me for decades. Thing is, he's never actually taken concrete steps to pursue his ambitions—until now." His eyes hardened. "Dallying with a powerful Greek goddess wasn't a smart move on Cair's part. Danu tolerates no outside interference in her realm, Keeper. My goddess knows I'm a good ruler, and I'm quite sure she'll prevent a forced change of leadership." He picked up a delicate coffee cup from the table and took a dainty sip, then placed the cup on its saucer with a click. "My foolish son's scheming means that things could get bloody—especially if others from outside this realm get involved in what is merely an internal Fae dispute."

A political tightrope stretched before Alex, twanging with pitfalls. Knowing she really wasn't cut out for this, Alex studied King Donal's expressionless face, thinking he'd make an excellent poker player. She'd have to be very careful with her words. "This dispute isn't just internal, though, Your Majesty, is it? Fighting has broken out among the Fae living in my realm, which disrupts the peace of the city under my protection. The Sylvan City Fae are taking sides—and we believe their anger is being stoked by outside provocateurs."

She took a risk. "Perhaps if we agree to keep our respective troublemakers under control, we could deescalate this situation?"

The king sipped his steaming coffee and studied Alex thoughtfully over the rim of his cup. She stifled a sigh, then reached for her cup and took a sip. She had to give credit where it was due: the Fae sure made an excellent cup of joe.

"Excellent coffee, sire. Perhaps you can tell me where you get it?" Alex said, then chided herself silently. Obviously, his servants couldn't just pop down to an Earth-side grocery store for supplies. *Or could they?* After all, a few Fae were allowed to use the distant Crossroads to travel between realms. However, it wouldn't be an easy or quick trip for the king's servants—unless they were making the trip using a much closer at hand illegally re-opened fairy mound? She cut off her musings and brought her mind firmly back to the task at hand, knowing she should be much more concerned with avoiding a war—and getting out of the Fae realm in one piece—than with where the king was getting his most excellent coffee beans.

"Whole Foods. Their store brand is excellent," King Donal explained with an amused chuckle, almost as if he'd heard Alex's internal musings. "I have a courier travel to the Crossroads and bring the coffee beans here from the earth realm once a month."

The king's lips pursed. "Or I did until recently, when Hecate had you lock down the Crossroads tighter than a drum."

Alex thought fast. The king definitely knew someone had reopened a fairy mound. After all, his courier must have used it to deliver her invitation to last night's ball, since the Crossroads were all locked down, and he knew it, but the wily Fae was pretending ignorance.

"I'll have to make a trip to my local Whole Foods, then. This coffee is amazing!" She replied politely, then took another careful step on the tightrope. "I'm sure we can come to an arrangement to reopen the Crossroads on a limited basis, as before, once we've reached a mutually satisfactory agreement about our respective concerns, Your Majesty. I'll be happy to relay any proposed treaty changes to my goddess if you agree to do the same to yours."

Silence stretched as the king finished his impressively enormous breakfast. Alex picked at the toast on her plate, her stomach in knots. She'd never paid much attention to politics when living in the human realm. Now here she was, brand new to the much more dangerous waters of supernatural politics and deep in negotiations with a Fae king to prevent a civil war. *Go figure.*

King Donal took a last sip of his coffee, then sat back, his dark eyes studying Alex intently. She met his gaze directly, her face showing none of her inner turmoil. Alex had learned how to play poker from the best. *Thanks, Aunt Maia.* The Friday lunchtime poker games her aunt forced her to endure each week were finally paying off.

"Alright, here's the deal, Keeper. You tell Hecate to keep that slut, Persephone, away from my son," the king bargained with a careful shrug, the many gaudy medals pinned to his robe clanking with the movement. "She can lock that bitch in the Underworld with that dolt of a husband of hers for all I care. In exchange, I'll keep my son confined to this realm and ensure I disabuse him of his desire to reign in my place. Further, if Hecate agrees to reopen the Crossroads, I'll ensure the very limited number of my people allowed to use them cause no further trouble when visiting your realm. I'll also inform Danu that she can stand down. Once Persephone is out of the picture, I'm sure my goddess will be open to an amicable settlement to this irritating dispute."

Alex was not at all sure the ancient goddess of the Fae would merely accept Persephone's absence in recompense for bonking the Fae prince and disturbing her realm with the threat of a coup. She also highly doubted the king's assurances he could control Danu, let alone his ambitious son. Plus, there was the matter of the re-opened fairy mound. However, agreeing to take the king's proposal to Hecate would at least buy them all some time—and hopefully get Alex and her team out of the Fae realm in one piece.

"I promise to present your proposal to Hecate upon my return." Alex informed the king, nodding firmly to back up her words. "I'm sure you'll want to consult with your advisors and goddess in the meantime. Perhaps—"

"We should meet again, Keeper, once the negotiations are complete," King Donal interrupted. "The next full moon occurs a fortnight hence, when my realm will celebrate my fourth Diamond Jubilee with a grand party. I'll have a messenger deliver an official invitation to your Crossroads within the next few days."

The hard glint in the king's eyes challenged Alex to ask exactly *how* the royal messenger would travel to the Earth realm since they'd both just agreed the Crossroads were currently locked down tight. She didn't take the bait.

"I'll be delighted to attend your jubilee party, Your Majesty." *Like hell she would.* "Hopefully, we'll also be able to celebrate a successful conclusion to our negotiations at the same time."

"I look forward to it," he replied, before nodding once and waving a dismissive hand. The iridescent glass wall separating Alex from her team disappeared, and the king strode from the room as quickly as his bulk allowed.

Alex's team rushed to her side.

"Are you alright?"

"What happened?"

"What did he say?"

Their concerned questions tumbled over each other.

"I'm fine," she assured them. "Let's talk about it later, after we get the hell out of here."

And so they did just that.

WITH EFFORT, Alex pulled her thoughts from her memories of that morning's meeting with the king and returned them to the present.

Larry eyed her with concern. *"You okay, partner? You were in your own little world there for a while."* As they had all agreed before entering the forest, her Familiar stuck to mind-speak.

"I'm fine, Larry. Just thinking about what to tell you guys regarding my meeting with the king." Alex heaved a sigh. *"I'm exhausted and really just want to get home."*

"No worries, Alex. I got the gist of the meeting from your memories just now." Larry snorted, then added, *"Boy, that guy is a real prick! I'm sure nobody but him will be happily celebrating his fourth Diamond Jubilee in two weeks. I'd bet he's been ruling four hundred years too long, in the minds of his unhappy subjects."*

Alex nodded absently, fully in agreement with Larry's comment about the unpopularity of King Donal's reign, then his initial words penetrated. *"Hey! Wait a minute! Did you just read my mind?"* She stopped abruptly and bent down so she could meet her Familiar's eyes head-on. *"Well, did you?"*

Larry cocked his head and returned her gaze, his dark brown eyes laughing at her dismayed expression. *"You were thinking hard and didn't have your mental protections up, silly, so you were broadcasting loud and clear."* He grinned at her and waved a paw at the others. *"Saves you from having to repeat yourself, though, doesn't it?"*

Sighing, Alex stood and resumed walking. She mumbled, "I always knew you guys could read my mind. Damned supernaturals! Can't mind their frikkin' own business and keep their minds out of mine."

Snickers behind her alerted Alex to her unintentional humor. *Well, fuck.* She closed her eyes and shook her head in defeat. To hell with it. If you can't beat 'em, join 'em. She addressed her team collectively. *"Anyway, you yahoos. What are we gonna to do about the king's offer?"*

"We're going to present it to Hecate, then discuss with her how we're really going to fix this situation." Conor's mouth tightened. *"We can't leave that bastard in charge of the Fae realm while his people starve and his cruelty foments revolution. Surely, Danu wouldn't want that either, if she really were paying attention. After all, the Fae people are technically her grandchildren. We'll have to get the gods to reason with her. She can't just hibernate in her crone's cottage in the woods for centuries at a time. She needs to be available to her people."*

Alex nodded her agreement, then trudged onward, hoping they'd reach the Crossroads before long. She needed a nap. And food. Breakfast had been ages ago, and she had eaten very little of it. They had all missed lunch completely. Her stomach growled; at least her appetite was back.

"I see blue sky up ahead," Larry barked, then raced up the path. "Last one out of the forest has to buy dinner."

The team made it back to the Fae Crossroads as the sun set in a fiery blast of red and pink. They traveled the ley line directly to the Crossroads temple, avoiding Hecate's domain in the In-Between. Alex didn't want to risk disturbing Hecate, figuring, rightly, that she was still entertaining an extremely drunk Danu.

Let the goddesses figure out their own affairs, Alex mused, snickering at her play on words. Then she sobered. If only the gods *would* sort this whole mess out between themselves. Then she could go back to concentrating on her Keeper training, visiting with her dangerous cousins, and maybe going on a second date with her sexy Hellhound Barghest Guardian.

Conor sniffed the air as they exited the temple. His twinkling eyes informed Alex that he had scented her arousal. She quickened her pace, determined to avoid that conversational minefield. "I'm starving. Let's go see what Henri can whip up for dinner."

No one argued with that.

19

THE TRUE HEIR

Alex slept late the next morning, exhausted from her journey and from dealing with her dangerous cousins upon her return. When Alex and her team had stumbled into the kitchen after their return the previous evening, they had found the Fates firmly ensconced around the farmhouse table. A delighted, if slightly nervous, Henri was serving the goddesses platter after platter of his specialties. Hungry and unwilling to retreat, the team had reluctantly joined the Fates for dinner.

The cousins regaled Alex with details of their visit to the In-Between several nights earlier. Apparently Hecate's generous hospitality had softened their ire at being excluded from the smaller team meeting afterwards. Lachesis explained she had especially enjoyed the modern magic called internet shopping. Alex had smiled to herself at their enthusiasm, while wondering how the hell Hecate got internet in the In-Between. And how the poor delivery guys were going to deliver the Fates' shopping bounty to Mount Olympus. Not her circus, not her monkeys, she had finally decided, before wearily downing the last of her dinner and toddling off to bed. She and Larry had collapsed onto their bed and fallen into a dreamless sleep immediately.

LARRY'S PAW on her arm disturbed Alex's exhausted sleep. *"Someone's in the room."* His urgent mind-whisper brought Alex immediately awake. She quietly extracted herself from the bedcovers and pulled the knife hidden under her pillow from its sheath. Bright sunlight filtered through gaps in the closed curtains, the shards of light informing Alex that it was mid-morning.

Larry crawled quietly to the bottom of the bed and peered over the edge. "Oh, it's you," he growled. "What are you doing here? Don't you know how to knock?"

A tiny, high-pitched, and rather irritated voice spiraled up from the floor. "I *did* knock, you pillock. I knocked and knocked, but no one ever answered, so finally I let myself in through the doggie door."

Larry snickered. "You used my dog door? Grenoble used it yesterday, too. I'm gonna start charging admission."

No longer fearing an attack, and with her curiosity awakened, Alex returned her knife to its sheath. She joined Larry at the side of the bed and peered over the edge. A tiny fairy paced back and forth on the patterned carpet, her wings fluttering slowly. The diminutive Fae wore a silky tank-top, cunningly tailored to fit around her iridescent wings, stylishly tattered jeans, and ridiculously high heels.

Alex's eyes widened when the fairy looked up and grinned at her. The creature's open mouth revealed a mass of needle-sharp teeth, above which sat a pert nose and gleaming, solid black eyes.

"Oh, there you are, Keeper. I have a message for you," the fairy said. She took flight, landing expertly on the bedside table closest to Alex. After a low bow, the fairy produced a tiny scroll, which she laid carefully on the table. She grimaced, before adding, "The royal invitation is small, I know, but I couldn't carry a full-sized one."

Alex's stomach sank. *Was this King Donal's emissary? Already?*

She had left the Fae realm less than twenty-four hours ago and had yet to speak with Hecate or meet with the posse to develop a plan to prevent a war for the Fae throne. Oh, and save the Fae from their asshole of a king. *Well, crap.*

"How is King Donal? He understands that I'll need a few days before I have an answer for him, right?" Alex studied the tiny fairy for any hint about the content of the king's missive.

Disgust creased the tiny fairy's expression before she schooled her face into neutrality. "Oh, this message isn't from the king, ma'am. It's from Princess Aine. She is Donal's daughter, and the rightful heir to the Fae kingdom. Her father exiled her to Earth several years ago, when he grew afraid of her popularity with their people. She would like a word with you."

I'll just bet she would, Alex reflected, both amused and disconcerted by the little fairy's words. *And so, another claimant to the Fae throne makes an appearance,* she mused.

"Would you like me to read the scroll?" The princess's royal emissary peered up at Alex questioningly.

Suppressing a sigh, Alex merely nodded.

Larry held up a paw. "Hang on, Flower, before you formally issue the princess's invitation, please give me a moment to consult with my magical partner privately." Larry's amused but wary gaze met Alex's, and he mind-spoke an explanation. *"Look, I know this whole Fae situation is turning into a royal pain in the ass, no pun intended. But you really should speak with the princess. She's our best hope for a positive outcome to this mess."*

Alex gazed at her Familiar through narrowed eyes. *"You recognized this fairy when you saw her, and you know her name, so I assume you two know each other?"*

Larry winced at Alex's clipped tone and nodded. *"Grenoble introduced us. He's known Flower ever since the princess moved here and purchased a cottage deep in the woods just outside of Sylvan City. Flower was the only Fae allowed to leave with the princess when King Donal exiled her."*

"You've known all along where the princess is hiding." Alex couldn't

keep the angry edge out of her voice. *"And you didn't bother to share that information with me or the rest of the team."*

Larry curled his lip in a sideways smile, but his eyes remained wary. *"No one ever asked. Besides, the princess's whereabouts really didn't matter before now, did they? Considering what's going on, I figured she would send for you soon, anyway."*

"Alright, I suppose." Alex closed her eyes and rubbed her forehead. *"But please tell me from now on when you meet a VIP supernatural living nearby, okay? That's 'need to know' information."*

"Okay. Will do." Larry placed an apologetic paw on Alex's knee. *"Sorry for not telling you sooner. I just assumed your aunt would mention it to you during one of your training sessions. Maia has known the princess since she arrived."*

Alex smiled and ran her fingers through Larry's soft fur. *"We're partners, remember? We've got to share intel. I'll have Maia fill me in better when I next see her."* She sighed and turned her gaze to the patiently waiting fairy.

"Apologies for the delay, Flower. I needed a private word with my Familiar. You can read the invitation now." Alex watched the tiny fairy break the seal on the scroll, fully expecting the blare of tiny trumpets. Every member of the Fae royal family she had met so far was very full of themselves. Why would the princess be any different?

Larry caught Alex's eye and snorted a laugh.

Flower cleared her throat, obviously seeking their full attention, the scroll now fully open in her hands. Both Alex and Larry sobered and gazed politely at the princess's messenger.

No trumpets. That boded well, Alex mused.

"Princess Aine, daughter of King Donal, and rightful heir to the Fae throne, requests the presence of Alex, Keeper of the San Antonio Crossroads and Priestess of Hecate, at afternoon tea on this day. Um, that's today. At three of the clock." Flower rolled up the scroll and regarded Alex with steady eyes, her sharp teeth just visible behind a practiced smile. "I'll return this afternoon to take you to the cottage, as it's quite hard to find—and dangerous if you attempt to find it without an escort."

Alex nodded, formally accepting the princess's invitation. Not that she really had much of a choice if she wanted to bring the Fae situation to a positive conclusion. "I'm honored to receive Princess Aine's invitation and look forward to meeting her." She just hoped the woman was nothing like her royal father or brother. The princess might be the Fae realm's only chance at a return to peace and prosperity.

Alex spent the rest of the morning deep in a strategy meeting with the posse. Everyone agreed the princess was their best hope of resolving at least a part of the Fae situation. There was still the small matter of Persephone's ill-advised affair with the Fae prince and an angry ancient Celtic goddess to contend with. *Sigh.* One step at a time. First, she'd meet with the princess and see what she had to say.

THAT AFTERNOON, Conor and Tyre insisted on accompanying Alex to the edge of the forest, but Flower would not allow them any further.

"Your guards must remain here, Keeper. The more people who know the princess's location, the greater the danger to her person." The tiny Fae fairy flitted anxiously between the edge of the forest and Alex. "Please hurry. We mustn't be late."

Alex glanced at her companions and shook her head, silently instructing them to remain outside of the woods. Once she obtained their reluctant agreement, she followed the little fairy down a narrow path between dense foliage. A flash of pink and white and the patter of paws informed Alex that Larry thought Flower's prohibition didn't apply to him. She hoped he was right.

The fairy led them on a circuitous route through the thick woods. Eventually, they entered a grassy clearing, in the middle of which sat an imposing stone manor. Alex studied the sprawling building in surprise. This wasn't a cottage, except perhaps by royal standards.

"Follow me," Flower said, then she darted around the corner of the building. "The tea is set up in the back garden."

When they rounded the corner, a lovely formal garden came into view. A flagstone courtyard near the center featured an open gazebo filled with brightly colored garden furniture. A slight figure rose from a chair and gave them a welcoming wave. "Hello there! So glad you could make it for tea. My chef makes the most delightful scones."

"I feel like we've stepped into one of those Victorian TV series the BBC does so well," Larry muttered. He barked and raced down the garden path toward the gazebo. "But who cares? Scones, here I come!"

Alex sighed and followed her excited Familiar at a more sedate pace. At least the princess seemed friendly. From a distance, anyway. She watched as the royal stooped to pet Larry upon his arrival at the gazebo. The woman seemed to understand Larry's greedy desire and immediately plied him with an enormous scone.

Alex studied the Fae as she drew closer. The princess wore a simple dress of flowing, gauzy white. A circlet of fresh flowers sat atop her long golden locks. Her silvery laugh danced on the breeze as she complied with Larry's waving paws and supplied him with a second scone. *"You better leave some for me, fur-ball,"* Alex chided her Familiar via mind-speak.

When Princess Aine stood and faced Alex, her beauty stole Alex's breath. Enormous aquamarine eyes dominated Aine's heart-shaped face, and a rosy glow graced her high-boned cheeks. The princess's full lips curved in an enchanting and welcoming smile. *It's a good thing the guys weren't invited,* Alex mused. She'd have had to spend the entire afternoon reminding them to close their mouths and not drool on themselves. *Jealous much?*

"Welcome to my cottage, Keeper Alex," the princess

murmured, holding out a slim hand in greeting. She gestured to a chair and added, "Please, sit. We have much to discuss."

THE FAE ROYAL fussed over Alex, plying her with tea, scones, jam, and cream, plus some golden, fluffy pastries called fairy buns. "We call them fairy buns because they are light enough for a fairy to carry," the princess said with a giggle. "Not because they resemble a fairy's actual, er, buns. Isn't that what you call an *arse* in this realm?"

A laugh bubbled up Alex's throat, and she choked on the bite of fairy bun she had just swallowed. After much coughing on her part and concern on the princess's, Alex finally regained her breath. "Um, in the United States, it's just called an ass. No 'r' needed."

The princess nodded solemnly, although her eyes twinkled with amusement. "Thank you for correcting my word usage. English is my fortieth language, and its regional intricacies give me the most trouble."

"Well, I think you do pretty good with English, princess," Larry cut in. "But I think your Goblin might need tweaking. Last time Grenoble and I were here for tea, you told him his thick, green skin was beautifully gross." Larry grinned winsomely up at the royal. "Oh, and can you please pass me another fairy bun?"

"In that instance, Larry, I meant what I said." The princess smiled down at Larry as she complied with his request for another sugary treat. "Goblins consider unattractive skin a highly desirable trait. By calling Grenoble's skin gross, I gave him a high compliment."

Larry nodded in understanding as he chewed on his sixth fairy bun. "That explains why he waxed lyrical about your kindness and wisdom all the way home that day."

Alex listened to her Familiar's easy, relaxed conversation with Aine and raised her estimation of the Fae princess. This woman was so unlike her egotistical, cunning, and traitorous royal family members. Her intelligence, wisdom, and kindness shone brightly. Maybe this Fae royal could bring peace and prosperity back to her realm. First, they'd have to depose the princess's father and keep her ambitious brother from taking his place. Oh, and avoid a war and appease an angry Fae goddess. *No biggie. Right.*

The princess's silvery laugh interrupted Alex's musings. "That's enough treats, Larry. I'm sure Alex doesn't want to travel home with a Familiar sick from overeating."

"How many times do I have to tell everyone?" Larry huffed in feigned frustration. "I'm a magical Familiar. I can eat what I like, and as much as I like." He took the rest of the fairy bun in his jaws and moved to the edge of the flagstone patio. "I'll just move my feast over here so you two can chat."

Alex felt the weight of the princess's appraising stare and met the woman's penetrating gaze. Aine's deep blue eyes contained wisdom, sadness, and a fierce determination. *Yes, this woman could lead the Fae out of their current troubles,* Alex reflected, feeling the first stirrings of hope.

Aine sat forward in her chair. "Do you mind if we speak frankly, Alex? I'd prefer to avoid small talk. We have little time before your Barghest and Indigo Fae companions lose their patience and enter the forest to search for you. We have much to discuss, and only a short time in which to do so."

Alex was all for cutting through the niceties. She preferred straight talk. Plus, the princess's comment about Conor and Tyre struck home. And Aine was right—those two nimrods would soon start searching for Alex, no matter how dangerous the forest was. "I don't mind at all, Princess Aine. I've never been one to beat around the bush, so I prefer that in others, as well."

"Please call me Aine. Here on Earth, my royal Fae heritage means very little," the princess replied with an easy grin. "Besides, that's what my friends call me. And I hope to number you among them soon. May I call you Alex?"

"Yes, please. Alex is fine ... uh, Aine." Alex stumbled over the princess's first name, initially uncomfortable with leaving out her title. "What is it you'd like to discuss?"

Aine smiled, her beautiful countenance glowing in the golden afternoon sunshine. Her smile didn't quite reach her eyes, where sadness and determination fought for dominance. "First, I would like to compliment you on your Familiar, Larry. He's very sweet. Hungry, but sweet." The princess sobered and glanced over at Larry. "I'm not sure how much he's told you, but you should know that he is one of the oldest and most powerful Familiars in existence."

"I keep telling her that, Princess, but I don't think she believes me," Larry interjected, rolling his eyes dramatically. "She even calls me fuzz-butt. If she truly respected me, she wouldn't do that, right?"

Alex turned an exasperated glare on her Familiar, who hadn't moved from his prone position on the sun-soaked flagstone. "I respect you, Larry. Always." She fought a grin and added, "Doesn't mean your butt isn't fuzzy, though."

Aine chuckled at their snarky exchange, then resumed her explanation. "I mentioned Larry's great power for one reason, Alex: to ensure you understand how powerful you are, not to mention your position as one of Hecate's priestesses." Aine's guileless expression belied her next statement. "Then there's your status as the only demi-goddess in history endowed with Primordial death magic."

Now we're getting down to brass tacks, Alex thought. She nodded mutely but didn't question how Aine knew about her newly discovered demi-goddess status or her death magic. Sylvan City was a small town, and word traveled fast.

Aine studied Larry contemplatively, then turned a troubled gaze to Alex. "Let me provide you with a brief history lesson about my family." She placed a delicate hand on Alex's. "Please know that I'm not complaining, as there is no point in doing so. I also don't want you to feel sorry for me, but you really need to know how our realm reached its current dismal state, and why I'm driven to change things for the better. Do you understand?"

When Alex nodded, Aine drew a deep breath, her gaze clouding with dark memories.

"My father has never been an excellent king, but neither was he a terrible one—until recently. Several centuries ago, Donal married my mother. She is—was a direct descendant of the last of the Tuatha de Danann. Ruling was in her blood, along with a deep desire to provide for the well-being of her people, the Fae. When the old king weakened with age, it was to my mother, not Donal, his own son and heir, to whom he delegated the kingdom's affairs."

Aine's lips pursed in disapproval. "My father caroused and avoided responsibility, while my mother ruled, both before the old king's death, and for centuries afterward. Donal was happy to let her—after all, he had all the trappings of royalty with none of the onerous duties." The princess sighed and shook her head. "Anyway, in due time, my mother bore two children: my brother, Cair, and me. In Fae culture, it is not always the oldest child who inherits the throne, but the one deemed most suitable. My mother trained me from an early age to rule one day. My brother grew resentful and regularly made his displeasure known, but my father ceded the decision to my mother—at least until her untimely death."

Aine bowed her head, surreptitiously wiping her eyes with a napkin. Her complexion remained rosy and her eyes clear, despite the well of grief they held. *Another beautiful woman who could cry 'pretty,'* Alex reflected wryly. Blotchy skin and red-rimmed eyes unerringly accompanied her tears, so she tried never to give in to them. Not always successfully.

Both women sat in silence for a moment, the only sound the gentle buzzing of the bumblebees in the surrounding gardens.

"So, your mother raised you as the heir to the Fae throne..." Alex prodded.

Aine took a breath and nodded. "Yes. Once I reached adulthood, my mother appointed me as the Fae Ambassador. She said it would benefit our people to have a more open exchange between the realms. For many years, I traveled extensively through the realms, arranged treaties, established supply lines, and more. My people prospered for a long time. Then, a decade ago, my mother died, and everything changed."

The air darkened as a cloud traveled across the sun, and Alex shivered in the momentary chill. She hid her sympathy but felt a kinship with this sad princess. While it had been her aunt, Maia, who had given her childhood love and meaning, not her mother, Alex knew what it was like to lose a loved one, along with the life they had planned for you.

Aine squeezed Alex's hand. "I knew you'd understand, Alex. I've known your aunt since my arrival several years ago. In fact, her friendship helped me climb out of a deep depression after my exile from the Fae realm. I'm sure losing your aunt at such a young age must have been devastating for you. Then, to discover that your mother had lied to you when she took you away from here, and that your aunt had been alive all these years. Until recently."

Sadness filled Aine's eyes. "At least you have her ghost. My mother disappeared into the Summerlands with her Tuatha ancestors when she died." She patted Alex's hand, then withdrew hers and leaned back in her chair. "Let me finish my story now, so we can avoid a mutual pity session, and I can get to my point."

"After my mother's unexpected death, my father had no choice but to take the reins of the kingdom. He was never fit to rule, but my mother's death left him even less so. Despite his many faults, Donal had loved my mother deeply. When she died, my father blamed Danu for allowing it to happen. He turned from the goddess and eventually from his people." Aine frowned in frustration. "The past few years have seen his rule worsen. He has fired most of his advisors and filled their positions with sycophants and strangers from outside the realm. Soon after, he limited access to the Crossroads, allowing only those in his new inner circle free travel. Then he stripped my Ambassadorship and had his guards confine me to the castle."

Aine's lips trembled, but she quickly firmed them. "Almost immediately after my mother's death, my father removed my heir status and named my brother as his successor. In the years since, the only way I had left to help my people was my Ambassadorship. When he took that, as well..." The princess's words ended on a choked sob.

Larry cocked his head and eyed the princess with sympathy. "Here's the rest of the scoop, Alex. About two years ago, the king's old advisors came to Princess Aine and begged her to challenge her father for the throne. They told her she had the support of the people, and that the army would back her. Before she could decide what to do, her brother discovered the plot and told the king." Larry paced over to the table and sat next to the quietly weeping princess, offering his unspoken support. "The king immediately had all his old advisors imprisoned or killed, then he exiled Aine to the Earth realm—"

"And that's where things have remained for the past several years, Alex." The princess had regained her composure, if not her sunny smile. "I've been using my contacts to stay informed about Fae realm happenings and to build a network of supporters." Her hand clenched around her teacup; the princess's white knuckles showed her tension. "We've been preparing for years, awaiting the right moment. My father's Draconian taxes and poor leadership have hardened the opposition. My brother's foolish affair with your goddess Persephone has awakened our goddess, Danu ... and she is very angry. The time has come for me to bring freedom and prosperity back to the Fae realm. And for you to prevent a war between the divine pantheons."

Aine's intense gaze radiated a steely determination. "I think we can help each other achieve our goals, Alex. Don't you?"

The two women stared at each other, each wrapped in their own similar thoughts.

Eventually, Alex smiled. "Yes, Aine, I think we can help each other. Let's get down to brass tacks about what needs to happen next."

The last of the sun's golden rays slanted low across the patio by the time the women had finished discussing their plans. An evening breeze ruffled the leaves on the trees surrounding the garden, while overhead, birds wheeled and darted, preparing to roost before the coming darkness.

Larry shot to his paws when a tiny, high-pitched war cry split the air. Flower flew across the patio and straight toward the woods. "We have intruders! Princess, please retreat to the house."

Aine called her attack fairy off. "Flower, you know as well as I do that it's only the Keeper's Guardian and her Indigo Fae guard in the woods. Please deactivate the perimeter defense magic. We don't want to disable Alex's loyal team members. After all, we will soon need their help."

Flower nodded reluctantly, then flew into the shadow-filled woods. Shortly after, an impatient and rumpled Conor, accompanied by a similarly disheveled Tyre, emerged. Both men bore deep scratches and minor wounds. Flower flew in front of them, scolding them firmly all the while. "I told you two to wait outside the woods, but did you listen? Noooo. Of course, you didn't. You have only yourselves to blame for your injuries. Pah! Stupid supernaturals!"

Larry and Alex snickered, and even the princess giggled, as the two warriors ducked their heads, dabbed at their wounds, and trudged behind the extremely angry fairy as she led them towards the patio.

"Hi guys," Alex addressed the two sheepish men. "The princess and I have finished our conversation. If you'd just waited a little while longer, I'd have returned, and neither of you would need a healer." She wrinkled her nose. "Or a bath. What magical mess did you two fall into? You smell foul."

Flower's fluted laugh floated through the evening air. She landed on the table and helped herself to a fairy bun crumb. "That's plain old unicorn shit you smell, Keeper. Nothing magical about it. The princess allows the local unicorn herd to use the woods and fields around the cottage for shelter and grazing."

Alex couldn't hold back her amusement any longer and burst out laughing. The princess and Larry joined her in merriment.

Conor straightened and drew his dignity around him. "When you are done, Alex, perhaps you could introduce us to the princess?" He glanced longingly back toward the forest. "And maybe we could get out of here before full dark?"

Aine sobered and addressed Conor directly. "Let's not stand on ceremony, Guardian. I'm Aine, princess of the Fae and rightful heir to the throne." She gestured toward Flower, who was busy gorging herself on the last of the fairy bun crumbs. "You've already met my emissary and Guardian, Flower."

Larry interjected. "Boy, do we have a lot of catching up to do, guys. These two have hashed out a plan. It's a pretty good one, but might need some tweaking." He glanced at the darkening sky. "Let's get back to the main road before it gets any darker. The unicorn herd spends the night in the woods and, believe me, you don't want to disturb a sleeping unicorn."

Conor nodded and held out a hand to Alex. "Let's go. We can discuss everything at tomorrow's posse meeting."

Alex remembered the ferocity of the unicorns during the battle at her aunt's funeral. They had fought hard alongside Alex and the posse to defeat her father's Regenerants. She shivered, not wanting to be on the wrong side of their wrath. She hurried to exchange farewells with the Princess, and they agreed to keep in touch.

20

THE IN-BETWEEN

It was a tense journey back to the estate, during which Conor and Tyre compared the injuries they suffered during their trek through the magically booby-trapped forest to find Alex and badgered her for information about her meeting with Aine.

Larry snorted and rolled his eyes, then muttered just loud enough for Alex to hear, "You'd think these two went up against a couple of pissed off dragons in order to save a damsel in distress." He smirked. "A couple of spelled thorn bushes and some unicorn poop doesn't make a heroic journey. And you're for sure no damsel in distress."

Alex smiled wearily at her Familiar and whispered her reply. "Their whining is getting on my nerves, too, bud. Let's ditch these guys and go for a walk once we get back to the estate. I need some time to think."

When they arrived at the Crossroads temple, Alex asked to be left in peace. "If you guys don't mind, I'm gonna stay here at the temple for a while. You two can head back to the house."

"But we need to talk—" Conor frowned.

"Keeper, we must—" Tyre's protest tumbled over Conor's.

"Leave her be, you two," Larry demanded. "She's tired of your moaning and wants some time to herself." He curled his lip and growled low. "Beat it, both of you."

Conor's mouth snapped shut, and he eyed Alex with concern. "Sorry about that, sweets. Are you okay?"

Alex nodded and sank down onto the temple steps. "I'm fine. Really. I just ... I need to think. Can we discuss my conversation with the princess at the next posse meeting?"

Conor exchanged a loaded look with Tyre, then nodded reluctantly. "Alright, Alex. But keep Larry with you, please. And call out if you need us."

"Will do." Alex watched the two men walk away, her gaze contemplative. Once they passed through the hedge leading to the garden, she rose. "Larry, I need to speak with Hecate. Can you stay here and keep an eye on things? I shouldn't be long."

"Sure thing, Alex. I figured that's why you wanted those two gone." Larry stretched out on the marble portico. "It's a nice night, and I just might have eaten one too many of those fairy buns. I'll rest my eyes right here."

Alex smiled down at her recumbent Familiar. "You mean you'll take a nap. Fine, but please keep one eye open in case there's trouble." She placed her hand on the stone of the nearest column, running her fingers across the intricate carvings covering the massive pillar.

"Sure thing, Alex. I'll keep an eye out," Larry muttered sleepily. *"I've already mind-messaged Grenoble. He's gonna raid the kitchen and join me here. Between us, we can handle anything that comes up."*

"I thought you said you were full—" Alex's chiding response ended abruptly when Hecate pulled her into the ley line. She closed her eyes and fought the nausea and disorientation that unaccompanied ley travel often caused her and clung to the stone pillar—the one constant between the earth realm and the goddess's expansive residence in the In-Between. Soon enough, the ley winds stopped blowing, and Alex opened her eyes.

"Welcome, Keeper. Apologies for not awaiting your formal request to meet, but we have much to discuss." Hecate reclined on a chaise near the massive fireplace. Intricate golden braids wound around the elegant goddess's head, glinting softly in the firelight. A simple jeweled tiara encircled her brow. Flames played across the goddess's regal features, highlighting her enigmatic expression. She waved a peremptory hand, encouraging Alex to join her.

Once her stomach settled, Alex released her grip on the stone column and joined the goddess by the fireplace. She sank onto a luxurious chaise opposite Hecate, glad to get off her feet after the past several days spent traipsing through various forests to visit Fae royalty.

Hecate smiled wryly and reached for a pottery jug on the low table between them. "Would you like some wine, Alex? It's Phoenician. Fortunately, my cellars are extensive, and Danu hasn't quite drunk me out of house and home during her visit. She's tried, mind you."

Alex held up a hand, refusing Hecate's offer of wine, then winced at the sharp edge in the goddess's tone. "Yeah, sorry about sending Danu here, ma'am, but I thought it would be best if you dealt with her directly. Goddess to goddess. Larry told me he messaged you to expect her—"

"Oh, I received his message, Alex, and I agree with your decision to divert Danu's attention from your mission to the Fae realm." The goddess squinted in the flickering firelight and rubbed her forehead, eyeing Alex ruefully. "However, as you no doubt realize by now, Danu can be ... difficult. And Larry's right—she drinks like a fish. I had a hard time even pretending to keep up with her. She's currently passed out in one of my guest rooms."

Hope raised Alex's spirits. "Were you able to come to an arrangement with her and talk her out of exacting revenge on Persephone for interfering with the Fae realm?"

"We came to a tentative agreement about that, but there's more at play here than a horny goddess's affair with a potentially treasonous Fae prince, as you well know." Hecate flicked an uneasy glance at the passageway along the far wall, then lowered her voice. "The walls have ears tonight, so we'll discuss your visit to the Fae realm and subsequent meeting with a certain Fae princess after we deal with Persephone's problem."

Alex didn't question how the goddess already knew of her meeting with Princess Aine. She knew Hecate kept herself informed through many channels—some magical, and others mundane. Supernaturals and gods were such gossips. *And those magically connected to you can read your mind, making keeping secrets even harder,* Alex reflected glumly, still not used to the mental intrusion. *Damn it.*

Hecate nodded at a guard, who stood upright and unobtrusive against the far wall. The steady flames from a torch affixed to the wall near his head touched the man's face, and Alex realized he was one of Tyre's Indigo Fae warriors. One day, she would ask Tyre how he and his men came to serve the powerful goddess of a different pantheon than their own.

"Braga, could you please ask Persephone to join us? Then give us some time alone. Once I'm done with her and have had a private chat with my priestess, you can wake Danu and guide her here." Hecate's command spurred the Fae into action.

As Braga left to carry out Hecate's wishes, Alex studied the goddess. Her stormy eyes and thinned lips told a story. Alex's stomach sank. Persephone was about to get the sharp edge of Hecate's tongue, with Alex bearing mute witness.

"Would you like me to leave while you speak with Persephone?" Alex asked hopefully.

Hecate's lips curved in a knowing smile. "No, Keeper. It was you to whom Persephone brought her problem, and you who must help solve it—whether you wish to or not. In fact, after I deal with Persephone, we need to speak further about a few additional responsibilities that I think you're ready to assume, now that you know about your demi-goddess status and have activated your Primordial power."

Oh, shit. Alex maintained a poker face but couldn't prevent an internal sigh. She realized immediately that Hecate must have known about her demi-goddess status right from the start. The goddess had told Alex more than once that she was special. Now, it sounded like her newly discovered demi-goddess status meant even more responsibilities. *Well, fuck.*

"I heard that, Keeper." Hecate's warning startled Alex out of her dismal thoughts.

"Sorry, Hecate."

"Apology accepted, Keeper. But please keep the swearing to a minimum. It disturbs my chi." Hecate straightened her blindingly white robes and sat up.

Goddesses have chi? Alex mused. *Who would have thought?*

When Persephone strolled into the chamber, the atmosphere thickened with tension. She feigned nonchalance, but Alex spotted worry in her eyes. The goddess with a problem poured herself a chalice of wine, then sat gingerly in the only other chair in the room. It was upright, wooden, and looked none too comfortable.

PERSEPHONE VISIBLY QUAILED under Hecate's steely glare. "I'm really sorry, Aunt Hecate. I didn't think—"

"That's right. You didn't think," Hecate snapped. She regarded her adopted niece with weary disappointment. "Persephone, dear, not thinking has caused you—and the rest of us—more problems over the millennia than just about anything else in all the realms. You 'didn't think' how it would affect your mother and me when you staged your kidnapping so you could flit away into the Under-world with Hades for half the year. You 'didn't think' we would move Mount Olympus to rescue you, unaware that you didn't need rescuing at all. And now there's this latest fiasco."

Persephone kept her head down during her aunt's lecture, sniffing and shrinking even further into the hard chair.

Hecate studied the cowed goddess for several silent moments, then shook her head in exasperation. "At least one good thing came of your feckless kidnapping ploy all those centuries ago. We created the Crossroads after your supposed rescue, when your mother and I—and you—used our combined magic to join the ley lines that run randomly through all the realms. No longer could gods be confined against their will by those more powerful than they. Free travel between the realms is now available to most, and this has reshaped all our lives for the better."

"So, Persephone, despite causing that original problem, something truly good came of your feckless actions." Hecate drew in a deep, cleansing breath, then gentled her voice. "I think that this current problem, your affair with Prince Cair, may also result in good—not that it excuses your reckless behavior. Your ill-advised actions in the Fae realm have stirred Danu from her slumber and spurred us into action. Until now, no one knew the extent of the Fae realm's troubles." The goddess flicked a glance at the hallway and lowered her voice. "Danu has obviously been neglecting her divine responsibilities by hiding in her woods for centuries while a corrupt king rules her lands, his traitorous son plots a war, and his people live in poverty, on the edge of starvation. She has a lot to answer for, as well."

During Hecate's speech, Persephone had straightened slightly. She dared to meet Hecate's eyes and whisper, "So, I'm not in trouble, then?"

"Oh, you're still very much in trouble, miss. Your actions in sleeping with the traitorous Prince Cair are reprehensible. You know better than to play your sexual games in another goddess's realm. Good may come of your recent actions despite them, not because of them. Do you understand me?"

The chastened goddess lowered her gaze to her lap and nodded, tears dripping onto her clenched hands. "Yes, ma'am. I'm really very sorry. Um, what happens now?"

"You will stay in your room here until your mother arrives. She's agreed to transport you back to the Underworld and to remain there with you for an extended visit. I have informed Hades of your impending return. He told me he's happy to provide accommodations to his mother-in-law—and you, of course, for an extended stay." The steel in Hecate's voice brooked no argument. "You will remain in the Underworld until we resolve the Fae situation successfully. Do you hear me, missy?"

A sly smile curved Hecate's lips. "Oh, and we've engaged the services of several preeminent therapists who are happy to provide marriage counseling for you and your husband. I had a pleasant chat with Mr. Jung during my visit to the Underworld yesterday. Mr. Freud is a tad pompous, but his views on sexuality have progressed nicely since he last walked the earth. They are both looking forward to working with you."

"Marriage counseling? Really?" Persephone sputtered an objection. "Hades and I have our issues, but we have an open marriage, as most divine couples do—"

Hecate clapped her hands sharply, cutting off Persephone's complaint. "Yes, dear. Marriage counseling. This isn't about how many people you each sleep with, but who—and how you both handle any complications that arise. Your fascination with 'bad boys', and his with 'bad girls' is obviously a cry for attention. Well, you'll both be getting a lot of that for the next long while."

Alex's shocked gaze swung between the two goddesses. *Oh boy, Persephone was really in the shit now,* she mused. A nervous giggle worked its way up her throat. She coughed to cover its escape, then could not stop. It was either cough or laugh—and she'd already witnessed one divine scolding today. She certainly didn't want Hecate's ire aimed at her.

By the time Alex recovered and looked up, Demeter had arrived. She stared down at her wayward daughter, arms crossed.

"Time to go, problem child. I'm so looking forward to some quality time with you and your husband over the coming months." Demeter pursed her lips. "I may even take advantage of Mr. Jung's services during his stay at the castle. I could use a sympathetic ear to unburden my family woes."

"Yes, mother," Persephone said meekly. She unfolded herself from the chair and stood, shoulders hunched, resignation in every line of her body, then flicked a resentful glance at Alex. "See what you've done, Keeper? This is all your fault. You were supposed to fix this mess. Quietly."

Alex's jaw dropped at Persephone's outrageous accusation. She leaned forward to defend herself when Hecate laid a restraining hand on her arm.

"No, Keeper, don't rise to her bait. She knows very well that this situation isn't your fault." Hecate flicked a glance at Demeter. "It would be wise to escort your daughter out of here before she gets herself in any more trouble."

Demeter merely sighed and nodded. The goddess placed a firm hand on her daughter's shoulder and steered them both toward the temple's column. Seconds later, she and Persephone disappeared into the ley line on their way to the Underworld.

21

CHILDREN OF THE GODS

After Demeter and her wayward daughter left, Alex and Hecate sat in silence for several minutes, both wrapped in their own thoughts.

"I'll have a glass of that wine now if you don't mind," Alex murmured. She reached for the jug and filled a goblet to the rim. The first mouthful of the rough, bitter wine brought tears to her eyes, but she persevered and swallowed half the glass in one go. The alcohol hit her stomach in a fiery wave, then sent warm tendrils through her body. She relaxed and sat back. "That's better."

Hecate smiled as she refilled her own glass. "Yes, I'm sure it is, Alex. But slow down, please. Phoenician wine packs quite a punch." The goddess chuckled and rubble her temple. "My aching head and Danu's drunken slumber are testament to its potency. Besides, we need to chat before I have Braga awaken Danu."

Alex suppressed a sigh. While she knew from previous experience that a chat with her goddess always came with strings attached, she couldn't muster up the strength to object, or care. Her head spun. *Damn, that wine was potent.*

"Throw 'em at me, Hecate," Alex urged. "What additional duties are coming my way?" Oops. Probably should show more respect, Alex mused muzzily, and I should definitely think before I speak. She sighed and forced herself to meet the goddess's gaze. A vague feeling of unease settled in her gut. What if the goddess was listening in on her thoughts?

Irritation and amusement warred in Hecate's narrowed eyes. "Yes, Keeper, I'm listening to your thoughts. And I'm fully aware of your tendency to speak before you think. I'd suggest, however, that you curb your disrespect." She pointed at herself. "Goddess here, remember? I expect my priestesses and Keepers to exhibit both restraint and wisdom at all times."

"Yes, ma'am," Alex replied. She nodded and then found she had trouble stopping. She eyed the half-empty wineglass in her hand, then hurriedly placed it on the table. "I think I've had enough of that stuff for a lifetime."

Hecate sipped her wine and smiled. "You'll need to get used to this stuff, I'm afraid. The gods love to drink, and it would be rude not to partake during formal occasions, Keeper. I'd suggest asking Conor to show you how to use your magic to reduce its intoxicating effect."

It took Alex a moment to parse the goddess's words. "Wait ... what formal occasions ... with what gods?"

Hecate pushed a small, ornately carved wooden box across the table towards Alex. "Open it, please."

Alex reluctantly picked up the box but hesitated to open it. Based on Hecate's serious expression, she knew that whatever the box contained, she wouldn't like it. The golden hasp opened easily; she opened the lid and gasped. A gleaming gold pendant lay ensconced in a rumple of stark white silk. Intricate engraving flowed across the pendant's surface. The carving showed a massive mountain soaring into the sky, its slopes reflecting in the still waters of a large lake.

She brought the pendant closer and squinted at it in the dim firelight. A temple sat on an island in the middle of the lake, and tiny, robed figures stood in a row on the temple's steps. She blew out an awed breath at the pendant's beauty, then her historian instincts kicked in and she looked up and met Hecate's eyes.

"This pendant dates back to ancient Greece, if not before. The quality of the carving is exquisite. I've never seen anything like it. I'm assuming the mountain is Mount Olympus, home of the gods." Alex studied the carving again. "The temple on the lake must be a Crossroads temple—"

Hecate's lips curved in a smile. "You're partly right, Keeper. Yes, the mountain is Mount Olympus. However, that temple pre-dates the Crossroads by many centuries. It's called the Temple of Hiereiai, and its priestesses are children of the gods. We have carefully selected each priestess over the millennia for their powers and talents. These women serve as intermediaries between the gods and their creations." The goddess studied Alex calmly, as if waiting for her explanation to register.

Alex studied the beautiful pendant in awe, then fear clenched her stomach. This was bigger—much bigger than just being priestess to a single divine being. If she was right, and the gods meant this pendant for her, it meant she was bound in service to all of them. Her vision blurred, and the box fell from her nerveless fingers, spilling the pendant and its intricate chain across the table. She slumped back onto the chaise and closed her eyes, as if doing so would negate the enormity of her new role.

"Exactly what does it mean to be a Priestess of Hiereiai?" Alex remained in her prone position but turned her head toward the goddess and opened her eyes.

Hecate's gaze held warmth and understanding. "It means you are now an Envoy of the gods, my dear. Unfortunately, your new role is not voluntary. Your Primordial ancestry, along with the newly discovered death magic you have inherited from your grandfather, Chronos, mark you as a demi-goddess. Unfortunately, I have no choice but to offer your services as an emissary to the wider divine community." The goddess pushed the pendant back across the table toward Alex. "You must wear this symbol of your position whenever performing official duties on behalf of the gods and when attending formal dinners on the Mount."

Alex reluctantly took the pendant from Hecate, then laid it on her chest and placed her hands over it. Strangely, instead of conveying the weight of additional responsibility, the pendant warmed against her chest. Something in her soul connected with the image etched onto the pendant. Priestess of Hiereiai. She was kin to the tiny forms standing on the temple steps. It felt right. Not easy, but right. Her dour mood lightened, but questions still tumbled around in her mind.

Abruptly, she sat up. "Okay, but what—"

Hecate chuckled and cut her off. "If only you had accepted your role as my priestess and Keeper of this Crossroads as easily as you've accepted your new position, Alex. It certainly would have made the past several months easier for you." She sobered. "I warn you. Your Keeper duties pale compared to your new role. You must study and train even harder over the coming months. However, we'll discuss this further at another time."

The goddess gestured to the Indigo Fae guard stationed against the far wall. "Please awaken Danu and escort her here, Braga. We're ready for her now."

Alex held up a hand. "Wait. Does this mean I'm no longer your priestess, or a Keeper? Will my new role take me away from here?" *From my home,* Alex thought with a growing sense of dread, *from my heart family.* She realized with a start that, as much as she might whine about her Keeper duties, and her sometimes intrusive and overbearing heart family, she had grown to love both with a passion. She wouldn't give up either of them without a fight.

Hecate smiled approvingly. "I see you have finally embraced your new life here, Keeper—and will fight to keep it. No, your emissary duties will not absolve you of your Keeper role, nor will they take you away from the estate or your heart family." She hesitated and added, "Well, your new role will require some travel, plus there are those formal dinners I mentioned earlier, but neither will require long periods away from your home or this Crossroads."

"Good," Alex said.

"Yes, it's good," Hecate agreed.

AFTER HER TENSE conversation with Hecate, Alex lapsed into silence and turned her gaze to the hallway down which Braga had disappeared to fetch Danu. Scuffling, swearing, and shouting echoed down the passage as the hapless guard cajoled the angry goddess towards the great-room.

"Take your hands off me, you brute. I don't know what Hecate was thinking, to send you for me as if I'm not an honored guest, but a mere servant." Danu's gruff voice continued to spew insults, even as she shuffled reluctantly into the room. She shook off Braga's supporting arm, staggered, then righted herself before collapsing onto the hard wooden chair Persephone had occupied earlier.

The Primordial goddess' rheumy eyes surveyed the room, then settled on Alex and narrowed in thought. "Haven't I seen you somewhere before? Oh, that's right, you're the one who intruded on my realm with some lame excuse about a royal pass to visit the king." The goddess sniffed and wiped her nose on the sleeve of her moss green dress. "Should'a killed you when I had the chance."

"Danu! Be nice." Hecate's sharp rebuke echoed around the stone chamber. "Remember, you are a guest in my realm, as is Alex. I will not tolerate rudeness towards me or my guests."

The ancient goddess of the Fae studied Hecate through slitted eyes, and her mouth worked as she fought to hold back a nasty retort. Finally, Danu pursed her lips and nodded once in curt agreement. Her restless gaze traveled to the wine jug and lit with greed. "May I have some more of that excellent Phoenician wine? Another glass or two would go a long way in helping me forget your guard's manhandling." A sly smile curved Danu's lips. "And it might even motivate me to overlook Persephone's illicit affairs in my realm."

Hecate waved a hand, and the wine jug disappeared, along with the still half-full goblets. "No, you may not. You've had enough wine, Danu. There are many things you should forget, but your responsibility to your people is not among them. We need to chat."

When Danu protested, an angry gleam lit Hecate's eyes, and her lips curled in disdain. "Would you rather we took this matter before the full Council of the Gods?" Hecate pointed at Alex. "We have an emissary of that august gathering right here. I'm sure Alex would be happy to report your abdication of divine responsibility to the Council."

Danu gaped at Alex in confusion.

Hecate threw Alex a meaningful glance and nodded discreetly at the pendant clasped in her hands.

Alex understood the goddess's subtle reminder and quickly placed the pendant around her neck. She'd worry about the full extent of her new role later, but it was time to leverage what she knew so far. Once the pendant settled into place, Alex ensured the ancient artifact caught the light from the fire and reflected a shimmering golden beam onto Danu's face. *So, there, you old crone. Envoy of the Gods here. Still wanna kill me?*

Alex directed a more politic verbal query to the goddess. She tapped the pendant and asked, "Do you know what this means, Danu? It signifies that I'm a Priestess of Hiereiai, and that makes me a representative of the gods. Wouldn't it be better to resolve the small matter of Persephone's interference in your realm amicably, just amongst ourselves? After all, who wants to trek all the way to Mount Olympus just to solve a simple territorial squabble?"

Hecate cut in. "The Envoy is right, Danu. What if we come to an agreement? We agree to keep Persephone out of your realm and away from the prince. You agree to overlook her ill-advised actions in your realm." The goddess gave a shark-like grin. "In addition, you will end your seclusion and resume caring for your struggling realm. After all, Prince Cair wouldn't have acted on his raging desire to overthrow his tyrant of a father if you'd been paying attention, would he?"

Silence stretched as Danu considered Hecate's offer. Flickering light from the fire highlighted the wrinkles etched into the divine crone's face. Finally, she gave an inelegant snort and shrugged. "Fine. Okay. I agree. Persephone is off the hook." The goddess shook her finger for emphasis. "But you must keep her out of my realm from now on. For the gods' sake, there's an entire universe of other royals and minor deities for her to sleep her way through without intruding on my realm."

Once Hecate nodded in agreement, Danu sniffed and wiped her nose on her robe. "I guess I'll head back to my realm and take stock of things. It's been ... a while since I checked in."

"No shit." The words escaped Alex's mouth before she could stop them, and Danu's angry glare pinned her in place.

Hecate interceded. "She's right, Danu. It's been too long since you monitored the happenings in your realm. Centuries, if I'm not mistaken."

Danu blew out a breath and nodded reluctantly. "When you've been alive as long as I have, time gets away from you."

"It's important not to let it," Hecate advised. Her wise gaze touched both of her guests. "As women with divine roles that affect the lives and wellbeing of those in our care, we must pay attention. Always. If our people suffer, and we do nothing, we are not worthy of our place."

Danu had closed her eyes during Hecate's speech. Alex wondered idly if she nodded off in the middle of it.

Suddenly, the ancient goddess leapt out of her chair and spun across the room, impossibly agile for one of her advanced age. "Time to go, folks. Places to be and things to do." Her merry cackle lingered in the air long after she left.

Alex heaved a relieved sigh. "Well, that went better than I expected. So she'll sort everything out, right?"

Hecate shook her head wearily. "No, Alex, she won't manage

this mess successfully without supervision. Danu has never been one to take decisive action. That's why it took divine intervention to get her to control her misbehaving creations, and why we had to force her to seal the fairy mounds. She's all fired up now, but that won't last long. Unfortunately, she's lazy and has a huge blind spot when it comes to her people. We—you—will have to prod her in the right direction to ensure a positive outcome that ends the suffering in the Fae realm."

"Gee, how did I not guess that?" Alex realized that her snarky tone might earn another rebuke, so she moderated her words. "I mean, what do I—we need to do next?"

"We need to stop Prince Cair from starting a war, depose King Donal, and place Princess Aine on the throne," Hecate replied succinctly. She reached for her wineglass and took a deep swallow. Then another.

When Alex realized the wine jug and goblets had reappeared on the table, she refilled her glass and immediately downed half of it. The rich, bitter wine went down much more smoothly this time. *She could get used to this ancient vintage.*

"That's all we have to do? Right, let me get right on that, Hecate." Alex murmured.

22

BAD NEWS

Alex woke early the next morning. The drama and discoveries of the previous day still lurked in the back of her mind as she yawned and stretched, but she resolved to worry about them later. She poked her still-sleeping Familiar. "Come on, sleepyhead. Let's go have an early breakfast."

Larry rolled over and sat up, instantly awake. "Did you say breakfast? You're on! I'll meet you in the kitchen." The little poodle hopped off the bed and padded to the door. "Maybe Henri will give me something to tide me over while you do your morning stuff."

Alex smiled as Larry's tail disappeared through the dog door. That dog could eat. She had better get ready quickly or there might be no breakfast left.

MUTED VOICES CARRIED down the hallway as Alex hurried toward the kitchen. She recognized the strident voice of Atropos and almost decided breakfast could wait, but her stomach growled, reminding her she hadn't eaten much at dinner the night before. She plastered on a pleasant smile and turned the corner into the kitchen. "Good morning, everyone." When conversation stopped abruptly and all heads turned to Alex, she wondered if she had toothpaste on her cheek or had forgotten to brush her hair. Discreetly, she wiped a hand across her face and patted her hair, then sat in the one remaining chair and reached for a piece of toast.

As she buttered her toast, the room's ominous silence told her she was still the center of attention. She looked up and realized that everyone's eyes were glued to the golden pendant around her neck. *Dammit.* She should have removed her newly acquired badge of office before coming down to breakfast.

Atropos broke the tense silence. She gestured to the pendant. "I see Hecate has finally acknowledged your demi-goddess status, cousin." The gaunt goddess snorted in derision. "It's about time. The fool should have inducted you as a Priestess of Hiereiai the moment your death magic activated."

The bite of toast in Alex's mouth turned to ash; she resisted the urge to react.

When Atropos suddenly yelped in pain and leaned away from Clotho, Alex had to smother a snicker. The kindly Clotho must have pinched her sister for being so obnoxious.

Clotho smiled brightly at Alex. "Congratulations on your appointment as an Envoy to the Gods, cousin. I'm so happy for you. Plus, it means we'll get to see more of you from now on."

"Um, thanks, Clotho," Alex replied, unease stirring in her stomach. Maybe she should have skipped breakfast. "What do you mean, we'll see more of each other?"

Lachesis answered for her sister. "Envoys must join the gods at their monthly Council meeting and dinner, cousin, in case any of the gods have business that needs tending to on Earth that they don't wish to handle themselves. That way, the gods can brief and dispatch an Envoy if necessary."

Clotho chuckled, adding, "Many of the gods are lazy, so they keep the Envoys hopping." She waved a piece of toast at Alex. "But, since you're new, I'm sure they'll give you time to settle in before your first assignment. Oh, and you're welcome to stay with us whenever you visit Mount Olympus for a Council meeting. Or anytime, really."

"We should have the new patio furniture by then," Lachesis added. Her eyes lit with remembered pleasure. "The nice salesperson at the furniture store even found cushions with equal-width stripes for us."

Alex merely nodded numbly and poured herself a cup of strong coffee.

Larry's soft fur brushed Alex's leg under the table. He sat on her foot in a show of support, then mind-spoke his reassurance. *"I know you're freaking out on the inside right now, Alex. But being an Envoy really is a good thing. We'll get to travel a bit. And the food on Mount Olympus is divine."* He snickered at his joke. *"No need to tell your cousins that you've already got your first Envoy assignment. Let's just get them shopped out and packed off back to Mount Olympus. We can deal with them another time. Having the Fates involved in this Fae realm mess is the last thing we need."*

Alex sipped her coffee, then snagged a sausage and held it under the table for Larry. "Sounds like a plan, bud—hey, watch out for my fingers!"

"Sorry. I'm hungry."

"You're always hungry," Alex griped.

Maia floated up behind Alex and laid a ghostly hand on her shoulder. "Don't worry, dear. Being an Envoy shouldn't interfere with your Keeper duties. Well, not much, anyway. Besides, you've got the rest of us here to support you. You'll be fine."

"Sure, Aunt Maia. I'll be fine." Alex's heart wasn't in her words, but she'd figure things out. She had to. And she'd need to rely on her heart family every step of the way. *Sigh.*

Henri placed a steaming, fragrant omelet in front of Alex. "Chives and mushrooms, plus sharp cheddar cheese. Just the way you like it, mon ami."

Alex's appetite returned in force. "Thanks, Henri. You're wonderful." She picked up her fork and dug in.

Spots of color appeared on the little French chef's cheeks. "It is my pleasure, Alex."

Atropos waved a peremptory hand. "Henri, I'd like one of those, please. It smells wonderful."

The chef nodded at the goddess and hurried to obey.

Alex savored the first bite of the fluffy omelet and suppressed a grin. Her normally rude cousin had addressed Henri politely ... and even said please. Who said you couldn't teach an old goddess new tricks?

With an inward sigh, she realized gaining Danu's cooperation wouldn't be that easy. She had her work cut out for her with the ancient goddess of the Fae. Hopefully, Danu agreed to pay attention to her people's plight. Alex and her team would need the ancient crone's help to stop a war and save the Fae realm from disaster. No biggie.

THE DINERS LINGERED over breakfast until a bumblebee buzzed into the room and flew in circles around the table. Hands swatted at the annoying intrusion, but the insect avoided every strike.

Alex recognized the angry mutterings and held up a hand. "Everyone! Stop! That's not a bee. It's Flower. She's a fairy in service to Princess Aine."

Flower made one more lap around the table, then landed next to Alex's plate with a practiced swirl, chattering with agitation, her words unintelligible.

"Slow down, Flower. I can't understand you," Alex said.

The fairy heaved several calming breaths, then nodded. "Sorry, Keeper. Apologies for my behavior, but I need your help. Princess Aine has been kidnapped."

Gasps of disbelief came from around the table.

Alex had a bad feeling about this. "Her brother, Prince Cair, took her. Am I right?"

Flower's shoulders shook as she sobbed silently. "Yes. He broke through our wards early this morning with a dozen of his personal guards. When the princess realized we were over-matched, she sent me out the window, instructing me to fly straight here and request your help."

Tears streaked the tiny fairy's face, and abject fear clouded her eyes. "He's a terrible Fae, Alex. He'll hurt her if she doesn't agree to his demands. I'm sure of it."

Alex's heart sank. She was sure of it as well.

ALEX SPENT the rest of the day in the barn, in conference with Conor and the core posse members. As night fell, the rest of the posse filed in and spread out on the risers ranged around the massive arena. Alex, Conor, Vinnie, and Maia sat at the long table that had taken up residence in the center of the former riding arena.

Hecate was conspicuously absent. Alex had visited the goddess earlier to explain their plan and had asked for the goddess's help. "I'd appreciate it if you could entertain my cousins this evening, ma'am. We don't want them interfering with tonight's posse meeting. After all, we *are* trying to avoid a war—and the Fates would only be too happy to start one."

The goddess had agreed to host the Fates for another evening of fine wine and food—and internet shopping—at her lodgings in the In-Between. Hecate and Alex had exchanged a conspiratorial grin, each knowing her offer would be irresistible. If there was one thing the Fates enjoyed more than war, it was shopping.

Billy the Squid was the last to arrive for the posse meeting. He quickly tentacled in, issuing an apology as he took his usual spot —the entire length of the far wall. "Sorry, Alex! I couldn't find my second favorite hat." He waved a tentacle at a human-sized cowboy hat perched precariously on his enormous head. "This one isn't as lucky as the one you smoked when you were learning your Keeper magic, but it's got pretty good vibes."

Alex remembered Billy's misguided attempt to help activate her magic shortly after her arrival. His plan had worked, thankfully, but she hoped never to view the arena from the top of its forty-foot-tall roof again. Billy was lucky that her newfound magic had only destroyed his lucky hat—and she had been lucky to survive the fall.

"No worries, Billy. Glad to hear you found your spare hat. We need all the luck we can get." Alex smiled affectionately at the well-meaning squid, then cast a glance around the gathered posse members and stood to address the crowd.

"Hello, everyone, and thanks for coming. As you may have heard, we have a new, uh, divine situation that requires our services." She gestured toward the others at the table. "We've talked about how to tackle things and have come up with some ideas. We'll open it up for discussion after the presentation. Any questions before we get started?"

The ghost contingent murmured urgently among themselves. When a richly-dressed female ghost stood, Alex suppressed a spurt of annoyance. Of course, Queen Elizabeth had a question— or, more likely, a command. "Yes, Liz? What is it?"

The ancient British royal peered down her nose at Alex, which was quite a feat, considering the top of her head barely reached Alex's chest.

"My question regards your cousins, Keeper. How much longer will they be staying? We would prefer if they departed prior to the next poker game. It is not acceptable for your bloodthirsty cousin to threaten us ghosts with soul annihilation each time she's called out for cheating." The ghosts ranged on benches near their de facto leader nodded in agreement.

Nonplussed, Alex eyed the queen. She'd gotten much better at handling the high-handed ghost over the past several months and was no longer cowed by her abrupt demands. "Liz, we're here to discuss a royal kidnapping, a coup attempt, and a war that threatens to decimate the Fae realm and spill over into this one. I'm afraid we'll have to address the length of my cousins' stay another time. I promise to have a word with Atropos about her behavior, though."

The ghost pursed her lips and retook her seat. "See that you do, Keeper. I'll not have our entertainment compromised, or our afterlives threatened by that jumped up—"

Vinnie slammed his hand on the table, making everyone jump. The stocky vampire smiled, showing off his razor-sharp canines. "Alright, Liz. That's enough. No need to tempt fate by insulting the gods."

Alex snickered at her uncle's unintentional humor. "Thanks, Uncle Vinnie. I'll take it from here." She drew a deep breath and spent the next hour explaining their plans.

Conor, Maia, and Vinnie, and even Larry contributed to the presentation. Once finished, Alex opened the floor for discussion. She rubbed her back and suppressed a sigh, expecting another hour or two of back and forth. After several minutes of silence, Alex noticed the posse members were nodding in agreement, their eyes lit with anticipation. What the heck? No one had anything to say?

"You have the posse's support, Alex," Larry murmured. "Remember, the posse did most of the planning for the mission to the Underworld, since you were new to your role at the time. But you've proved yourself several times over since then." He nudged Alex with his wet nose. "They trust you now."

Trying not to let her shock and delight show, Alex merely nodded at the gathered crowd. "Okay, then. If no one has anything to add, then we need to discuss volunteer duties."

Once everyone had their assignments, the crowd quickly disbursed. The search team remained behind, deliberately small, to remain both agile and unobtrusive.

They gathered around as Flower alighted on the table. The fairy had calmed down considerably since her arrival that morning, but she still vibrated with anxiety.

"Flower, can you please share your thoughts about where the

prince might have taken Princess Aine?" Alex gave the floor to the tiny Fae.

Flower cocked her head in thought. "As you have probably realized, I'm magically connected to the princess. I usually know her thoughts and location almost as well as she does. However, there's something blocking our communication." The tiny fairy threw up her hands and shook her head. "I can feel her misery, but it's muted and her location is hidden from me. I've tried and tried, but I'm not able to—" her voice broke, and she wailed in despair.

Conor eyed the distraught fairy thoughtfully. "I think we should begin our search for the princess in the local area. Cair may not have taken her far. We know he has supporters in Sylvan City, so we'll start by identifying them and searching their homes and businesses."

Maia verbalized everyone's silent concern. "I just hope the idiot hasn't taken her back to the Fae realm. I wouldn't put it past King Donal to kill two heirs with one blow. If they are in his realm, the king's spies are probably searching for the pair already. Donal's got to know it would threaten his rule if Prince Cair forced his sister to cooperate with his plans for a coup."

Fresh wailing filled the air, the volume impressing everyone. Flower might be small, but her lungs were mighty in their grief.

23

COFFEE CAN BE BAD FOR YOU

Several days later, Alex dithered over breakfast. She wasn't sure if that morning's planned trip into San Antonio to take her cousins to the Farmer's Market was a good idea or not, but it would at least take her mind off the current state of Fae affairs. Her cousins' new outfits had helped with that, as well. When the trio had trooped into the dining room for breakfast arrayed in sleeveless sundresses covered with massive, violently colored flowers, the room had gone silent and wide-eyed. Fortunately, Maia had saved the day be complimenting the goddesses on their shopping success to date.

Alex vowed to have a word with Conor about taking her taste-challenged cousins to better stores from now on. Ugh.

She sipped her coffee and picked at the last of her breakfast, musing glumly over their failure to locate the princess. For the past several days, her team had searched everywhere, with no success. They had questioned every local Fae and searched every nook and cranny in Sylvan City. The river trolls had searched the deep caves lining the lake's waterline, while various other supernaturals had concentrated on investigating any lead, no matter how small. Unfortunately, it had become increasingly clear Prince Cair must have spirited his sister back to the Fae realm. Alex knew this meant a return trip through the Fae Forest, and a conversation with Danu to secure her support in the search.

Appetite gone, Alex pushed her plate away with a sigh and idly tuned in to the chatter around the kitchen table.

Lachesis was raving again about the quality of the food served at the manor house. Earlier in the week, Chef Henri had told the goddess that he did much of the food shopping at the weekly Farmer's Market at the Pearl. She had insisted on visiting the market, stating that the food on Mount Olympus was nowhere near as tasty, so she wanted to take back some fresh produce and breads for her chef to use.

Alex toyed with her toast, her lips curved in amusement at Lachesis's excitement about their upcoming visit to the market, then her cousin's intent penetrated her gloomy musings. It seemed the goddess didn't just want to purchase fruit and bread; she actually had plans to 'acquire' several of the Farmer's Market vendors and bakers and bring them to Mount Olympus to train the extremely inadequate ones there. *Holy crap. Another disaster in the making.*

It took almost an hour to convince Lachesis that she couldn't go around kidnapping humans these days, and certainly not those living in her Keeper cousin's proverbial backyard. After Alex explained the concepts of modern guns, armed police, arrest, and jail, Lachesis finally relented—but only once Atropos told her sister that she wouldn't use her scissors of Fate on local law enforcement to save her from being arrested.

"I'd spend too much time laughing my ass off at you getting handcuffed and carted off to the local prison, sister," Atropos told her, eyes glittering with malicious pleasure. "Of course, I'd rescue you. Eventually. But not before you missed at least several days of Henri's fabulous cooking. I'm not sure what they serve to prisoners these days, but I imagine it's not very appetizing."

Alex watched as Lachesis considered Atropos's comment. The small, birdlike goddess couldn't weigh over ninety pounds, soaking wet, but she ate like a horse and had the palate of a gourmand. Alex made a silent promise to give her chef a bonus for his extra efforts and superb cooking. Henri's skills had been heavily tested over the past week. Besides her three divine cousins, several other groups had recently arrived, so the poor man was preparing food for double the usual number of Crossroads guests. The manor's ghost residents, fortunately, didn't count, but Alex knew they hung out in the kitchen occasionally just to sniff Henri's latest creations and give him unwanted recipe advice about food they couldn't eat.

When Henri placed another steaming dish in front of Lachesis, the goddess smiled and thanked him sweetly for his latest culinary offering. When she leaned forward and placed a delicate hand on the chef's sleeve, a horrible thought struck Alex.

"Lachesis—um, cousin," Alex waved her hand to get the goddess's attention. "You can't have Henri, you know. He's mine." Alex spotted Henri's startled face and amended her statement. "Uh, I mean, he's the Crossroads chef and an extremely valuable member of our team. We don't want to lose his wonderful services, so I'd appreciate it if you didn't try to, um, hire him away from me —the Crossroads." No point in mentioning that she suspected Lachesis wouldn't think of actually *hiring* the shy French chef. She'd merely pack him up with her luggage—kidnapping is such a loaded word—when she and her sisters finally departed for Mount Olympus. Which would not be a moment too soon, Alex brooded.

Clotho spotted the brewing argument over Henri's services and intervened. "Lachesis, sister, we can't just kidna—I mean, hire staff away from Alex. After all, she is our host, and that would violate the rules of hospitality. Plus, she's our cousin, remember?"

Alex wasn't sure how much weight the 'cousin' reference would have with the acquisitive goddess, but her Aunt Maia had drilled the obligations of Crossroads hospitality into her. Even gods must behave themselves and observe the rules when visiting a Crossroads—if they ever wanted to be welcomed back.

Lachesis sighed and nodded reluctantly. "You're right, Clotho.

It wouldn't be seemly to ... er ... hire any of Alex's most excellent staff away from her Crossroads."

The acquisitive goddess smiled winningly at the flustered French chef. "But Henri, if you ever tire of the demands of catering for a busy Crossroads, please do consider coming to work for us. It's just us three goddesses, rattling around in our mansion on Mount Olympus. We don't entertain much—"

"Lachesis! What did we just discuss?" Atropos's rebuke cut through the air. The goddess's ancient scissors of Fate appeared on the table next to her place setting. She stroked them lovingly, the threat in her actions real.

Alex wasn't sure if Atropos's scissors would have any effect against a divine being, let alone her sister goddess, but the implicit threat seemed to penetrate Lachesis's food-driven frenzy. The tiny goddess bobbed her head in apology. "Sorry, sister. I just can't help myself." She shrugged in resignation and gazed longingly at the culinary magician. "Henri, I must regretfully withdraw my offer of employment, I'm afraid."

The now-perspiring chef suppressed his relief, but Alex noticed it. "Henri, thanks for everything. I'm glad you'll be staying with us for the foreseeable future. Please let me know if there is anything you need, either in the kitchen or personally." She vowed again to give the poor man a substantial raise.

The rotund chef bowed politely. "You are most welcome, Keeper Alex. I do truly enjoy working here, first for your aunt and now for you. I have no desire to leave this Crossroads, either willingly, or..."

Unwillingly, Alex silently finished the sentence for him. She realized Henri had taken Lachesis's implied threat to kidnap him for his services seriously. He knew as well as Alex that no one could stand against the whims of Fate.

~

HALF AN HOUR LATER, Alex waited with her excited cousins on the mansion's front steps while Conor went to get the estate's limo. When the limo pulled up, the Fates piled in the back, Alex having called dips on the front passenger seat.

As the car exited the gates, Conor explained they'd be able to park quite close to the Farmer's Market, at a friend's house. "Parking downtown can be tough. Fortunately, Davos wanted an underground garage, and his dwarf friends love to dig." Conor grinned. "They got a bit carried away, and now have parking for a couple dozen cars."

Alex envisioned Davos and his dwarf buddies getting together for a casual brew and an evening of digging and grinned at the thought. She had met Davos once when he dropped off crates of his craft beer at Vinnie's restaurant. The dwarf was short and stout with scruffy chin hair that resembled a hedgehog hanging from his face. He sported several tattoos and wore a stylish fedora. Alex was sure he fit right into the San Antonio hipster scene, where he owned and ran a highly rated brewpub.

The Fates kept their faces glued to the window during the drive, commenting all the while on the many changes to the human world since they last visited. Eventually, Conor slowed and pulled to the curb in front of a stately old-fashioned townhome. "We're here, everyone. Why don't you all hop out? Give me a minute to park in the garage, then I'll join you and we can all walk over to the Farmer's Market at the Pearl."

Everyone climbed out and waited on the curb, Alex watching in amusement as her cousins gaped at the downtown scenery. It had likely been a while—if ever, since this trio of ancient goddesses had played tourist. She pointed to the right, toward a narrow side street. "I think we can reach the Farmer's Market that way, but let's wait for Conor. He knows this area better than I do."

Almost as much a tourist in San Antonio as her cousins, Alex studied the stylish and varied buildings around her. She'd been too busy since her arrival to do much sightseeing, but she vowed to change that—once she rescued the princess and prevented a war in the Fae realm. If she did.

When Conor joined them, he pointed to the same narrow road she had. Alex felt a burst of pride at correctly identifying the right way to the market, but it fled as Conor led them through several increasingly narrow streets and alleyways. She quickly realized they'd be lost without his expert guidance.

As they walked down yet another alley, live music curled in the air enticingly. Soon, they emerged into a large, sunlit square filled with market stalls and bustling with people, dogs, and bicycles. A herd of tethered bikes rested to one side of a massive metal sculpture that burbled with water flowing from multiple levels into a large basin at the base.

"That fountain looks like the one we have in our courtyard," observed Clotho.

"But it's shinier. And I like the sound of it better." Lachesis eyed the fountain longingly.

Atropos rolled her eyes at her greedy sister. "It's shinier because it's not over a thousand years old, you dingbat. And you liked the sound of ours well enough when you 'liberated' it from that sultan's courtyard after the fall of Alexandria, remember?"

Alex shared an amused glance with Conor. Apparently, Lachesis's sisters had been dealing with her magpie ways for millennia. Conor urged the group forward toward the busy market square.

After spending an hour listening to her cousins oooh and ahhh over the massive market's many culinary treasures and ensuring they actually paid for their purchases and didn't try to stuff a preferred vendor or two in their bulging shopping bags, Alex was exhausted. Shopping with her divine cousins was tiring, and she had had a late night.

She smiled tiredly at Conor when he arrived back from taking the Fate's latest acquisitions to the car. The patient Barghest stooped to relieve her cousins of yet more shopping bounty. While Conor chatted amiably with her cousins, a cute little coffee shop across the street caught Alex's eye. She yawned widely and decided she desperately needed a Spiced Chai. Henri, for all his culinary skills, couldn't make a good Spiced Chai to save his life, insisting that coffee was the only 'real' morning beverage.

With the image of a frothy, spicy chai in her mind, Alex detoured toward the coffee shop. As she entered, she sniffed the air appreciatively and thanked the gods when a stool immediately opened up at the counter. She slid onto the stool in the busy cafe and caught the eye of a barista. "Large spicy chai, please."

"Is that for here or to go?" The harried barista smiled at her, his hand already reaching for the lever of the steaming, gleaming beverage machine.

"For here, please." Alex was sure Conor could handle her cousins by himself for a few minutes. Hopefully.

"Make her drink to go, please." The gruff order came from a man standing close behind Alex, startling her. The knife pricking the skin of her ribs through her t-shirt startled her more, though. When the barista eyed Alex questioningly, she nodded stiffly. "What he says. Make it to go, please. Sorry for the confusion."

When the barista turned away to grab a disposable cup, the man with the knife whispered in Alex's ear. "Good choice, Keeper." He threw some money on the counter, then grabbed her arm and pulled her close, the knife following his every move. "Once he gives you your drink, we'll both just mosey on out of here like nothing is happening. Agreed?"

Alex knew she didn't have a choice. While she could call her Keeper staff and disarm her attacker before he wounded her, she knew the rules of fight club. Never let the humans see your supernatural powers. She could tell that the man holding her arm was Fae, so he likely had some impressive supernatural powers of his own. She'd just have to wait until they were out of the coffee shop and away from prying human eyes to attempt her escape. Nodding reluctantly, she murmured, "Agreed."

Once they exited the coffee shop, Alex peered through the swirling crowds, hoping to spot Conor and her cousins, but they were nowhere to be seen, so she let the man force-walk her down the nearest empty alley. Good. No one around. Just as she prepared to call her Keeper staff, a nondescript compact car pulled up beside them and its trunk popped open.

Alex spotted the sticker of a well-known rental car company on the rear window and curled her lip. "Really? A subcompact? I'm assuming Prince Cair put you guys up to this. Couldn't he afford to rent you a decent-sized kidnap vehicle? Or don't you guys rate a nice car?" Alex regretted her smart mouth when the Fae behind her shook her angrily and shoved her towards the open trunk. *She damned well could not keep her mouth shut for anything. Sigh.*

After thirty minutes of bouncing around in the back of the tiny vehicle, Alex's leg cramped yet again. She cursed the compact car's uncomfortable trunk space. You really would think Cair could have coughed up for a larger getaway car for his thuggish Fae warriors. She twisted her wrists again, but the ropes held tight. Her kidnappers may be foolishly loyal to an idiot traitor prince, but they sure could tie a knot. Damn it.

Alex knew she could have called her Keeper staff and fought off the kidnappers before they tied her up and shoved her in the trunk, but had decided at the last minute not to. Even now, she could escape with a little finagling; it might be hard to wield the Keeper staff with her hands tied together, but it could be done.

However, she and the posse had been hunting unsuccessfully for the prince's bolt hole for almost a week. Since the kidnappers didn't immediately try to kill her, Alex figured the prince wanted her delivered in one piece—at least initially. Why not let his Fae co-conspirators bring her to the prince instead of chasing him across the realms? Hopefully, this unplanned journey would lead her to the princess at the same time.

The small vehicle bounced across yet another pothole, and Alex winced as the rough carpet underneath her rubbed her cheek raw. Sometimes, she questioned her impetuousness and wisdom. Oh, and her smart mouth.

24

FANCY SEEING YOU HERE

The scent of strong coffee woke Alex from a nightmare. She pushed back the dark dreams and opened her eyes, squinting in the sunlight streaming through a row of windows. Slowly, she took stock of her body. Nothing broken. Good. Just a few rope burns on her arms and legs, and an enormous lump on the back of her head. Her fingers gingerly explored the swelling and came away sticky with blood. Ugh. She wiped her hand on the rough blanket underneath her and sat up.

"How do you feel this morning, Keeper?"

Princess Aine's gentle query told Alex several things at once. She had obviously been successful in finding the princess's prison but had failed spectacularly at discovering exactly where that was. And now she was imprisoned alongside Aine. The last thing Alex remembered was the uncomfortable car ride in the trunk of her kidnapper's tiny rental car.

"Uh, not feeling so good. But thanks for asking, Aine," Alex muttered, gratefully accepting a mug of coffee from the princess and sipping the steaming brew. "Ohhh, that's good."

She took her time with the rich, black coffee, silently thanking the princess for waiting patiently while she recovered. By the time the coffee was gone, she had a decent caffeine buzz going.

Lowering the mug, she surveyed the room, pleasantly surprised to discover a nicely decorated space. She sat on one of the two small beds set against the wall opposite a row of light-filled windows. The large room also held a table and chairs, along with a high-backed couch set in front of a roaring fireplace. A minimalist kitchenette was squeezed into a nook to one side of the massive fieldstone chimney breast.

After a full circuit of the room, Alex's gaze fell on the princess. Aine sat quietly on the bed opposite her, sipping from a matching mug. Apart from a yellowing bruise on her temple, she appeared uninjured.

"Are you okay? Your idiot brother didn't hurt you, did he?" Alex queried.

Aine gingerly touched the bruise on her forehead and gave a ghost of a smile. "I'm fine other than this. I could heal the bruise, but I want my brother to see it when he visits, as evidence of his brutality." The princess lowered her hand and sighed. "Not that my injury will disturb him. Since a child, Cair has had a cruel streak, always delighting in hurting those weaker than him."

Determined to brighten the mood, Alex replied, "Well, that ends now, Aine. My team has been searching for you for days. Now that I've found you, we can figure out an escape plan."

Brows raised, Aine eyed Alex quizzically. "Escape to where? Do you know where we are? Even if we escape from the house, my brother's guards patrol the grounds, while Dark Fae in his service have filled the surrounding forest with harmful magic."

Crestfallen, Alex pondered their dire situation. "So where exactly are we, then?"

"This is one of the royal hunting lodges. When my father banished Cair from court, he was sent here to keep him out of trouble." Aine shook her head sadly. "Of course, my brother has used his years here, hidden deep in a forest at the northern edge of the realm, to plot and plan—well out of the sight of the king and his spies."

Alex tried not to panic. She almost regretted her impulsive

decision to allow the prince's men to kidnap her. What a fool she had been. If Aine couldn't escape, what had made her so sure she would succeed where the powerful Fae princess had failed? She had let everyone else's high opinion of her magical abilities lull her into a false sense of her own skill level. *Sigh.*

She knew she had a shit-ton of magical potential—she was a demi-goddess, for goodness' sake—but her training hadn't yet reached a stage that would allow her to tap into even a tenth of her abilities, that much she was sure of, and that was mostly her own fault. For months, she had pushed away Conor's efforts to train her on ley line travel and avoided even thinking about her necromantic magic, to say nothing of her newly discovered divine heritage. She vowed to allow her cousins to help her learn how to use her Primordial death magic—sooner rather than later. If she ever got out of this place.

Closing her eyes, Alex heaved a defeated sigh. Death magic. Demi-goddess. Envoy to the Gods. Plus, her Keeper heritage. The walls of duty and responsibility threatened to tumble down and crush her under their combined weight. *It was a lot.* Then she smiled at her unwitting use of a phrase she had shared with Conor frequently over the past several months. He'd always agree, saying, '*Yes, it's a lot, Alex, but I'm here to help you, as is everyone here.*'

Warmth filled her, and hope followed. She'd get out of this mess and take the princess with her. Then, they'd defeat Cair and move on to the king. Alex studied the strong, kind Fae princess opposite her. With this woman on the throne, the Fae kingdom would prosper. Getting her there in one piece, though. That would take teamwork.

"Are you hungry? I can fix some breakfast." Aine stood and bustled over to the kitchenette.

"I'm starving. I'll help you, but first—is there a bathroom in this place?" Alex hoped the answer was yes. She didn't relish the thought of using a chamber pot. Plus, she really needed a bath.

Wordlessly, Aine pointed to a door beside the bed. "Through there." She smiled. "One good thing I'll say about my father: once they invented modern plumbing in the human realm, he quickly modernized the bathroom facilities in all the royal properties."

Alex's mood brightened when she opened the bathroom door and beheld a marble palace, complete with a soaking tub, a glassed-in rain shower, and a sleek, modern toilet. "Your dad may be an asshole, but he sure knows how to pull off a great bathroom." Aine's silvery laugh followed her as she closed the door and turned on the shower.

ALEX SAT at the small table across from Aine and polished off the last of a truly great omelet. With a pang, she remembered the last omelet she had eaten, sitting in her kitchen surrounded by her heart family. Henri's rosy-cheeked face floated through her mind, while the memory of the feel of Larry's fur against her leg strengthened her determination to escape.

"Thanks, Aine. Your cooking is almost as good as my chef's." Alex realized the princess might take offense at the comparison and reddened in embarrassment.

Aine merely smiled, then stood and began clearing the table. "I'm not insulted, Alex. My mother was a superb cook. She often shooed the servants out of the kitchen and prepared our meals herself." Sadness clouded the princess's eyes. "She insisted I needed to learn almost every job in the castle. She said if I didn't know how ordinary things worked in the real world, I'd make a poor ruler, and our people would suffer for it. My father often rebuked my mother for what he called her 'common ways.'"

Alex's estimation of Aine increased. A wise and caring mother had obviously brought the princess up right. Memories of childhood cooking classes with her Aunt Maia surfaced. Her own wholesome childhood had ended shortly after she reached adolescence, when her mother kidnapped her, told her that her aunt was dead, and hid them both away from the supernatural world.

"As for my father ... well, you've met him." Aine's bone-dry words snapped Alex out of her revery. "As you so succinctly put it earlier, he's an asshole."

"Yeah, sorry about that." Alex grimaced. "I mean, he *is* an asshole, but it's not polite to remind a child of her parent's, er, shortcomings."

Aine burst into delighted laughter. "Oh, Alex. You are so funny! I knew we'd be great friends as soon as we met." The princess sobered, and sympathy filled her eyes. "After all, we have so much in common ... including arrogant, egotistical, and downright evil fathers."

Alex stared at Aine in shock. "You know about my father, then." Memories of Talon's cruel eyes and hurtful words surfaced. Closing her eyes, Alex shook her head sharply as the sound of her father's final, agonized scream echoed in her mind. She had been the one to end his soul during the battle with Nyx in the Underworld. Determinedly, she banished the still painful memories of her father's betrayal.

"He would have killed you if you hadn't ended his soul first, Alex. You did what you had to do to save those under your care." Aine placed a gentle hand over Alex's, where it lay clenched on the table. "It's what I'll have to do as well."

A protest rose to Alex's lips, but she swallowed it back. As personally painful as the battle in the Underworld had been, she had indeed done what she had to—and it had inadvertently activated her death magic and alerted the gods to her demi-goddess status. She sighed, wishing again that she hadn't spent the past several months suppressing her new powers and avoiding dealing with her role in her father's death.

Alex nodded. "Yeah, my father would have killed me if he'd had the chance. But he betrayed me long before that. Many times. He was an evil man." Her spirits lightened as she spoke the words aloud. She *had* done what she had to do to save herself and her people.

Aine squeezed Alex's hand. "Ditto."

SOMETHING warm and fuzzy brushed against Alex's leg. She shrieked and jumped out of her chair, fully expecting to see a rat or mouse. Instead, the liquid brown eyes of her poodle Familiar stared up at her.

"Hi Alex. How's it hanging?" Larry's muzzle opened wide in a grin, then he sniffed the air. "Is that bacon I smell? There wouldn't be any left for me, would there?"

He turned begging eyes on the princess, who laughed and handed him the remains of her breakfast. "Hello, Larry. Still hungry, I see."

"Always," Larry mumbled as licked the last of the egg from the plate, then eyed the table hopefully.

Alex recovered from her initial shock. "Are the others here too?" Hope burgeoned. "Can they help get us out of here?"

Larry shook his head. "I got here by jumping a ley line, so no, the others aren't here. It would take too much energy for me to bring them this far." His long pink ears drooped. "They are on their way, but it's going to take them time to get here. The Fae realm only has a couple of Crossroads, thanks to Danu's sulking about the whole closing of the fairy mounds thing. That's all she would allow in her realm. The closest Crossroads is a day's travel away, or more."

Confused, Alex asked, "Then how did you get here?"

"I told you. I jumped a ley line." Larry huffed, then fixed Alex and Aine with a narrow-eyed glare. "Listen, what I'm gonna tell you guys next is top secret. Agreed?"

Alex and Aine shared a perplexed glance. "Agreed," they chorused.

Larry waved a disdainful paw at his poodle body. "Despite outward appearances, I'm a magically powerful Familiar." He gave them a serious look. "Here's the secret part. My magic allows me to form a magical bridge to pretty much any ley line, and jump into it, without having to use a Crossroads." He yawned and sprawled on the hearthrug. "Takes a lot of powerful magic, though, and it's not a common skill. In fact, I know of only one or two other supernaturals who can do this. Even most gods can't do it—only the Primordial ones, and there's just a handful of them." He closed his eyes and sighed wearily. "Jumping a ley without a Crossroads makes for a dangerous and wild ride."

Reluctantly, Larry sat up and shook himself from nose to tail. "Lemme finish my report before I fall asleep, then I'll leave. I can't get caught here, or the prince will know there's a hole in his defenses. Unfortunately, I can't take you both with me, because I had to use too much power to get here." He yawned, and added, "Jumping leys is hard enough. Doing it between realms at the same time—now that's really tough. I'll for sure need extra treats to regain my strength."

Aine reached for the last of the bacon and placed it on the floor next to Larry. "You are indeed a powerful Familiar, Larry. I've only met one other supernatural who could jump into a ley line without a Crossroads and live to tell the tale."

After gobbling up Aine's offering, Larry eyed the princess and nodded slowly. *"Two. You've met two,"* he said cryptically.

After a brief hesitation, Aine glanced at Alex and nodded. "Yes, you're right. Two."

Alex's stomach dropped as understanding dawned. "You mean I can jump a ley line? That can't be right!" She shook her head in denial. "Hell, I can't even use a damned Crossroads without help."

"You mean you won't use a Crossroads without your beau Conor holding your hand." Larry snorted in derision. "Get a grip, Alex. It's time to spread your wings."

Indignant, Alex replied, "I've spread them lots since we arrived in San Antonio! Don't forget, I knew nothing of the supernatural world before I got here a couple of months ago."

Patiently, Larry prodded her. "Yes, you knew some things. Not everything, of course, but a lot. You spent your childhood learning about the supernatural world from your aunt. When your mother kidnapped you, she paid that black witch to suppress your memories, but you've got 'em all back now. Right?"

At Alex's reluctant nod, he added, "And now's the time to take flight, Alex."

"Even if I knew how to jump a ley line, I can't leave the princess here, now that we've found her," Alex protested. Normal ley line travel through a well-constructed Crossroads made her nauseous and dizzy. The thought of forcing herself into a rushing river of magic midstream terrified her. "I couldn't possibly jump into a ley outside of a Crossroads. I wouldn't know where to start."

Larry rolled his eyes. "I'm not telling you to jump into a ley line right now, you idiot. You'd probably kill yourself if you tried. You need to stay here for now and stall if the prince shows up. Conor and the rest of the team are on their way here. They left the Crossroads as soon as we figured out where you were, but they won't get here until nightfall."

A rich golden glow wafted from Larry's fur. He pressed his warm body against Alex's leg. "Here, take some of my magic. You look like hell."

"Gee, thanks, fur-ball." Alex smiled affectionately down at her Familiar. She let the warmth of his magic soak into her bones. And her heart.

A peremptory knock on the door startled everyone. "Princess Aine, Prince Cair is on his way to the lodge. Please prepare yourself for his presence."

Larry bid them a quick farewell, then disappeared as quickly as he had arrived. Alex marveled at her Familiar's powerful ley line magic. *She could never do that. Could she?*

Alex and Aine cleared the table, then took turns in the elegant bathroom. After Larry left, Alex had discovered a backpack on her bed. Upon opening it, she sighed with pleasure. It contained her Keeper outfit, along with her favorite pair of kick-ass boots. Larry must have carried them through the ley line. She sent a silent thank you to her loyal and thoughtful, if irascible, magical partner.

25

DEADLY MAGIC

Aine and Alex sat at the table and waited for Prince Cair's arrival, each wrapped in their own thoughts. The blare of trumpets had already announced the prince's arrival at the lodge. It was only a matter of time before he demanded entry into their room.

"Have you seen your brother since he kidnapped you?" Alex queried Aine. "How did he manage it, anyway? Aren't you both evenly matched in magical power?"

"I've not seen my brother since he and his men attacked my home in the Earth realm," the princess replied. "How he captured me was simple." Aine closed her eyes and gingerly rubbed the greenish-yellow bruise on the side of her face. "Cair has never been afraid to use violence to get his way. While I fought his men with magic, he approached from the rear and knocked me over the head."

Aine sighed and met Alex's concerned gaze. Despair and hope fought for dominance in the princess's troubled eyes. "In the past, my brother has defeated me with cunning. That's how he convinced the king to exile me from the Fae realm. I'm sure Cair was the one who whispered poisoned words about me in my father's ear. This time, he resorted to violence—and it worked."

She shrugged. "If it had been a fair magical fight, I'd have won, and he wouldn't have captured me."

Alex considered. "You're saying your magic is stronger than his, correct?"

The princess nodded. "Yes. Much stronger. However, I'm handicapped by my mother's insistence on training me to fight fair and honorably as a child."

"You might want to consider whether your principles are more important than your life—and that of your people," Alex warned her.

Aine's lips curved in a sly smile. "Oh, I've had plenty of time to consider that over the past week, Alex. This time, I will fight dirty—and win. Plus, you're here to help—"

A hard knock on the door interrupted Aine's words. Both women jumped at the intrusion, then glanced at the door in trepidation. Things were about to get dicey.

"I'm coming in, dear sister, whether or not you are ready." The thick door muffled Cair's words, but the mockery in them came through loud and clear. The prince knew he had the upper hand.

The door burst open, and the handsome Fae prince Alex recognized from the Beltane ball strode into the room. He was taller than she remembered, but his long, golden blond hair and elegant attire remained the same. The last time she had seen Cair, two of the king's guards were dragging the red-faced prince from the Beltane ball after his father had unceremoniously banished him from court—yet again. The smug smile and arrogant tilt of Cair's head informed Alex that the prince knew he held all the cards this time. *That's okay,* she mused. *I've gotten pretty good at playing poker lately.*

Cair strode forward and sat on the couch, facing them. He crossed one booted leg over the other and leaned back as if totally at ease. Alex saw the tension in his shoulders and the tightening of his jaw, though, and knew the prince wasn't as relaxed as he tried to appear.

"Merry Meet, sister. I do hope you are finding your stay at the lodge comfortable?" Cair addressed his query to Aine, ignoring Alex completely.

Aine nodded stiffly. "You mean my imprisonment? Yes, the rooms are adequate, as I'm sure you know. However, let's not pretend I'm here willingly."

When Aine kept her gaze firmly on her brother, Alex realized the princess was attempting to keep the prince's focus on her. *Smart.* It gave Alex the opportunity to study the man for weaknesses, and maybe come up with a plan for escape. She flicked a glance at the phalanx of guards crowding the hallway and realized the futility of her hopes.

"Now, now, let's not start off on the wrong foot, sister," Cair said. "Unfortunately, your presence in the Earth realm, along with the protection of your attack fairy and your herd of unicorn friends, gave me little chance to approach you directly." The prince's sneer belied his words. "I brought you here merely so we could discuss a few things and come to an amicable agreement."

"What things?" Aine's face remained calm, but Alex noticed the princess's hands clenched her dress under the table, out of sight of her brother's gaze.

Cair's affable smile didn't reach his flinty eyes. "As you have no doubt realized, our father is no longer fit to rule—if he ever was. Our people groan under excess tithes, while their cupboards are bare, and their children starve. If we band together, we can depose him and restore a fair and just rule to our lands."

Thick tension filled the air. Alex held her breath, waiting for the princess's response and willing to support her either way.

The princess laughed derisively. "Fair and just are words that have no meaning to you, brother." She raised her eyebrows inquiringly. "I'm assuming you wish to rule, despite our late mother's wish that I take the throne when father can no longer rule? And what are your plans for me if I go along with your desires and deliver the support of my people?"

Cair sat forward, his amiable air slipping as a snarl overtook his flushed features. "Our mother is long dead. Her wishes are irrelevant. This kingdom needs a firm hand—one only I can supply."

With effort, the angry Fae relaxed his aggressive posture and leaned back against the couch. "Come now, sister, we must deal with today's realities, rather than dreaming about the past. I have the support of most of the army, and I've made inroads with the nobility. Plus, as I'm sure you have noticed when you explored the idea of escaping from here, my magical firepower is formidable."

Aine spoke softly. "You are forgetting one important thing, brother. You do not have the support of the common people—and I do. And I wouldn't be too sure about the army's loyalty to you, either." She folded her hands on the table and leaned forward, as if to impart a confidence. "There is no way I'd ever agree to support your ascension to the throne, Cair. I'll die before I let that happen to our people—and I'll take you with me to the Summerlands when I do."

Silence thrummed as the royal siblings stared at each other mutely, neither willing to give way.

Finally, Cair growled and leapt to his feet, his face a mask of fury. He covered the space between the couch and the table in an instant, but Aine did not cower; instead, she braced for her brother's anger. A sharp slap rent the air.

The princess stifled a groan at the impact but remained seated, a trail of red trickling from one corner of her mouth. Aine's slow smile revealed blood-stained teeth. "As always, Cair, your first response is violence when you don't get your way. That is the mark of a weak, flawed man—and one not fit to rule this magnificent realm."

Aine's goading words pushed the prince over the edge. He grabbed her arm roughly, forced her to stand, and then shook her violently. "You bitch! I'll kill you if you don't agree to support my plans!"

The princess's silvery laughter floated on the air. She threw her arm out to the side, and the door slammed closed. A violent red cloud of magic formed a swirling barrier around the entryway, sealing the protesting guards outside, and leaving Aine and Alex to face off with a madman.

The prince shouted incoherently and launched himself at his sister, sending them both tumbling to the floor.

The pair rolled around, each fighting for their lives. Alex's estimation of Aine's fighting prowess rose when the princess kneed her brother in the balls. She used his momentary disability to scramble away from Cair and lever herself onto a bed with her back against the wall. Her heaving chest and blood-covered face evidenced the fury of their fight.

Aine threw a pleading glance at Alex. "I can't beat him in a physical fight, and my magical powers are constrained here. He must have nulling wards in place. I'm lucky I could block the door, but the magical barrier won't last."

THE FURIOUS PRINCE crawled inexorably across the floor towards the bed, leaving a trail of blood in his wake. His gaze remained fixed on his sister, and his eyes held her imminent death.

Alex noticed the red magic swirling around the door was slowing and becoming translucent. There was little time before Aine's ward fell and her brother's guards flooded the room. *Fuck.* She rose and instinctively called her Keeper staff but wasn't really surprised when it didn't materialize.

Helpless rage filled Alex as the mad prince edged closer to his injured sister. Red-hot anger coalesced inside her, and a deeply buried corner of her soul she had been keeping locked cracked open. Tendrils of gleaming black smoke swirled from the molten lava within until they filled Alex's soul. Her vision became crystal clear, hyper-focused on the object of her rage.

The prince had reached the bed and was using the blanket to pull the princess away from the wall and closer to him. Aine scrambled back against the wall, but there was nowhere for her to go. Soon, a royal brother would kill his sister, and her death would plunge the Fae realm further into darkness.

Instinctively, Alex raised her arm and pointed at the prince. She didn't have her Keeper staff to direct magic, but quickly realized she didn't need it when inky black tendrils of power coalesced around her outstretched fingers. She focused her magic on the traitorous Fae prince. Raven-black fingers of magic curled lazily from Alex's outstretched hand and swirled ominously across the flagstone floor, reaching inexorably for the prince. As the first wisps of magic touched him, Cair stiffened and screamed in agony.

Alex's focus almost broke at the pained sound, so eerily like her father's last cries, but she shook off the painful memories. If ever a man truly needed to die, it was this one.

The prince's cries grew weaker. He clutched his chest and fought for breath.

"Alex? Alex! Stop! Please." Aine's words seemed to come from far away, but their insistence finally broke Alex's concentration. The dark tendrils of magic surrounding the prince faded, leaving him sprawled on the floor, gasping for air, his fearful gaze fixed on Alex.

Aine drew Alex towards the table and made her sit. "That's enough, dear. I think my brother now has a good idea of the power of my allies. But I need him to live long enough to be tried for treason in open court, so justice can be seen to be done by our people." Aine's eyes shone with compassion, but fear lurked in her gaze as well.

Alex nodded numbly. She knew that her own eyes also contained abject fear. Her Primordial death magic was terrifying.

Plus, she had promised the Fates she wouldn't use it again until properly trained. Breathing out a relieved sigh, Alex realized she was lucky she hadn't killed the princess and half the guards in her magical fury.

Hopefully, her divine cousins understood the necessity of her actions, or she might face their deadly magic, so like her own.

26

LEARNING THE HARD WAY

The room's door slammed, startling Alex from her dismal musings. She glanced at it and saw nothing but the dark wood of the door's thick panels. Gone were the red swirls of Aine's protection magic that had prevented the guards from interfering while Cair's life ebbed away during Alex's death magic attack.

The lock clicked firmly into place, the prince's cruel laughter echoing in the hallway outside. "That was a grave mistake, sister. You should have let that bitch kill me. Don't think you'll get another chance."

Cair commanded his guards to double their presence. "And get those blasted mages here. Tell them I need stronger null wards around this room, or their lives are forfeit."

"Yes, Your Majesty." Quick footsteps hurried away to obey.

A thud shook the door. "I'll deal with you two later. I've got other irons in the fire." The prince's faltering footsteps as he retreated revealed he had yet to fully recover from Alex's magical attack. He wouldn't give them another chance to overpower him, at least not while they remained imprisoned.

Aine sighed and sunk into the chair across from Alex. "He's right. I should have let you kill him. He won't put himself in a position of weakness again. Blast my stupid honor!" She placed her head in her hands and lowered it to the table, shoulders shaking as she wept.

Alex studied the crying princess thoughtfully. Aine was the Fae realm's only hope of a return to peace and prosperity. They couldn't count on Danu to intervene. That ancient goddess had already proved herself an unreliable ally and a Primordial who neglected her people.

Fuck it. They couldn't wait for Conor and the rest of the team to show up. Alex knew that the next time she faced the prince, one of them would die. She had to make sure that it was the prince, and not her, that took an unscheduled trip into the afterlife. But she needed backup and a strategy to confront the prince. Only then could she deal with the king.

The only way forward was to escape the lodge and bring the princess with her. And the only way to do that was to jump into a wild ley line midstream. *Double fuck.* Alex mused, then smiled affectionately in reminiscence. Uncle Vinnie had a lot to answer for. Her foul mouth was completely his fault.

"Come on, Aine. It's time to blow this popsicle stand."

The princess raised her head, confusion replacing the despair on her face. "What is a popsicle stand? And why would anyone blow on it?"

Alex burst into laughter. The princess's unintentional humor broke the tension in the air. Once her mirth resolved, she explained. "A popsicle is a type of frozen dessert on a stick. In many Earth cities, there are small stalls set up where people can buy popsicles, hold them by the stick, and eat them as they walk around." With a final chuckle, she added. "Although I'm not sure why anyone would blow on a popsicle. They are cold enough as it is." She snickered. "In fact, the word 'blow' sometimes has a much cruder meaning on Earth than it apparently has here in the Fae realm."

Aine nodded in understanding. "Thank you for the explana-tion about popsicles, Alex. I'll have to try one next time I'm on

Earth. They sound delightful." The princess's mouth curved in a sly smile. "And you'll have to explain Earth's vernacular meaning of 'blow', so I fully understand my faux pas."

Reddening, Alex nodded. "Sure thing. But how about we get out of here first?"

"And how do you propose we do that?" Aine asked, then her eyes widened. "Oh. The ley lines. But I thought Larry said it was dangerous."

"Maybe so, but can you think of another way?" Alex raised her hands and shrugged.

Aine's shoulders drooped in defeat. "No, I can't."

"The ley lines it is, then."

Alex stretched herself out on the floor and laid her hands on the cold flagstones. She was unsure why she did this, but it seemed the right thing to do. Closing her eyes, she flexed her hands and pushed her magic past the flagstone floor and deep into the earth. After a desperate search, she felt a faint tingle of ley energy and reached for it with her Keeper magic. The image of a small ley line floated into her mind's eye. This wasn't the rushing river of magic she was used to. The ley's weak pulse of energy swirled in a shallow, sluggish stream. *Damn it! How the hell am I supposed to jump into that? It'll cut us off at the knees!*

Out loud, she confidently told the princess, "I've located the closest ley line. Time for us to go."

Aine's trusting gaze fixed on Alex. "What do you want me to do?"

"Uh, grab my hand and lie next to me." Alex shifted over to give the princess room. Once Aine complied and grasped her hand, Alex blew an anxious breath. "Are you sure you want to do this? I've never jumped a ley line before, and Larry said—"

Aine squeezed Alex's hand. "I am familiar with some Earth colloquialisms. This one seems appropriate." The Fae princess grinned and said, "How about you shit or get off the pot?"

Alex snorted with laughter, then turned her attention to the distant ley line. "Okay, but don't say I didn't warn you."

HER SOUL WAS BEING TORN APART; she was sure of it. The pain was excruciating. Body arcing, she screamed in agony. Flames of gold and crimson magic burned her up from within. Aine's firm grip on her hand was the only thing that kept Alex from losing consciousness.

Alex pulled on her last bit of energy and commanded her dueling magics to work together instead of fighting each other. "Please, please, pull it together, guys. I need you both to get us into that ley line." She latched on to the distant flow of the tiny ley line with her golden Keeper magic and begged the blood-red flames of her demi-goddess death magic to allow her entry into the ley.

The fire inside her soul consumed her mind.

"ALEX? ALEX! WAKE UP, PLEASE," a panicked voice pleaded. "I need you to wake up now!"

At first, it seemed too much effort to respond. Echoes of pain called to her, encouraging a return to oblivion. Then a deluge of icy cold water slapped her in the face. Alex sat up, sputtering. The princess stood above her, holding a dripping bucket.

"What the hell did you do that for?"

"I've been trying to wake you for the better part of an hour. Nightfall is almost upon us." Aine peered anxiously into the gloom. "Your ley jump landed us behind the barn in the far field. But come darkness, the guards will increase their patrols. We must get to the woods, where we can hide." She gestured across the field.

Alex shook her head to clear it and peered at the distant tree line. Nausea roiled her stomach, but she swallowed back the bile. They needed to move. She rose unsteadily to her feet. Aine's arm around her waist kept her upright as she regained some equilibrium.

"Thank you for saving my life, Alex. I owe you a great debt," Aine whispered, smiling in gratitude. Her eyes held a firm promise. "You may call on me anytime, if ever you find yourself in need."

"Hold that thought." Alex extracted herself from the princess's supportive arm, staggered, then found her footing. "Let's get away from this place first and then find the rescue team. We've got a kingdom to save."

They crouch-walked through the tall grass of the field, freezing at each sound and fearing discovery. Finally, they reached the thick undergrowth of the forest and crept under the shelter of the massive trees.

Alex shivered as they moved further into the trees. These woods had an ominous air—even more forbidding than Danu's gloomy forest to the south.

Aine stopped and held up a hand. "There is a boundary ward up ahead. It's powerful. I'll need to break it before we proceed." Her lips thinned. "Let's just hope we're out of the range of my brother's null wards, so I can use my magic."

The ward split in a flash of violet light, momentarily blinding Alex.

"His mages used black magic to create this ward," Aine muttered. She strode forward, her face set in anger. "The null wards in our room also reeked of black magic. That rat bastard."

Alex followed the princess, glancing down at the broken ward as she passed. The twisted, ugly mass of metal hung from a bush, black smoke still swirling lazily around it.

"I know your brother is an asshole, but what about his using black magic sets you off so much?" Alex queried, her interest roused.

Aine glanced over her shoulder, her gaze fiery. "Black magic is not native to the Fae realm. It relies on the use of iron as a conductor. Iron alone can injure or kill most Fae under the right circumstances. When imbued with magic, it's even more deadly. Our first queen banned iron from the Fae realm millennia ago."

Alex mused on Aine's explanation as they crept through the forest. Several more black magic devices required disarming, slowing their progress.

After a particularly hairy experience with a powerful device designed to cover anyone who crossed its path with molten iron, Alex voiced her thoughts. "All these black magic booby-traps mean someone must have brought the iron here illegally, along with some non-Fae mages, to work it. I'm pretty sure they didn't use a Crossroads to do that. Any Keeper would have stopped them."

"My father must have brought in the mages, and the iron, through the fairy mound he had re-opened," Aine explained. "My brother doesn't have the connections—or the power—to re-open a fairy mound or to import such deadly things without the king intervening. I figure Cair has quietly stolen some of the iron, and recruited some mages, from my father."

"So much to unpack there, Aine," Alex muttered. "So, you know about the unsealed fairy mounds? And you know your father has been importing deadly mages and black magic through them. What else do you know—and what were you planning to do about it?"

Aine stopped and threw out a hand to prevent Alex from continuing. "Shhhh. I hear something up ahead. Quickly now, take cover. We can address my spies and plans for a royal coup at another time, okay?"

Alex gave Aine serious side-eye. "Okay," she murmured, "but you owe me an explanation. I'm beginning to think that at least some of what's happened since Persephone fell into bed with your brother is down to you. Am I right?"

"Perhaps," Aine whispered, smiling enigmatically. "My wise mother taught me well."

❧

THE UNDERGROWTH to one side of the narrow deer trail they had been following shook, its leaves rustling in the still air. Alex and Aine crouched further into the brush on the far side of the path. Alex's eyes widened when a huge, midnight black muzzle and familiar amber eyes peered out of the undergrowth.

"Conor, is that you? You scared me to death!" Alex shook her finger at the now-grinning Barghest as he emerged from the bushes and padded onto the path.

The undergrowth rustled again, and several other familiar figures appeared.

Relieved, Alex rose from her uncomfortable crouch and joined her team. "Tyre, Braga, it's good to see you both." She nodded at the half dozen other posse members present. "Thanks for coming, everyone."

"Ow! Stop that!" Aine, who had followed Alex onto the path, waved her arms wildly. "Flower, knock it off! That hurts."

The tiny fairy finally landed, perching on the thick fur between Conor's ears. She waved her pin-sized sword at Aine a final time, then sheathed it, fixing her mistress with a narrow-eyed glare. "I warned you of the growing danger to your safety, Your Majesty, but you wouldn't listen."

The angry fairy stamped her foot on Conor's head, the impact thankfully softened by his thick fur. "Instead, you stayed your hand until it was too late—then look what happened! That oaf of a brother of yours kidnapped you and dragged you off to his dungeon. Don't ask me to rescue you again because I won't do it."

Alex stifled a grin. Flower hadn't actually done any rescuing. Neither had the rest of the team. She had gotten herself and Aine out of the prince's prison, thank you very much. Okay, maybe Larry helped—rather a lot, she admitted. Speaking of the furball, where was he?

Anticipating her question and fighting a grin of his own at Flower's antics, Tyre explained. "Larry remained at the San Antonio Crossroads, Alex. He's fine, just really spent magically after jumping the ley here line to find you. He needs to rest for a while."

Alex breathed a relieved sigh. "Thanks, Tyre. I was worried about the little guy."

"What about me? Weren't you worried about me?" Conor asked, amusement twinkling in his amber eyes.

Alex glanced down at Conor, expecting to see his Hellhound form, then realized she was looking at his now very human feet. *Oh crap*. She kept her gaze below his knees, afraid to let it travel any higher. When Conor shifted from his furry Hellhound Barghest form back into his human one, clothes didn't magically reappear.

Conor snorted a laugh. "You can look up, Alex. I'm not naked."

Alex allowed her gaze to travel higher and realized Conor had donned a pair of shorts and a shirt. Disappointment warred with her embarrassment.

"We can do the naked thing later. In private," Conor murmured with a sly grin. He winked at her. "Once this situation is over, just say the word."

Warmth pooled in Alex's stomach and reddened her cheeks. She turned away and started up the path. "Oh, shut up, Conor. Let's go, everyone."

A silvery Fae voice carried on the night air. "Time to blow this popsicle stand."

Alex snickered at Aine's words, then picked up the pace. The princess was right. It was.

27

TAKING CHARGE

After a relatively uneventful journey back from the Fae realm, Alex and the posse reached the San Antonio Crossroads just before dawn. Maia fussed over Aine, offering her an elegant suite in the manor house, which the weary princess accepted. The rest of the team disbursed to get some much-needed rest.

Alex trudged wearily to her room and tumbled onto the bed with a sigh. The warmth of the room lulled her towards sleep. Larry snored at her side, still not fully recovered from his ley line jumping escapade.

But worry about the coming posse meeting, at which the team would rework their strategy considering new events and information, kept Alex from drifting off. King Donal's fourth Diamond Jubilee was only a week away. The king's invitation had been waiting for Alex upon her return to the Crossroads. Would she go? Should she? Was the king aware that his son had kidnapped Alex and his daughter? If so, did he know they had escaped? So many questions. And no answers.

After rolling over, she pounded her pillow into shape, trying to get comfortable. The political tightrope she walked yawned over an alligator-filled ravine. If she failed to traverse it, or made the wrong move, she'd be far from the only one to suffer. The Fae realm would either remain under the tyrannical rule of a corrupt king or, worse, descend into a bloody war for the throne.

ALEX WOKE late in the afternoon at the sound of a hesitant knock.

"Are you awake? I brought you some dinner."

Conor's muffled words woke Larry, who raised his head from the bed. "Dinner? Did someone say dinner?" He yawned widely, then licked his chops. "I could eat."

"You can *always* eat, Larry." Alex petted her Familiar's head affectionately, then crawled out of bed and headed into the bathroom. "Can you please ask Conor to put the food on the dressing table? I'm gonna take a shower." Before closing the bathroom door, she shot a warning look at her greedy Familiar. "And don't touch my plate, fluff-ball! I'm sure Conor brought something for you, too. Plus, there's kibble in your bowl."

Larry grumbled at the rebuke, then hopped off the bed and headed for the dog door. "I'll tell him he can come in. He'd better have brought a plate for me. I don't like that new kibble you bought. It's square. You know I prefer round pieces."

Alex shut the door on Larry's complaints and eyed herself in the mirror. Her naturally olive skin was pale. Red rimmed her deep green eyes, while her normally lustrous long black hair resembled dry straw. *Damn, girl. Better work some magic before tonight's meeting*, she reflected wryly.

After a long, hot shower, and a makeover triage attempt, Alex opened the bathroom door to the tantalizing aroma of New York-style pizza. She smiled, sure that Uncle Vinnie had a hand in tonight's delivery menu. He had always offered her pizza to solve any childhood traumas.

"Conor's a smart Hellhound," Larry told Alex. "He brought two whole pizzas. Otherwise, there might not have been any left for you."

She nodded in silent agreement, already well into her second slice of the heavenly pizza. "You're right; he's pretty smart. And you'd have been a fried Familiar if you didn't leave me any of this pie."

LATER THAT EVENING, Alex scolded Larry as they walked through the gardens, heading to the posse meeting. "If you don't stop yawning, I'm gonna send you back to the room. We need to be alert and have our collective shit together tonight."

Larry grinned up at her. "You mean *you* need to have your collective shit together. I'm just along for the ride."

"Oh no, you don't, Mr. Ancient Magical Familiar." Alex glared at Larry to emphasize her words. "You're older than dirt. I'm sure you've helped your previous magical partners more than once when they had a sticky situation like this one. And I know you've seen a battle or three. Am I right?"

Larry's eyes darkened with memories. Then he shook himself off and pranced toward the barn's wide entrance, throwing a cheeky grin over his shoulder. "I suppose I might know a thing or two that could help. But you'll have to ask nicely, girlfriend."

The packed arena quieted when Alex walked into the barn. She hid her rising panic behind a businesslike facade. *Fake it till you make it,* she reminded herself.

"Good evening, everyone. Thank you for coming. We have a lot to get through tonight, so let's get started." Alex strode to the table in the middle of the arena and joined those already seated. Maia and Vinnie sat on her left, while Princess Aine and Tyre sat to her right. Flower stood at attention on the table, directly in front of Aine.

She scanned the faces of the attendees. Off to one side of the arena, a bevy of goddesses reclined on massive, throne-like chairs. Besides Hecate and Demeter, her cousins, the Fates, were also present. When Clotho smiled and gave her a thumbs up, Alex realized she had yet to speak with them about her use of death magic against Prince Cair. While she hadn't killed him, she very easily could have. She had most definitely broken her promise not to use death magic until properly trained. *Sigh.* That meant at the very least that the Fates would be here a while longer. She wouldn't get away without their training on how to control her lethal magic.

The silent expectation in the air brought Alex's attention back to her audience. Posse members, along with a dozen ghosts, filled the wooden risers against the walls, everyone eyeing Alex expectantly. The only one missing was Billy the Squid. He was patrolling the lake near the open fairy mound, so he could warn them of any new intrusions from the Fae realm. They didn't want any unexpected Fae guests during tonight's meeting.

"Don't worry, sweets. You've got this." Conor's soothing, mind-spoken words calmed Alex. *"Do you want me to start the meeting?"*

Alex mind-spoke a reply. *"Nope. I'm good. I sat there like a bump on a log while you guys did all the planning for the battle in the Underworld. You can't carry the whole weight again. After all, I'm the Crossroads Keeper, right? Saving the world is part of the job description."*

Conor grinned at her. *"Not the entire world, Alex, just your part of it. Oh, and the Fae realm, and—"*

"Oh, shut up, you jerk. Just what I need—more pressure." Despite her sharp rebuke, Conor's teasing words helped center Alex. *Game time.* She took a deep breath and addressed the crowd.

Alex explained everything that had happened since the posse last met, including her and Aine's kidnapping and their eventual escape. It had been less than a week since the posse last met, but felt much longer. As she wrapped up her summation, mind-spoken advice from Larry prompted Alex with a recommendation, and she agreed with his suggestion. It would be a wise move to let everyone hear from the only Fae royal who could permanently resolve their current misbehaving goddess situation and, hopefully, bring peace and prosperity back to the Fae realm.

"Next, before we get into any strategic planning, I'd like to introduce you all to Princess Aine. She is King Donal's daughter, and until a few years ago, was heir to the Fae throne. But King Donal exiled the princess to our realm. Since then, the princess has lived quietly in the forest outside of Sylvan City."

Aine rose and smiled at the expectant crowd. She waved at the audience, several of whom waved back and shouted enthusiastically.

"Hi Princess!"

"Good to see you here today!"

"Sorry to hear about your kidnapping!"

Alex realized that at least some of those present already knew and liked the princess. Others eyed Aine with curious, but stoic, gazes, obviously as in the dark about the Fae royal living in their midst as Alex had been until the princess's invitation to tea had arrived several days ago.

When Aine spoke, her silvery voice played a magical word melody in the air. "Hello, everyone. Endless thanks for your welcome. I count those amongst you whom I have already met as good friends, and I look forward to meeting the rest of you, so we can be friends, too." The princess smiled, her lovely face lit with kindness, while her eyes contained the wisdom of the ages. "I'm so happy to be here, among friends, both old and new."

The curious, reserved expressions of most in the audience dissolved into smiles, then laughter. Soon, everyone was clapping enthusiastically. Even the ghost of Queen Elizabeth summoned an approving smile.

Alex realized Aine must have used her Fae powers to lighten the tense atmosphere and encourage support. *Huh. Persuasion magic. Who knew?* She cocked her head and considered. *That could be very useful.*

Tyre's mind-spoken voice interrupted Alex's musings. *"You do not have persuasion magic, Keeper. It is a uniquely Fae power. However, you have those who can use it on your behalf."* He gestured discreetly to himself and the two other Indigo Fae warriors standing at attention behind him.

While Alex digested this interesting tidbit, Aine gestured for calm and resumed speaking once the audience had quieted.

"Friends, I stand before you in entreaty. My people suffer and starve under the cruel yoke of a corrupt king, while his son works to precipitate a bloody war for the throne." Crystal-clear tears streaked the princess's lovely face. "Our goddess, Danu, is blind to the needs of her people. She hasn't responded to our cries for help and has remained hidden away in her woods for centuries. Yet, she quarrels jealously with your gods because one of them dared have an affair with a debauched Fae prince who seeks to use his lover's divine power to take the throne. While a war threatens the Fae realm, which will certainly spill over into your community, the gods argue and posture over imagined slights. What are we to do?"

The princess's eloquent plea captivated Alex, along with the rest of the audience. The crowd buzzed with excitement, then erupted into applause and excited chatter.

Alex realized Aine had neatly manipulated the situation. By mentioning the dispute between the gods, she tied the safety of the Crossroads and Sylvan City to the ugly situation unfolding in the Fae realm. *Well done, Aine,* Alex mused silently.

"Thank you, Alex. Don't forget, for several centuries, I served my realm as a diplomat." Aine smiled conspiratorially at Alex's shocked expression. *"Yes, I'm that old. And yes, I can mind-speak with you. You are correct—I used just a touch of persuasion magic on the audience. Not enough to interfere with their free will, of course."*

Alex nodded mutely. *Damn it.* Another supernatural who could read her mind. She might as well just buy an enormous bulletin board and scrawl her thoughts across it for everyone to see. It would save her at least some of the constant mind invasions.

Aine nodded and smiled at the crowd, then retook her seat. She resolutely avoided Alex's accusing gaze, but mind-spoke a reply to Alex's unspoken concerns. *"Not everyone can read your mind, Keeper. Just those with a magical or life connection to you. You saved my life a few days ago, remember? Without your intervention, my brother would have killed me that night. If you hadn't jumped the leys and gotten us both out before his return, we both would have perished."*

She met Alex's gaze, her eyes solemn. "That makes us sisters now, my dear."

"Oh." Alex realized her mouth hung open in shock and snapped it shut, then closed her eyes and heaved a sigh. Here was yet another heart family obligation. Then she brightened; if her new sister was a princess, did that make her one, too? And did she really want to be one?

The princess's silvery laughter floated on the air, letting Alex know the Fae royal was still present in her mind. Aine grinned at her and spoke aloud. "Our sisterhood doesn't make you a princess, Alex. But once I'm on the throne, I can certainly award you a royal title or two, if you like."

Larry snickered. "Duchess Alex. No, Countess Alex. I helped. Hey Aine, does that mean I get a title as well?"

The Fae princess grinned down at Larry, then stroked his pouffy head. "Does Sir Larry work for you, Familiar?"

Tail thumping the floor with excitement, Larry barked aloud. "Absolutely!"

After that, with the posse now fully on board, Alex and the team dove into planning a winning strategy.

One ancient goddess to appease—and then spur into action on behalf of her people.

One bloody civil war to prevent.

One throne to take.

Not much at all. Right?

28

JUBILEE JITTERS

Alex winced as Princess Aine adjusted her headpiece one last time. "Why do I have to wear this stupid thing? It's not *my* fourth Diamond Jubilee we're celebrating."

The princess drove in one last bobby pin, then stood back and admired her handiwork. "There, that looks perfect on you. For royal events in the Fae realm, all nobility and guests must dress for the occasion, Alex." After a brief pause, Aine grinned slyly and mind-spoke her true thoughts. *"Just what occasion they'll be celebrating tonight will come as a surprise to many, though, I'm sure."*

Alex glared at her reflection in the full-length mirror. The almost translucent Fae gown she wore clung to her every curve, revealing way more skin than she was comfortable with. The gown's deep emerald color set off her green eyes, making them appear large and mysterious. She had to admit that the princess's borrowed dress looked great on her—but its tight, low-cut fit would certainly interfere with tonight's planned activities. She threw up her hands in exasperation and mind-spoke a reply to her companion. *"And just how the hell am I supposed to fight in this thing? Why can't I wear my Keeper leathers? They're perfectly presentable."*

Aine gently pushed Alex away from the mirror and replied to her mind-spoken objections out loud. "Stop whining and let me finish getting ready. I need the mirror." The princess studied her reflection critically, then nodded with satisfaction. As she fastened a stunning sapphire necklace around her neck and donned matching earrings, she mind-spoke a reminder. *"While I have warded this room for silence, Alex, I don't trust my father not to have other methods to spy on us. We must behave as if our only reason for being here is to celebrate my father's fourth Diamond Jubilee. Do you understand?"* Aine gazed at Alex in the mirror with a mute plea for cooperation. *"If we are to have any chance of success tonight, we must let our plan play out."*

Alex sat gingerly on the massive, canopied bed and nodded mutely. She wasn't sure their plan would work—but it was the only one they had come up with that had a chance of success—if everything went according to plan and everyone involved did their part.

At the posse's planning meeting the previous week, Aine had revealed she had spies throughout the castle, including several highly placed members of the king's Council. That was how she had known about the reopened fairy mound—and how she had finagled an invitation to her father's fourth Diamond Jubilee.

Aine's 'man on the inside' had convinced the king to invite his only daughter—despite her exiled status—along with his disgraced son to the celebration as a show of strength. With both his children present to witness his fourth coronation, King Donal's power would be unassailable. Or so the king had been advised.

The past week had sailed by while messengers came and went from the Crossroads as the princess and the posse cemented alliances and laid plans. Alex had quickly realized that Princess Aine had been planning a bloodless coup for quite a while. She already had the support of most of the army, except the king's personal guard. Several of the Council members also supported her plans, as did many of the most powerful noble families. Oh, and the benevolent princess had the devotion of the common people—almost all of them.

Most of the Fae wanted King Donal gone—but they knew his

dissolute and treacherous son hungered to take his father's place on the throne. Unfortunately, they also realized that any attempt by Cair to usurp his father by force would cause a bloody civil war.

Everyone already knew that Princess Aine offered the Fae kingdom's only hope for a peaceful transition of power. Over the past decade, the ambassador princess had quietly woven alliances and gathered evidence of her father's corruption, even after her exile. She had always promised a bloodless coup, and a fair and prosperous rule. Many of those attending tonight's celebration were on Aine's side—but not everyone. The king's guard, along with his most loyal Council members and members of the nobility who benefited from the king's corruption, all presented a major threat to tonight's plans.

"Our plan will work, Keeper. It has to." Aine's confident assurance drifted into Alex's troubled mind.

It had better, Alex brooded. After the posse meeting the previous week, Alex had accepted the king's formal invitation to the Jubilee, and then carefully chosen a retinue chock full of powerful posse members. Her team had traveled to the Fae realm the previous day, stopping for a while in Danu's woods to have a forceful discussion with the recalcitrant and unreliable goddess.

When Alex and Aine had reached the king's castle the previous evening, the staff had welcomed them as honored guests. They were assigned adjoining rooms even more luxurious than the one Alex had on her previous visit. Each suite had a large bedroom that opened onto a shared parlor. Upon their arrival, Aine had discovered over a dozen listening devices in their rooms. Partnering with Larry, they had deactivated the listening devices and set a privacy ward around the whole of the suite. Exhausted, they had both fallen into bed and slept dreamlessly.

The following morning, servants delivered a delicious breakfast to their doors. Both women kept to their rooms and sat silently for much of the day, deep in mind-conversations with their co-conspirators, who ranged freely around the castle and grounds. After a final enlightening exchange with Conor regarding his investigative success, Alex admitted to herself that having the power to communicate over distances via mind-speak *might* just make up for its intrusive nature. *Might.*

After a late lunch, Alex and Aine had napped until it was time to prepare for the evening's festivities.

WITH EFFORT, Alex returned her mind to the present. Knowing that any further excuses about appropriate attire for a royal coup would be in vain, she reluctantly rose from the bed and joined Aine in front of the mirror. Their eyes met in its reflection, each gaze filled with trepidation—and a fierce determination.

By midnight, there would be a new queen in town.

BY PRIOR AGREEMENT, the team gathered in Alex and Aine's parlor so they could travel as a group to the throne room for King Donal's Jubilee Ceremony. Tension filled the crowded room; tonight's plan needed to go like clockwork, or none of them would live to see another dawn.

Seemingly unconcerned with the outcome of their planned coup attempt, Conor grinned at Alex, his heated gaze gliding over her skimpy gown. "We should attend more Fae events together, sweets. You look amazing."

Despite the pleasant warmth that Conor's compliment evoked, Alex rolled her eyes. "Now is *so* not the time, Conor."

"Tonight, then. After the party. Your place or mine?"

"Knock it off, you two. You're making me nauseous." Larry gave a pretend gag, then barked a laugh. "Honestly, though, the sooner the two of you get it on, the sooner the rest of us can relax. You're both way too tense. But it'll have to wait until after we take care of things here first. After that, you two can hit a home run anytime." The little poodle grinned up at Alex's flaming face. "Just gimme a heads up, though, so I can make myself scarce when you do."

"And so we all know who won the bet," Tyre interjected, his calm eyes twinkling at Larry.

Alex's forehead wrinkled in confusion, then she gasped when illumination struck. "Wait a minute—do you guys have a bet on when Conor and I, uh, ... you know?"

Judging by the lack of eye contact and smothered grins amongst her team, Alex realized that, yes indeed, her team had a betting pool on when she and Conor would finally have sex. The fiery blush on her face deepened, and her eyes narrowed.

"Listen, you lot. When—or if—Conor and I get it on is none of your damned business. I know most of you will be able to tell, because of the whole mind connection thing, but I'm warning you —if I sense even one of you listening in when ... if we sleep together, I might just have to test my death magic on your ass. Got it?"

Subdued nods greeted her rebuke.

"Yes, Alex."

"Sorry, Alex."

Alex threw everyone one last glare, then snarled at her Familiar. "I'd bet you're the fleabag who started this whole thing, aren't you?"

Larry just grinned and wagged his pink tail.

When Aine giggled merrily, Alex threw up her hands in defeat and headed for the door. "Let's go. No time like the present to ... well, you know."

Everyone followed her meekly enough, but Alex heard more than a few smothered chuckles behind her as she opened the door and swept into the hallway.

"I hate you guys."

"No, you don't. You love us," Larry snarked. Then he pranced ahead of the group and led the erstwhile heroes down the marble halls and toward a political battle with the highest of stakes—their lives.

29

HERE COMES THE KING

Trumpets blared as Alex and the others entered the vast expanse of the Great Hall. A liveried servant approached them and bowed low. "Keeper Alex, King Donal extends his thanks for your attendance at his re-coronation."

The servant turned to Aine and bowed again—not quite as low this time. "Princess Aine, your father has reserved a seat for you on the royal stage." He gestured to the far end of the massive room, where a raised platform contained an impressive golden throne. Two much smaller silver thrones flanked it, but all were currently empty. A phalanx of the king's personal guards stood at attention along the back wall behind the stage.

Deep unease settled in Alex's stomach, and she shared a fleeting glance with Aine. *How much did the king know of their plans? Was this his way of dividing and conquering—thwarting the coup before it had even begun?*

The princess merely smiled at the servant and nodded agreeably. "How thoughtful of my father. Please inform him I'll be happy to join him for the re-coronation ceremony—once it is underway."

It looked like Aine had adroitly side-stepped the royal summons—until a scarlet-coated member of the king's guard appeared at her side. "I'm afraid we must insist, princess. The king wishes his children to take their seats before the event begins." The guard gestured politely, but firmly, toward the platform. "After you, Your Highness."

Alex squeezed Aine's hand and mind-spoke her reassurance. *"Go ahead. We've got this. Just ... be ready when the shit hits the fan, okay? Then it'll be your turn to act."*

Aine flicked a glance at Alex and gave her an almost imperceptible nod before gracefully preceding the guard toward the trio of thrones, her back straight and step firm.

Alex and her retinue edged their way as far toward the front of the gathered crowd as they could. When they broke free of the last group of tightly packed courtiers, Alex spotted three rows of benches set in front of the largest throne. A group of stone-faced, scarlet-robed Fae occupied the benches, facing toward the crowd. Each sported a sheathed sword at their waist, and more than a few wore quivers of lethal-looking arrows slung from their shoulders. Long wooden bows rested next to each of the archers.

"That's the full Royal Council." Tyre mind-spoke his explanation to Alex and the rest of the team. *"Their position in front of the king's throne is likely no accident. Normally, Council members sit on either side of the main dais—and they are never armed in the king's presence."*

"Well, shit." Alex mind-spoke her reply, her heart sinking. *"Looks like the king has been one step ahead of us the whole time."*

Tyre's lips curved in a small smile. *"Don't despair yet, Alex. My men and I are more than a match for the Council. Indigo Fae warriors, remember? Plus, we have many allies here tonight, remember—including several members of the Council itself."*

BEFORE ALEX COULD REPLY, a deafening blast of trumpets heralded the king's arrival.

The stocky royal appeared from behind a heavy velvet curtain that Alex surmised hid a back exit from the Great Hall. King

Donal's silken robes glittered with gold embroidery, while a cloak of purple velvet swung around his short, stout form. A heavy golden crown, completely covered in glittering jewels, sat firmly on his head. After a theatrical pause while his courtiers clapped and bowed, the king slowly approached the golden throne and lowered himself gingerly onto its padded surface.

"He's gotta keep a steady head," Larry mind-spoke to Alex. *"If that crown tilts, the weight of it could break his neck."*

Alex pursed her lips and mind-spoke her dry reply. *"We can only hope."*

She glanced up at Aine, seated on the much smaller throne next to the father who had stolen her heritage and exiled her to another realm. The princess's calm, blank countenance hid what must surely be turbulent emotions. On the other side of the king, Prince Cair slouched on a throne identical to his sister's. The petulant prince didn't bother to hide his scowl.

Once the trumpets ceased, the tallest of the Council members stood. Alex studied the man's arrogant expression, richly-embroidered robes, and the gleaming gold medallion hung around his neck, surmising that this must be the head of the king's Royal Council, Councilor Jerrold. If Aine was correct, this man was her father's closest ally. The princess had told Alex that Jerrold was one of the Fae her father had brought in from the Earth realm when he fired almost the entire Council several years previously. It was after Jerrold's arrival that things had gone from bad to worse in the Fae realm.

A servant hurried up to Jerrold and handed him several gilded scrolls. With a sneer and a careless wave, the chief Councilor dismissed the servant, who scurried away, relief clear on his face.

Councilor Jerrold raised a brow and cast icy eyes over the crowd. Immediately all murmuring ceased, and silence reigned in the massive space. Once satisfied he had the room's full attention, Jerrold spoke. "Welcome, everyone, to this august occasion. I speak for the full Council tonight, as we celebrate the fourth Diamond Jubilee of our beloved King Donal. For six centuries, this realm has prospered under his wise and benevolent reign. Tonight, we recommit ourselves to King Donal and recognize his divine right to rule our kingdom for another century."

Jerrold then unrolled the largest of the scrolls and read off a long list of the king's titles, awards, and accomplishments, his deep, monotonous voice droning on and on.

"*Divine right, my ass.*" Larry mind-spoke his cheeky commentary. "*Another century of this idiot's corruption and there won't be anything left for him to rule.*"

"*Quiet, Larry!*" Alex scolded, unsure if the crowd held any whose powers allowed them to listen in to her Familiar's silent words. "*Just—be ready when the time comes.*"

"*Yes, ma'am.*" Larry's body tensed in anticipation. "*Just say the word.*"

Alex tuned back into the proceedings and realized that Jerrold had finally finished his dry recitation. He rolled up the scroll and handed it to one of the other Council members, all of whom had risen from their benches and each of whom seemed poised for action.

Jerrold unrolled one of the smaller scrolls and consulted it. When he glanced up, his dark eyes gleaming with triumph, Alex's heart sank. *Jerrold knew something was up.* She was sure of it.

"Before we continue the ceremony, there are a few matters of importance we must address." The tall Fae gestured toward the king's guards, several dozen of whom were arrayed against the wall behind the raised platform containing the thrones. Several guards broke ranks and positioned themselves next to Prince Cair's mini throne. The prince sat up, his eyes wide and worried.

Jerrold gave Cair a disdainful glance, then read from the small scroll in his hand. "It has come to King Donal's attention that his son, Prince Cair, has been fomenting a rebellion. When the king brought his concerns to the Council, we investigated. This proclamation contains our findings."

The prince shot up from his throne, a denial on his lips.

King Donal glared at his son and shouted. "Silence!"

The prince quailed at his father's command and allowed the king's guard to push him back into his seat. Cair's expression was thunderous, but fear lurked in his eyes.

"As I was saying," the councilor doggedly plowed on, "we investigated the king's charges and found ample evidence of the prince's plot. Therefore, the Council hereby finds Prince Cair guilty of treason. Sentencing and punishment shall take place tomorrow morning."

When the guards lifted the terrified prince from his chair, Jerrold shook his head. "No, leave him in place. The people need to see justice done—and they will. But first, the prince should remain present to witness the abject failure of his little rebellion."

"I'm going to be next, Alex." Aine's calm voice sounded in Alex's mind. *"This is just political theater—grandiose, but not unexpected."*

"Well, it shouldn't be unexpected," Alex mind-spoke her sharp reply. *"I thought you had a couple of Council members on your side. Why didn't they warn us?"*

"There are several Councilors sympathetic to our cause, Alex. However, I suspect they were not aware of tonight's exhibition." Aine nodded slightly, her eyes fixed on Councilor Jerrold's broad back. *"Jerrold is a wily old fox. I'm sure he kept this 'investigation' from the full Council. He likely suspects one or more Council members are not as loyal to the king as he is."*

"And he's right. They're not, but that doesn't help us now," Alex replied. *"So, what do we do now?"*

"Watch and learn, Alex." Aine smiled slightly and rose from her throne. A discreet movement of her hands stopped the approaching guards in their tracks. The princess turned to the king and sighed. While it appeared she was speaking solely to King Donal, Aine's voice carried easily throughout the room. "I'm so sorry it has to come to this, Father. However, most of those present this evening know that *you* are the primary royal traitor in this room. You have betrayed our people for decades, ever since the death of your wife, our fair and rightful ruler, Queen Maeve, and your rule has become increasingly cruel and corrupt of late. "

The king stared at Aine, mouth open in shock. He rose quickly, both hands supporting his massive, wobbling crown. "How dare you, woman! Guards, arrest her! She's a traitor!"

The princess gestured again, and most of the guards hesitated briefly. Then all hell broke loose. Soldiers poured into the room from all sides. Shouts and screams rent the air, while swords clashed, and arrows flew.

The Council members scattered, some running to the king's aid, while others tried to stop them. The rest fought their way through the soldiers toward the curtain-covered door on the back wall, intent on making their escape.

Alex slid her sword from its scabbard and waded into the fight alongside her team. She was determined to reach the princess, who remained alone on the raised dais, facing off with her furious father. Streams of powerful magic arced between them, momentarily blinding Alex. When her vision cleared, she despaired. Scores of fighters blocked her way. She'd never reach the princess in time.

Hopefully, Aine had the magical power to defeat her father. Otherwise, all would be lost.

30

DIVINE INTERVENTION

lex spotted a stealthy figure creeping along the far wall toward the raised throne platform. The man's scarlet Councilor's robe concealed a crossbow. Alex caught the gleam of a gold medallion and recognized Jerrold. Gaze fixed intently on Princess Aine's back, his deadly intentions were clear.

Gasping in horror, Alex realized she was too far away to defend her new friend from Jerrold's attack. She also feared that mind-speaking a warning to the embattled princess might be a deadly distraction. While Aine and her father appeared almost evenly matched, distracting her would give the king an advantage.

Alex almost despaired at the scene, until tendrils of magic swirled up from the red-hot pit of death magic normally buried deep within, and she took unthinking, instinctive action to protect her friend. Pointing her sword at Jerrold, Alex pushed her magic through the sword and commanded it to end the threat to the princess. A stream of crimson magic shot from the tip of her sword and arrowed through the air, before enveloping the treacherous Councilor.

Horror filled Alex when a familiar scream of anguish ripped from the dying Councilor as her death magic overtook him. The wooden crossbow in Jerrold's hands vanished in a puff of gray ash, and his body arced in agony, black smoke pouring from his robes. The man's knees buckled. In seconds, only ash and tatters of velvet remained where the Fae had previously stood.

Nausea threatened, but Alex swallowed it down. She would deal with the consequences of using her terrifying death magic later. She sprinted forward, her path now strangely clear of fighters. Huh. *Look what fear of a little death magic could do,* she mused distractedly.

When she reached the raised platform, Alex's fear returned in full force. Princess Aine now fought not one, but two powerful magical attackers. Her brother Cair had joined their father, and both threw increasingly powerful bolts of magic at an obviously weakening Aine. So far, the princess had stood her ground, but battling the two powerful men was taking a toll on her.

Fuck. Too bad the king had prevented his soldiers from removing Cair earlier, Alex brooded. She raised her sword but feared using her death magic again. The battle between the royal family was moving too fast; she might take out Aine if she timed her magical shot wrong. *And where the hell was Danu? At their meeting with the goddess in the Fae Woods the previous day, Danu had somewhat reluctantly agreed to help them.*

Alex gazed helplessly at the chaotic scene around her. *Now what do we do?*

~

"Now, we end this charade, Keeper," Danu said. "Told you I'd be here."

Alex swung around, stunned to see the ancient goddess standing behind her. Danu grinned at her, then raised her arms and snapped her fingers.

Silence immediately descended; the battle had stilled.

The Primordial goddess of the Fae clapped her hands and cackled in delight. "See? I've still got what it takes."

Alex gazed around the massive room in awe. A hazy green

magical mist filled the air, freezing the fighters in mid-action. Swords about to slice into an opponent remained inches from their skin. Arrows hung in mid-air. Grappling fighters remained frozen in each other's fierce embrace. Larry's jaws remained clamped in place on a guard's crotch. *Ouch.*

"Wow. That's pretty impressive." Alex eyed Danu with a mixture of respect and irritation. "But why couldn't you have shown up a little earlier? Like we agreed."

Danu pursed her lips and stuck her chin in the air. "I showed up when I was good and ready, child." Then the goddess grinned at Alex conspiratorially. "Actually, I've been here since that pompous prick you just ashed started his speech. I just wanted to see how things played out."

"You're incorrigible. People have *died* here tonight." Alex growled in frustration.

The ancient goddess nodded agreeably. "They did—but no one who didn't deserve it. And there will be several more deaths before this night is over."

Alex's gaze swung to the Fae royal family. The king and his son were frozen side by side. The arrogant men wore matching hateful expressions; their weapons aimed directly at the princess. Aine's beautiful face showed her fierce determination, but dark circles under her eyes spoke of pain and exhaustion. She had little left to give. If Danu had not stepped in, the Fae princess would have given her life for her people in vain.

"I wouldn't have let that happen." Danu's disgruntled objection brought Alex's gaze back to the goddess. "I just wanted to see what the princess was made of." The goddess snorted and shook her head. "Of course, I should already have known. Her mother was a great queen—one of the best, and Aine is her mother's daughter. If I'd been paying attention these past few centuries, things would never have come to this."

"So, you admit you've been neglecting your people?" Alex grimaced and dropped her gaze as soon as the words left her mouth. *Would she ever learn to think before she spoke?* One did not just go around accusing ancient Primordial goddesses of abandoning their duties. Even it was true.

"Oh, don't be a smartass with me, Keeper," the goddess shot back. "Or I may just add an extra supernatural to my death tally tonight."

Alex reluctantly returned her gaze to the goddess, breathing a silent sigh of relief when she saw Danu's wide grin.

"Hah! Got you!" The goddess cackled with delight. After a thoughtful pause, Danu tilted her head and added, "You know, Persephone might just have done me a favor by sleeping with that idiot prince of mine. I haven't had this much fun in centuries."

Alex stared mutely at Danu, rolling her shoulders to work out some of the tension stored there. She was so freaking glad there was no familial relationship between her and this crazy goddess. That she knew of, anyway. Alex's cousins, the Fates, were model family members in comparison.

"How do you know we're not related?" The goddess asked, a wicked twinkle in her rheumy eyes. "I could be your great-grandmother, for all you know."

"Goddess, I hope not," Alex blurted. She covered her mouth, eyes wide. "Oops, I mean..."

Danu merely snickered and said, "We'll have to have a family reunion sometime." She turned her attention to the frozen tableau around them. "But first, let's sort out this bloody mess, Keeper."

The ancient goddess hobbled over to the frozen royals, then studied the king with an annoyed frown. "Royal inbreeding. Humph. Should never have let Maeve marry this arsehole. His mother's mother married her cousin, as did his mother."

Danu shook her head in disappointment, then shot Alex a glare, a spark of remembered anger shining in her dark eyes. "If your lot hadn't forced me to recall most of my people to the Fae realm and close the fairy mounds, this might never have happened. An injection of human blood every few generations used to sort things out nicely."

Alex rolled her eyes. This goddess was as bad as her cousins.

"Listen, Danu, you can't just go around kidnapping humans—or anyone else." She hung on to her patience by reminding herself that divine beings had a very different moral code—and came of age in very different times.

"How about this?" Alex bargained with the goddess. "If you help us close the unsealed fairy mound, we can discuss allowing more of your people to visit Earth through my Crossroads. Then they can do the dating thing, like everyone does these days." She eyed Danu and shrugged. "If your people can convince someone to marry them and join them in the Fae realm—of their own free will—then it's all good. Deal?"

"Deal," the goddess agreed with a sharp nod. "Gotta move with the times, right? Now, back to the present."

Danu placed a gnarled hand on King Donal's arm, and Alex gasped in shock when the king simply ... disappeared. His crown still hung in mid-air, creepily calling attention to his missing body. "Wha—What did you do?"

"I created the Fae and their ancestors, the Tuatha de Danaan, dear," Danu explained, "I can uncreate 'em just as easily." The goddess reached out and touched the frozen prince, who simply disappeared, as had his father, the king. Dusting off her hands, Danu nodded in satisfaction. "Problem solved. Now let's have a word with the new Queen."

As the goddess reached for Aine, Alex yelped and leapt forward. "No, wait!" She crashed into the princess, pushing her off the dais. They both landed in a heap on the hard marble floor behind the raised platform.

"While I appreciate your quick action to save me, Alex, perhaps you could remove your hand from my breast?"

At Aine's dry request, Alex quickly removed the offending hand and scrambled back, away from the now unfrozen princess. "Uh, sorry. I didn't mean to—"

Aine's silvery laugh echoed in the still room. "No worries, sister. All is forgiven." The princess tried to stand, then sat back with a pained grimace. "I'm still a little weak from using all that magic. Could you help me up, Alex?"

Alex climbed painfully to her feet and helped Aine up, then they quickly straightened each other's rumpled gowns, both eager to prevent a wardrobe malfunction with the skimpy Fae formal wear.

"If you two are quite done, I'd like a word." Danu sat on the edge of the raised platform, her short legs dangling over the side. The goddess eyed the two friends with amused interest. "Or would you prefer to get a room?"

Aine grinned and shook her head. "We're done. And, as you well know, Alex and I are just good friends."

"Suuuure, you are."

The goddess's baiting words irritated Alex. "That's enough, Danu. You said you had something to say?" She gestured pointedly at the enormous room's still-frozen occupants. "Maybe we could get on with things before all these people get stuck like this?"

Danu pursed her lips and admired her frozen handiwork. "That almost never happens." She chuckled and rapped her knuckles on the wooden platform. "But you're right, Keeper. We should get on with things. I don't want my realm to suffer a second longer without a competent ruler on the throne." The goddess hesitated, then gave Alex a narrow-eyed appraisal. "Much as it pains me to do so, Keeper, I must admit your actions in this situation are commendable. You risked your life, and that of your team members, to right a festering wrong in my realm. One that I ignored for too long. I guess I owe you one."

Alex hid her shock, merely nodding at the ancient goddess. She realized that being owed a favor from Danu could come in very handy one day. After all, a favor owed to a certain Greek goddess had gotten her into this mess in the first place. As favors go, Alex figured she definitely got the better end of this deal. A Primordial goddess now 'owed her one.' Pretty cool.

Danu cackled and jumped to her feet. "Enough of this nonsense. Time for me to finish the job." The goddess motioned to

Aine, who stood quietly at Alex's side, a dazed expression on her lovely face. "Come here, girl. Join me on the dais. Time you received a very overdue promotion."

Alex marveled at the divine crone's sudden agility, then a thought struck her. All the other gods and goddesses she had met were young and attractive—despite their many millennia. Perhaps Danu chose to appear as an old woman? She shook her head in puzzlement. *Why would an immortal goddess choose to appear as a wizened old woman, though?*

"Because then everyone underestimates you, Keeper. Old people are seriously underrated, don't you think?" Danu's simple statement rang true. Because it was.

31

THERE'S A NEW QUEEN IN TOWN

In the stillness of the frozen room, Aine sat on her late father's massive golden throne, her face expressionless. Alex perched uncomfortably on one of the smaller thrones, as the goddess had directed.

Danu hopped up from the last throne and snatched the king's abandoned crown from the air. "Let's get this show on the road," she crowed, then snapped her fingers. The lingering green mist disappeared and, as suddenly as it had stopped, the battle resumed. Shouts and screams split the air as swords clashed and arrows resumed their flight.

"ENOUGH!" The goddess's divine command echoed from the walls, startling the fighters into stillness. All eyes flew to the thrones on the dais, where sat a new queen, an old goddess, and a confused Keeper. Shock and awe seemed to be the audience's primary emotion. Almost everyone dropped to their knees, heads bowed. The few who remained standing, still poised to battle for a dead king, were quickly subdued.

When silence finally returned, Danu addressed her people. "I'm ashamed of you, Fae children of the Tuatha de Danann. And I'm ashamed of myself, too." The goddess grimaced. "Sometimes evil creeps in gently. Minor acts of unfairness to others are overlooked. Corruption that benefits us is glossed over. All the while, evil blackens our souls a little more each time we look away."

She cast a stern eye over the crowd. "There will be no more looking away—for any of us. No more sleeping on the job. This realm has suffered under the yoke of a cruel and corrupt king for too long. His traitorous son has threatened civil war for almost as long. Many of you have been complicit in this ugly situation—no matter whose side you were on—even if you merely looked the other way. That is over now. For all of us. Do you hear me?"

Heads bowed, still kneeling, murmurs of ashamed assent swept through the cowed audience.

"Yes goddess. No more looking away."

"You are right, Danu."

"We apologize."

"Good. Let's get on with things, then." Danu nodded sharply, then gestured for everyone to stand. The goddess waved the glittering crown in the air theatrically. Once she had everyone's attention, she placed the crown firmly on Aine's head. "I don't have the time or energy for a flowery speech. Here's your new queen, duly appointed by me. Your goddess. You will respect and obey her as my representative. Do you hear?"

The old crone placed her hands on her hips and eyed the crowd. "Well? I don't hear you agreeing!"

"Yes, goddess."

"We understand, goddess."

Once satisfied with the crowd's response, the ancient goddess of the Fae grinned, then snapped her fingers and disappeared, leaving her last words to hang in the air. "See you in the Summerlands, my children, if not before..."

An electric moment of shocked silence descended, then everyone started talking at once.

"SILENCE!" For the second time that evening, the sharp command echoed around the walls.

Shocked into obedience, the crowd shut up and eyed their new queen uneasily.

Queen Aine gracefully rose to her feet and clasped her hands, the heavy crown remaining in place on her long, golden hair. Her warm gaze swept the room, and she smiled. "I'm delighted to accept this crown, and the responsibility that goes with it, direct from our goddess. As your queen, I will work hard to return peace and prosperity to our realm—and you will all help me." Steel entered the new ruler's voice. "Anyone who attempts to hinder me will feel the edge of my sword. Do I make myself clear?"

After a tense moment of silence, the crowd erupted, clapping and shouting with joy.

Cries of 'Long live Queen Aine!' Echoed in the air.

As the raucous cheers continued, Aine reached for Alex's hand and pulled her to her feet. She leaned over and whispered, "I damn well *better* live long. My corrupt father and idiot brother left me a huge fucking mess to clean up."

Alex chuckled. "You better not let my Aunt Maia hear you swear like that. She might threaten to wash your mouth out with soap."

Aine's silvery laughter sounded. "Oh, she has threatened me with that punishment more than once, sister. I always tell her it's all your Uncle Vinnie's fault."

"You too?" Alex replied, laughing along with the new Fae queen.

"Oh, I almost forgot." Aine gestured to the crowd for silence.

Once the room quieted, the queen tugged Alex forward, then invited the rest of Alex's team to join them on the dais.

Larry was the first to respond. He hopped easily onto the raised platform, then pranced over and sat at Aine's feet. "Is this the part where I get a treat?"

Aine smiled down at Larry and murmured, "Title first, Familiar. Then we feast."

"Sounds good to me," Larry replied with a gleeful grin, his canines gleaming white in the flickering torchlight.

The queen addressed her attentive court. "Alex and her team are the genuine heroes tonight. Without their selfless support, we might not have succeeded in throwing off the yoke of tyranny that has burdened the Fae realm for far too long." Aine strode over to one of the soldiers who were hovering near the dais and held out her hand for his sword. The awed man quickly unsheathed his sword and handed his new queen, hilt first. Aine held the sword high, then gestured to Alex and her team and issued her first royal command. "Please kneel to receive your honors."

The first title went to Larry. He barked with delight when the queen knighted him. "Sir Larry! From now on, everyone has to call me Sir Larry!"

Alex grinned at her Familiar's joy. Obviously, a title meant much more to him than it would to her. Based on Alex's recent experiences, she knew that new titles always came with new responsibilities. Always. When Queen Aine placed the sword on Alex's shoulder, she called her a sister of the realm, awarded her the king's hunting lodge—the one where the prince had held them both prisoner—and gave her the title of The Keeper Countess. Alex stifled a groan and swore quietly.

Next in line, Conor threw Alex a sideways grin and snickered. "Suck it up, Countess."

"Fuck you, soon-to-be Sir Conor."

After the honors came the feast. And oh, what a celebration it was. The Fae sure knew how to party. And eat.

Everyone in the castle slept late the next morning. Considering no one had gotten to bed until the first pale streaks of dawn tinted the sky, it was not surprising.

Alex woke just before midday with a pounding headache. She groaned and rolled over when the maid opened the curtains, allowing bright sunlight into the room. She sat up slowly, holding onto her head in case it fell off. Through narrowed eyes, Alex noticed Larry had absconded at some point.

A slender maid Alex had not seen before stood at the foot of her bed, balancing a silver tray in her small hands. The woman smiled shyly and bobbed a careful curtsy. "Countess, I have brought you a light meal. Would you like me to place it on the table by the window, or would you prefer to break your fast in bed?"

The maid's formal address brought the events of the previous evening rushing back. Alex rubbed her gritty eyes and sighed. "Please, just call me Alex—or Keeper, if you prefer. Countess is a bit much for me." She pointed at the table. "Please put the tray over there. I'd like to clean up before I eat."

Alex slid out of bed and padded toward the bathroom. As she went to shut the bathroom door, she realized that, while the maid had obeyed her and placed the tray on the table, the woman had made no move to leave. "You can go now. I appreciate the food."

"I'm so sorry, Your Highness, but I'm bidden to stay. The house-keeper has assigned me as your personal maid." The willowy Fae bit her lip anxiously. "It would be unseemly for the queen to allow a member of the nobility to be without a personal servant."

Your Highness. Alex had forgotten about that. Queen Aine had called her 'sister' the previous evening when handing out honors after her abrupt coronation. She stifled a sigh, realizing she'd put the maid in a difficult position. While she would prefer less pomp and circumstance, asking a servant to disregard protocol was not fair to them. *Damn it.* She still had so much to learn. Every time she thought she was getting a handle on her new supernatural life, the gods threw her a curveball in the form of another task, title, or both.

"That's okay, er..."

"My name is Morgan, Your Highness." The maid curtsied again, and Alex fought not to roll her eyes in frustration.

"Morgan. Thank you again for bringing me some food." Alex had an idea. "However, I am concerned about my Familiar, Sir Larry. I haven't seen him this morning, and I'm sure he is as hungry as I am. Please find him and ensure he is fed an enjoyable meal."

Alex held her breath, waiting for Morgan's response. Thankfully, the maid merely smiled and nodded. "Yes, Your Highness. I will find Sir Larry and bring him to the kitchen for a hearty meal."

"Oh, I'm sure he'll appreciate that." Alex smothered a chuckle as Morgan bobbed yet another curtsy and retreated, closing the door quietly behind herself. Alex was damned sure Larry had already eaten at least one breakfast, if not two. She was equally sure the little chowhound would be quite happy to enjoy a third.

Shortly after the maid left, Alex slipped into a steaming, scented bath and laid back with a groan. After browsing the array of magical bath salts lined up along the stone ledge next to the massive tub, she had selected a lovely hot pink one that reminded her of the color of Larry's ears. As the warm, scented water soothed her headache, her thoughts turned to the events of the previous few weeks.

It felt like months since her first date with Conor at her Uncle Vinnie's pizza restaurant. She remembered trying not to grin while her adopted uncle threatened her date with dire consequences if he didn't treat her right. The evening had been lovely ... until a weeping goddess with a problem had rudely interrupted their evening, setting the events of the past several weeks in action. So much had happened since then.

Persephone's problem—an affair with a treacherous Fae prince —had led directly to the reawakening of an ancient Fae goddess and a royal coup, just not the one the amorous prince had had in mind.

Idly, Alex wondered what had made the Persephone think of involving Alex and her team by calling in a favor Alex wasn't even sure she owed.

Soon after that came the extremely coincidental invitation from King Donal to visit the Fae realm and attend his Beltane celebration. Maia had told Alex at the time that it was a first. No Keeper had *ever* been invited to attend such an important royal event in the past.

Then, within a day of Alex's return from, a Fae princess had invited her for tea and a talk. Princess Aine had already known about everything and had been happy to help Alex and her team come up with reasonable—if dangerous—solutions to the brewing situation.

Damn it! Alex shot upright when she realized the truth. Cooling water slapped against the side of the tub, and she shivered. That wily royal had been orchestrating events from the very beginning. She wrapped herself in an enormous, fluffy towel and shook her head at the Aine's audacity and cunning. *She was sooo going to have a serious talk with her 'sister', the new Fae queen.*

Alex fumed as she ate the delicious brunch the maid had dropped off earlier. The meal's temperature briefly distracted her. She had spent at least an hour getting ready, and yet the food was still piping hot. *Huh. Magical food warmers. Cool.*

ONCE SHE HAD FINISHED her meal, with no sign of Larry or the rest of her team, Alex realized she needn't put off her confrontation with Aine any longer. She dressed and went in search of the queen, finally locating her in a small antechamber off the Great Hall used for the previous evening's celebration.

Queen Aine nodded to acknowledge Alex's presence before issuing brief commands to a short, round man Alex recognized as one of the late king's Councilors. "After that, Magnus, please consult with the remaining Councilors—the ones not dead or in the dungeon, that is—and gather a list of potential candidates to fill the empty Council seats."

"Yes, Your Majesty." The man nodded and bowed obsequiously, then walked backwards to the door, intent on leaving to carry out the queen's wishes. Alex hastily moved aside to allow him room to turn and exit the room without running smack into her.

Once the Councilor had trotted away, Aine waved Alex into the room. The queen studied Alex intently, then her lips curved in a sly smile. Her deep blue eyes twinkled with humor as she rose from behind an enormous, elegantly carved desk. "Close the door behind you, sister, and join me by the fire."

Soon, they were both ensconced in comfortable armchairs near the roaring fire. Alex rebuffed Aine's attempts at hospitality, instead crossing her arms and frowning at her erstwhile friend. Sister. Whatever. "We need to talk, Aine. I'm beginning to suspect you've been behind this whole affair right from the beginning. Am I right?"

The new queen's delighted laughter confirmed Alex's suspicions.

"Oh, Alex. It took you long enough to figure it out." Aine's wise eyes regarded Alex warmly. "Now that the gods have appointed you as their Envoy, it is critical that you learn how to play the game of politics, my dear. You have much to learn—and I'll help you do so. My many years as an Ambassador for this realm taught me much."

Alex shook her head, brushing off Aine's offer of help. She pursed her lips and studied the queen through narrowed eyes. "So, you admit instigating your brother's affair with Persephone? How did you do it? And why?" Alex tried to keep her voice neutral, but she knew her anger showed.

Aine merely gave her a sly smile. "It was quite easy to ensure Persephone crossed paths with my brother. Cair is ... was a very attractive man, and very devious. I was sure he'd immediately see the advantages of having an affair with a powerful goddess. Plus, everyone knows Persephone sleeps around, and word soon reached her that my brother was very good in bed. In fact, I made sure it did." The queen grinned, her eyes twinkling with ribald humor.

Alex snorted a laugh. "Okay, I'll give you that one. Even so, why—"

Aine's gaze sobered. "You have a right to know why I involved you, my new friend, so I'll explain. In order for my plan to free the Fae realm from my father's tyranny and my brother's scheming to work, I needed help from a powerful ally. My sources assured me your magical powers far exceeded those of your Keeper predecessors. Word reached me after your decisive victory in the Underworld that your divine ancestry featured Primordial death magic —and that you may have inherited it. I realized then that the time for action had arrived. I knew that, with your help—and that of an angry goddess or two—I could save my people."

The queen raised her eyebrows questioningly, her gaze steely. "Would you not have done the same for your people, Keeper?"

Alex considered the new Fae queen silently as the minutes slipped by. She had searched out Aine today to get some answers. Perhaps she had all she needed. Nodding slowly, Alex admitted, "Yes, I would have done the same for my people."

The thick tension seeped from the air, and both powerful women sat in contemplative, but comfortable, silence for a long time.

Eventually, Alex threw her hands up in the air and groaned. "And what the hell am I supposed to do with a hunting lodge in the back of beyond in the Fae realm?"

Aine grinned at her, a wicked twinkle in her eyes. "I can think of a thing or two, sister. After all, privacy really matters when romantic relationships are ... consummated."

Alex groaned, covering her face to hide a fiery blush. "Don't tell me you've conspired with the rest of my team and placed a bet on when Conor and I will, uh, do the deed, too?"

The queen rolled her eyes. "Oh, Alex, stop being such a prude."

THE JOURNEY HOME

The journey home was uneventful. Well, except for the ominous news Alex shared with the team as they trudged wearily through the Fae Forest toward the distant Crossroads.

Alex sighed. "I'm going to have a word with Hecate and the queen. Danu, too. Maybe we can come to an agreement and get a Crossroads put in near the castle. This day-long slog through Danu's creepy woods every time we visit the Fae realm is getting old fast."

Larry padded slowly along at Alex's side. "Sounds like a plan." He grinned slyly. "While you're at it, you should also ask Hecate for a Crossroads near that hunting lodge the queen gave you. I think it would make a great love nest for you and—"

"Oh, shut up, fur-butt," Alex snapped. She blushed and hoped Conor hadn't heard Larry's suggestive comment.

"Let's worry about extra Crossroads plans later," Conor said. "We've got quite a few other things to discuss before we get back to our Crossroads." His words held no sign he'd heard Larry's snide insinuation, but the merry twinkle in his eyes revealed that he most definitely had. "Alex, I know you met with the queen this morning before we left the castle. Want to share?"

Alex's stomach dipped when she recalled her conversation with Aine. After their brief verbal jousting, the two women had talked for several hours about the fallout from the late king's cruel reign. In the end, they had both agreed there were more malign forces at work than just a corrupt king, and that these dark forces had contributed to the Fae realm's subjugation. They suspected the tentacles of evil infecting the Fae realm reached into other realms, too. They had won this battle, but others were coming. Soon.

Alex rolled her shoulders, trying to work out some of the tension that had settled there.

"It would be best if you shared your thoughts with us, Alex," Conor prodded. "We can tell from your inner turmoil that dark clouds lie ahead."

"Why don't you just read my mind?" Alex snapped, but instantly regretted it, knowing Conor and her team were currently allowing her mental privacy when they didn't have to. "I'm sorry, Conor. It's just ... a lot, you know?"

Conor slowed his pace, threw his arm around Alex's shoulders, and gave her a sideways hug. "Yeah, sweets, I know. It's a lot."

Feeling marginally better after Conor's show of support, Alex grinned reluctantly. "I say that a lot, don't I? But it *is* a lot. And more keeps coming."

"You can handle it, Alex. You're the strongest person I know," Conor assured her.

Alex shook her head. "No, I'm not that strong. Not by myself, anyway. Fortunately, I've got you lot of miscreants to help me, though."

Everyone immediately assured Alex they had her back, while also expressing mild outrage at being called miscreants. Her team's good-natured banter helped center Alex. Conor had mentioned that dark clouds lay ahead, but she knew it was more like they were in the storm's eye—and turbulent times lay ahead. She needed to bring her team up to speed.

"Okay, guys, so here's the scoop." Alex sat on a fallen log in a small clearing to one side of the path. The team joined her, forming a semicircle around her.

"You all remember the Chaos Council, right?" At everyone's confused expressions, Alex explained. "The Chaos Council is a shadowy criminal organization with realm-wide reach. We learned a bit about them during the battle in the Underworld. For over a decade, Nyx has used her grandson, Morpheus, to leverage his powers over dreams and nightmares to influence criminals to join her earth-based Council. Nyx has been playing a long game. Her plans for the Chaos Council remain unclear, but I'm pretty sure that, at the very least, she sees the Council as a criminal welcoming committee for if—when she finally breaks out of her prison in the Underworld and makes it to Earth."

"But you instructed your father's—your—Regenerants to take Nyx back to her prison on the edge of the Underworld and keep her there," Tyre protested. "Since she's currently stuck in a Regenerant body herself, her divine powers are constrained. Correct?"

Alex nodded, then pursed her lips. "That's all true, Tyre. But we don't know how long my command to the Regenerants will hold ... or if Nyx can escape them somehow. After all, she's escaped before. That's how we got into that whole mess in the Underworld with her and my father, remember? When he used his necromantic powers to create the Regenerants." She shivered at the memory. Her father had used his dark magic to insert the souls of dead criminals into dead human bodies. The magic had altered the bodies: changing them to resemble the souls that inhabited them and animating the bodies to resemble living beings. All under her father's command, of course—until his death at Alex's hand, when she had inadvertently used her death magic to destroy his soul and take command of his undead army.

"The bottom line is this: we know that Nyx's followers run the Chaos Council. At the very least, it seems the group's goal is to commit crimes and sow chaos, both on Earth and in other realms." Alex heaved a sigh, then reluctantly continued her tale. "The queen had her guards question her father's Council members last night. Almost half of them are—were Chaos Council members."

Gasps echoed around the clearing, and everyone started talking at once. Alex patted the air, asking for quiet. When the team showed no signs of obeying, she shouted for silence.

Once she had everyone's attention, Alex told them the rest of the bad news. "When King Donal fired almost his entire Council several years ago, he brought half a dozen Fae here from the Earth realm and gave them Council seats. It appears most of these new Fae Councilors were members of the Chaos Council." Alex shrugged philosophically. "Um, I say 'were' because the queen executed all of them this morning, after discovering their treachery. Apparently, these new Councilors had been draining the royal treasury for years. Aine's people can't locate the missing funds, although it appears most of it left the realm and is now in the hands of this damned Chaos Council."

During Alex's explanation, Tyre had picked up a stick and begun poking angrily at a circle of squat mushrooms. "Did the king know?" The Indigo Fae warrior answered his own question. "*Of course*, he knew. How could he not?" After decapitating the mushroom circle, he threw the stick far into the woods.

Alex eyed her Fae friend with sympathy. "Queen Aine says her father definitely knew. It seems the king wasn't a member of the Chaos Council himself. Instead, he made a deal with the devil. Almost a decade ago, Donal's grip on power was weakening. Years of his unwise rule had fomented much discontent among his subjects. He feared a coup by either—or both—of his children. Then the Chaos Council's earthbound Fae stepped in and offered the king a deal. Let us into your realm, pay us handsomely, and we'll keep you on the throne."

Larry scratched his ear, then shook his head, pink ears flapping. "But how could they do that? Most earthly Fae aren't as strong magically as those who live in the Fae realm. That's mostly why they stayed on Earth, despite Danu's recall, in the first place."

Conor answered for Alex, his face grim. "With the Chaos

Council's support—and with the help of a god or two, the earthly Fae could back up their promise to Donal. We know that Nyx and her co-conspirators are behind the Council, even if she's out of commission at the moment."

"Yup," Alex agreed. "They are. Somehow, one of them must have opened that fairy mound the king was using to keep his nefarious dealings secret. It's sealed back up tight now, though. Danu honored her promise." Her lips curved in a satisfied smile. "Nothing's getting through those damn fairy mounds for the foreseeable future."

"Sounds like we've got work to do." Larry cocked his head, then nodded decisively. "Gotta figure out who else is on this Chaos Council and take 'em out."

"Yes, Larry, we do. But that's a problem for another time." Alex pushed herself to her feet and trudged back to the path. "Right now, I just want a warm bath and a hot meal. Let's go, guys."

Conor placed a restraining hand on Alex's arm. When she looked up, the turmoil in his gaze unsettled her. She thought she was the one with all the bad news. "What is it, Conor? Just tell me."

"Just before we left for the Fae realm, one of my informants contacted me. I had tasked him with keeping an eye on your mother. Just in case—"

"Just in case she gets on her broom and flies to San Antonio to kill me," Alex interrupted, her words bitter. "Well? Spill. And we'll deal with why you didn't tell me about this until now after we get back."

Conor cocked an eyebrow. "Sure thing, sweets. I figured we had enough on our plates with the brewing war in the Fae realm, so your mother could wait. Anyway, my informant told me he recognized someone your mother recently met with."

Alex gave Conor serious side-eye. "Who? Tell me!"

"Morpheus."

Darkness wavered at the edge of Alex's vision, but she fought it back. Memories of the last time she saw the god of nightmares tore through her mind. Morpheus had just killed her friend. He had been sneering down at her while she knelt on the filthy floor of a prison cell in the Underworld, holding the cooling hand of Greta, the river troll. Alex had threatened she'd kill him. Before he disappeared, Morpheus had merely smiled and promised that he'd return the favor one day.

Larry's furry body pressed against Alex's leg. The soothing warmth of her Familiar released Alex from her painful memories. "I'm okay now, bud. Thanks."

"No problem." Larry's worried brown eyes met hers. "You sure?"

"Yep. I'm just dandy," she replied, a bite to her tone. "My evil mother is in league with a god who has promised to kill me. That god is the grandson of a powerful goddess who also wants me dead. And all of them are involved with this Chaos Council that wants to take over the world. What could possibly be wrong?" Alex shook off Conor's arm and stalked down the forest path.

"Well, when you put it like that..." Conor said, jogging to catch up with Alex's fast pace.

"How else is there to put it?" Alex sped up. "Let's get back to the Crossroads. Looks like I'm going to have to up my magical game—and take my cousins up on their offer of death magic training sooner rather than later."

THE LAST HAND

The exultant goddess slapped her cards down, face up, on the table. "Royal Flush! Read 'em and weep! I win again!" Atropos grinned and reached for her winnings. The small pile of potato chips in the center of the table left crumbs as she gathered them together and deposited them in her already overflowing bowl.

Alex grinned. Ever since her aunt had given Atropos lessons on how to play and win at poker—without cheating and threatening to kill anyone who called her out on it, the goddess had been on a winning streak. The few times she didn't win, one of her sister Fates did, much to the other player's quiet relief. The gruesome scissors of Fate hadn't appeared at the weekly poker game in almost a month. *And the Fates were leaving the next day. Yay!* Alex did an internal happy dance at the thought of her divine cousins' imminent departure.

"Another game?" Lachesis asked, handing her losing hand to her sister, Clotho, and reaching for the chips and dip. "We've only played three games, and you know I prefer it when things end with even numbers. Oooh, these potato chips are so delicious! I'm going to order a bunch of them from Hecate's magical shopping box to take back home with me." The diminutive goddess nodded to emphasize her words, then crunched happily on her chips.

Clotho smiled benignly at her sister, then expertly shuffled the cards for another game.

My freaking goddess cousins are now card sharks, Alex mused. She devoutly hoped the trio didn't start up a poker game between the gods upon their return to Mount Olympus. A loss at poker might just spell disaster among the competitive, amoral, and short-tempered gods.

"I think we'll have to start a weekly poker game at our house," Lachesis mumbled, her mouth still full of chips, dashing Alex's hopes of a poker-free Mount Olympus.

Clotho agreed enthusiastically. "Alex, you'll have to join us for a game when you come to stay at our house next month for your meeting with the Divine Council."

Conor laid a restraining hand on Alex's leg under the table. "Don't say anything you'll regret, sweets. They *are* family, after all —and rather deadly, if you recall. Plus, you know you've got to make the journey. As an Envoy, you cannot refuse a summons from the gods. They might have a mission for you or want to brief you on your duties. Or both. They might even have some information about the Chaos Council issue." With a final comforting squeeze, Conor removed his hand and gathered up his cards for the next game.

Alex made use of her poker face and collected her cards with an internal sigh. She'd spent much of the last month with her cousins, learning how to control her death magic. After returning from her successful mission in the Fae realm, she had asked the Fates to train her right away. Once the goddesses learned of her unauthorized use of death magic, both to injure Prince Cair and then to kill the traitorous Counselor Jerrold, they had immediately agreed. Fortunately, her new cousins had agreed that her actions had been necessary and hadn't called her out for breaking her promise not to use her Primordial death magic until she had some training. In fact, after their last training session,

Clotho had smiled at Alex approvingly and told her she now knew enough to be less dangerous to the universe. *Comforting thought, Alex reflected wryly. I've got magic that can destroy tens of thousands of souls in seconds, but at least now I can control it. Mostly. Sigh.*

"Cheer up, Alex! And pay attention—it's your turn." Larry's mind-spoken words interrupted Alex's morbid thoughts. *"Remember, you've got your second date with Hunky McHunkerson this evening. I'm thinking tonight might be the night you two lovebirds to get it on. Don't worry, I'll make myself scarce."*

Alex threw her grinning Familiar a narrow-eyed glare. *"Conor and I are going out for dinner. That's all. I promise you we are not going to—"*

"Don't make promises you can't keep." Conor's amused, mind-spoken words interrupted Alex's promise. *"Besides, I hear the members of the 'when are Conor and Alex going to get it on' betting pool are getting antsy. Perhaps we should put them out of their misery."*

Alex quickly played her hand, keeping her head lowered to hide her flaming face, then silently rebuked her friends. *"Will you two knock it off? Conor, when—if—we sleep together, it won't be so that some idiot can win a freaking bet. Tonight is dinner. That's it. We'll see where it goes from there. Don't make me regret saying yes to a second date."*

"Pay attention, Alex." Maia's gentle rebuke brought Alex's attention back to the poker game. "Your cards are showing."

Alex quickly pulled her hand up, so that her cards were no longer visible to the other players. "Sorry, Aunt Maia."

"And so you should be, Keeper." Queen Elizabeth's sharp complaint cut through the air. "It's bad enough that the ghostly participants at this poker game have had to play for potato chips instead of haunting rights at Vinnie's bar for the last several weeks." The ancient, ghostly monarch regarded Alex with pinched lips. "You know we ghosts can't eat our winnings, even if we win—which we haven't since your cousins learned to play. The least you can do is keep your end up and play the game as if you've got a brain. Who knows? One day, maybe you'll learn how to play properly, and it'll be an actual challenge to beat you."

Larry snickered, while Conor turned a chuckle into a cough at the queen's blunt remarks.

Loath to rise to the queen's cattiness, Alex bit back a tart reply, then she spotted Atropos. The skeletal goddess faced the royal ghost, an enormous, blood-encrusted pair of scissors in her outstretched hand.

"Take that back, you old hag. That's my cousin you're talking about," Atropos snarled, snapping the scissors meaningfully at the ghostly queen. "No one talks to my cousin like that."

"I win!" Lachesis shouted. "Four of a kind! That means I win, right? No one else has a better hand than I do, right?" The exultant goddess gazed around the table, challenge in her eyes.

After a tense moment, the other players dropped their cards on the table facedown and shook their heads.

"Looks like you win, Lachesis," Maia said, gesturing toward the potato chip bowl in the middle of the table. "Why don't you and your sisters take your winnings out to the terrace? I'll have Henri mix up some of that lemonade you like and bring it out to you."

Lachesis nodded agreeably and reached for the half-full potato chip bowl.

Clotho gently placed a hand on Atropos's scissor-waving arm. "Put those away, dear. I'm sure Liz didn't mean to insult our cousin." The motherly goddess nodded encouragement at a frowning Queen Elizabeth. "Did you, Your Majesty?"

"Of course not." The royal ghost smoothed her face and grimaced a smile, flicking a nervous glance at Alex. "I was just teasing the girl."

Larry suddenly leapt to his paws, then ran around the table, barking madly. When he reached Grenoble's chair, he jumped up and pushed the little goblin out of his booster seat. Grenoble howled and gave chase. The crackling tension in the air soon dissipated as the speedy duo chased each other around the room.

"Thanks, Larry." Alex sent a mind-spoken thanks to her wise and speedy Familiar.

"No worries, Alex." Larry threw his magical partner a quick grin, then raced toward the door, leading his growling opponent into the hallway. *"Grenoble and I are gonna head to the kitchen for a snack. Play-fighting makes a dog—and a goblin—hungry."*

As the sounds of the lively chase receded down the hallway, Alex dared to glance around the table, sighing in relief when she realized Atropos had sent her deadly scissors of Fate back into the ether—or wherever the heck she kept them.

Picking up the chips and dip, Alex said, "Come on, cousins. Let's head out to the terrace and wait for that lemonade my Aunt Maia promised."

As she led her now-cooperative cousins towards the patio, Alex was surprised to find that she'd miss the quirky trio when they departed the next day. Well, she wouldn't miss their presence at her aunt's weekly poker games, or Atropos's deadly scissors, but she had gotten to know the trio over the past month. The Fates could be a bundle of fun when they weren't threatening to kill you —or someone else—on your behalf.

She grinned and ate a chip.

ALEX TOOK another slow sip of the rich burgundy wine and nervously studied the wavering reflection of the almost full moon reflected in the pond. She and Conor had enjoyed a delicious dinner in downtown San Antonio, at a fancy restaurant along the Riverwalk. Recalling their disastrous first date, when a distraught goddess with a problem had interrupted their meal, they had both silently agreed to avoid her Uncle Vinnie's Italian restaurant for their second. No reason to tempt fate. After dinner, they had lingered over coffee, laughing, and chatting easily until almost midnight.

Upon their return to the estate, Conor had suggested a stroll in the gardens. When they reached the pond, it hadn't surprised Alex to find a bottle of wine and two wine glasses perched on the pond's wide stone containment wall. *Barghests sure are strategic thinkers,* she mused. *They must get it from their Hellhound ancestors.*

Conor edged closer along the wall, put his mouth to her ear, and whispered. "You're right. I'm a planner. I'm also a shifter." He nuzzled her neck, inhaling deeply. "And I can smell sexual attraction, remember?"

Despite herself, Alex shivered in anticipation. Out loud, she said, "Get out of my mind, Conor. And get your shifter nose away from me."

"I'll get out of your mind if I can get into your bed. Tonight. Now." Conor murmured. He stood and reached for Alex's hand, a slight smile on his face.

Stunned, Alex gazed up at the handsome man. Barghest. Whatever. Despite his blunt request, she saw both heat and vulnerability in his intense gaze. Conor was willing to take a chance on them. Was she?

Placing her hand in Conor's outstretched one, Alex smiled and stood. "Yes. Tonight. Now." Then she led him toward her room.

As she and Conor fell onto the bed together, Alex heard a distant bark in the back of her mind. *"Yes! I win the bet! I knew it!"*

"Get the fuck out of my mind, fur-face. And that goes for the rest of you who share a magical connection with me." Alex growled. *"Everyone leave. Now."*

The silence in her mind was deafening. Now that the low hum of the magical connections she shared with her heart family was notably absent, Alex almost missed its reassuring, if sometimes annoying, presence. Almost.

As Conor did wonderful things with his lips, Alex moaned in pleasure. She'd worry about her newly expanded heart family's shared magical connections—and her upcoming meeting with the gods on Mount Olympus—another time.

Tonight was her time. And Conor's.

THE NEXT BOOK in this series is called Demeter's Dilemma. For more information about this book, along with information and purchase links to all my books, please visit my website at:
www.samanthablackwoodnovelist.com

YOU CAN JOIN my VIP Reader's Club newsletter for the latest information on upcoming releases, bonus content, discounts, links to multi-author book fairs, and more.

REVIEWS ARE ALWAYS APPRECIATED. *If you enjoyed this book, I would be grateful if you could spend just five minutes leaving a review on your favorite vendor's website.*

- WOOFS & Wags, Samantha Blackwood

ALSO BY SAMANTHA BLACKWOOD

The Crossroads Keeper Series

Prequel - Larry's Familiar Tale

Book 1 - Hecate's Heir

Book 2 - Persephone's Problem

Book 3 - Demeter's Dilemma

Book 4 - Hades in Hot Water - Coming Soon

Book 5 - The Chaos Council - Coming Soon

Book 6 - Nixing Nyx - Coming Soon

The Kitchen Witchery Series

Book 1 - The Maple Muffin Murder

Book 2 - The Lemon Croissant Corpse

Book 3 - The Damson Danish Death - Coming Soon

Join my VIP Reader's Club to receive a free copy of Larry's Familiar Tale, the prequel to the Crossroads Keeper series, and to receive news about upcoming releases, bonus content, Larry's Life Blog, multi-author book fairs, reader discounts, and more.

For more information about my books, purchase links, and newsletter signup, please visit my website at:

www.samanthablackwoodnovelist.com

ABOUT THE AUTHOR

Samantha Blackwood writes fiction books in the urban fantasy, supernatural, and paranormal mid-life cozy mystery genres.

She lives near the beach in sunny Portugal with her husband and their pack of rescue dogs. She has worked professionally with dogs for most of her life and proudly claims the title of 'Crazy Dog Lady.' Her friends and family don't disagree...

Of course, she couldn't imagine not including dogs in her writing, so there's at least one sassy, snarky canine character, based on one of her own dogs, in each of her books.

She has a lot of fun giving her fictionalized fur-kids magical abilities—and voices. We all know dogs don't really need human words to communicate, but it's nice—and hilarious—to hear them tell us exactly what they think!

For more information, please contact the author.
www.samanthablackwoodnovelist.com
sam@samanthablackwoodnovelist.com

Find her on social media.
Facebook.com/samanthablackwoodnovelist
Instagram.com/samanthablackwoodnovelist
Pinterest.com/samanthablackwoodnovelist

www.ingramcontent.com/pod-product-compliance
Lightning Source LLC
Chambersburg PA
CBHW060916190726
48286CB00002B/530